South of Heaven

Ali Spooner

South of Heaven

Ali Spooner

Affinity
eBook Press
NZ
2016

South of Heaven
© 2016 by Ali Spooner

Affinity E-Book Press NZ LTD
Canterbury, New Zealand

1st Edition

ISBN: 978-0-908351-91-6

Editor: Angela Koenig
Proof Editor: Alexis Smith
Cover Design: Irish Dragon Designs

Acknowledgments

I would like to thank my fans for following my stories, providing great feedback and encouragement. Writing wouldn't be so much fun without you. Thanks to Affinity, Irish Dragon for the cover art and the team of editors, readers, and publishers who continue to help me grow as a writer.

Dedication

To Haeden. You will always be the keeper of my heart. Thanks for your unconditional love.

Table of Contents

Also by Author

Chapter One

Kendra Drake sat on the end of the pier gazing out across the Gulf. The western sky filled with hues of red, orange, and gold as the sun sank toward the horizon. Gulls swooped and dove between a boat's wake as a late day shrimper headed for home. *Heaven can't be much better than this.* She took a long pull from a bottle of Corona and placed it beside her on the time-worn wood of the pier, then took an envelope from her breast pocket. Her heart raced as she pulled out the enclosed letter.

She read the letter for the tenth time that afternoon, the smile still plastered to her face. The state Fisheries Commission had taken two months to review and approve her application for a license to fish for Royal Reds.

Kevin, her father, had decided to retire after thirty years at the helm, and her objective was to take their small shrimping operation to the next level. Her family had thrived on the brown, white, pink, and rock shrimp caught locally off the Northwest Florida shores, but her dream was to move to deeper waters during the Royal Red season. Only captains with a special license could fish for the cherished red shrimp, sought after by every seafood restaurant and market along the Gulf coast. The special license she now held excitedly in her hands.

†

1

Earlier in the day, returning from the morning run for browns, she saw her father approaching down the pier. The years of hard work shrimping had taken a toll on his body, and they showed as he painfully limped toward the boat. The grin he was wearing as he waited for her to dock let her know he had good news to share with her. When the crew had them tied off, Kevin stepped aboard. As the crew began unloading, he met his daughter in the wheelhouse.

"I do believe this is what you've been waiting for." He handed her the envelope and waited for her response.

Kendra looked at the return address and smiled up at him.

"Go ahead. What are you waiting for?"

Her hands trembled with excitement as she pried the envelope open and pulled out the one page letter. Her eyes traveled down the page to where the license number was located, and she let out the breath she had unconsciously been holding.

"We got it, Dad. We got a license to fish reds."

"I knew it would come," he replied with a smile of pride. "You've been out fishing the boys around here for two years now."

Even the weathered wrinkles of his face could not hide the tear that slid down his cheek. Kendra stepped forward and hugged him tightly.

"Don't forget, old man, you taught me everything I know."

"You were an eager learner, and that brings me to my next bit of information."

"More good news?" she asked.

"I think it is, or can be depending on your decision."

"That sounds serious. What's up, Dad?"

"I got a call this morning from an old army pal of mine in North Carolina. He's also a shrimp man and has a daughter a few years younger than you that he hopes will take over his business one day."

"That's good, but how does that affect us?"

"His daughter, Lindsey, has got in a bit of a bind. Her father thinks it's time for her to leave town for a while to let some things cool down a bit."

Kendra cocked her head at him. "Trouble with the law, would we be harboring a fugitive?"

Kevin chuckled, "No, nothing that serious. It's more of a personal nature. I'll let her tell you about it herself, and if you want to hire her to replace your old man on the crew, then it's your decision. I do think you need one more seasoned hand since you're going to be out longer in deeper water going for the reds."

She let his words sink in for a few long seconds. "When does she arrive?"

"Lindsey will be here this weekend. If you don't think she's right for your crew, then we'll send her home."

Kendra knew her father wouldn't ask this of her if it weren't important. She was also glad that he would allow her to make the decision without any pressure. The last thing she needed was a troublemaker, especially if they would be out on the water for nearly a week at a time. She had no time as captain to deal with emotional baggage from either male or female hands.

He was right though, she did need to hire another deckhand, especially for the extended trips, and finding another man to be gone from his family all week would be difficult, even though the pay for reds would be better than local shrimping.

"We have a week left on the browns before the reds' season begins and we head out for our first trip for reds, so if she seems like she might be a good fit when I meet her, she'll have next week to prove she can handle the work."

Kevin smiled at his daughter. "That's only fair, Captain Drake."

She returned his smile. "You'll always be Captain Drake."

"I'll be Captain at home, but the boat is all yours now."

"Thanks, Dad. The boys have the weekend off so I'll be home once we get the haul delivered and the boat cleaned."

"Get hungry. I've got some huge steaks marinating."

"Oh, you've got my mouth watering already. Do I need to bring anything home?"

"I've got beer on ice, but you can clean up a batch of those blue crabs in your pot. They'll make a great appetizer while the steaks cook."

"That's an easy request."

"I'll see you at the house then." He smiled and left the wheelhouse.

Kendra followed him to the pier and watched as he made his way back to his truck. The crew was bustling around the deck, bringing tubs of iced shrimp to the dock just as the delivery truck arrived.

Her first mate, Harvey, walked up to her with a clipboard, handing it to her for a signature. "Sixteen hundred pounds is a good way to end the week."

"Yes, it is. We also got good news, so gather the boys after they load the truck and I'll tell everyone at once."

"A reds license?" he asked. Harley was the only one of the crew to know she had applied for the license.

She nodded with a smile.

"All right," he hollered, and went to help the others load.

†

Kendra walked back into the wheelhouse to finish some paperwork while the crew unloaded the day's catch. She was writing out paychecks when Harvey knocked on the doorframe to get her attention.

"We're about to start the cleaning, Captain. Did you want to talk to the crew first?"

"Yes, thanks, Harvey." She followed him out on deck where the men had clustered together.

"What's up, Captain?" Charlie asked.

"Thanks for another great week, boys. We only have one more week of browns to go."

"Then what, Captain?" Charlie asked.

"Well, about two months ago, I applied for a license to fish for Royal Reds and today we received word that we were granted a license."

"Oh, hell yeah," Charlie hollered. Even the youngest of her crew knew the value of the prized shrimp.

"So, after next week, we'll have three months to catch all the reds we can." She grinned.

"I can finally replace my old truck," Harvey declared.

"I can promise you much higher paychecks once we start catching reds. It'll make more time away from home but worth the investment."

"Out on Monday and back the following Saturday?" Charlie asked.

"Sooner if we fill up our freezers faster," Kendra answered.

"What freezers?" Harvey asked.

"The ones that will be installed next week after we get back to harbor. I've had them ordered and ready for weeks now, with faith that we'd get the reds' license."

"That sounds really good, Captain." Harvey grinned.

"We will also have a new crew member working with us next week, to see if she can hang with us."

"Did you say she?" Charlie asked.

"Yes. A friend of Dad's from North Carolina is sending his daughter down to learn from us. So if she works out next week, she'll be joining us for red season."

"It'll be nice to have an extra set of hands. We've been working short since Captain Drake retired," Harvey reminded her.

"Especially if they're attached to a cute girl," Charlie joked.

"You better not let your wife hear you talking like that," Bobby teased, bringing a round of laughter from the crew.

Kendra shook her head at their antics. "Do any of you have questions?"

When none came, Harvey set the crew to task. "Let's get to work cleaning the boat while the Captain writes us some big checks. We all need to have a good weekend."

"I'll second that," Charlie grinned.

Kendra returned to the wheelhouse to finish calculating and writing out the paychecks while the crew prepared the boat for the night. As with each Friday night, the tradition was to pass out checks with a cold Corona to start the weekend off for her crew.

She pulled out a tub with a six-pack of iced down beer and passed out checks while Harvey gave each man a beer.

When everyone had a beer, Kendra raised hers in the air. "To the reds we will be catching."

"Amen to that, Captain," the crew cheered.

†

After the crew finished their beer, they left for home. Harvey was the last to leave. "Are you headed home soon?"

"In just a bit. I promised Dad I'd clean some blue crab to bring home, and I have a few other things to finish."

Harvey grinned. "I heard you earlier. I've already cleaned your crabs and they're in a bucket of ice in the back of your Jeep. Bobby carried them out for you."

"Thanks, Harvey."

"If there's nothing else I can help with, I'm going to head for home. Congrats on the license. I know you've wanted this for a long time."

"It will take us to the next level financially. Dad always hoped to add another boat to the fleet, so maybe this will make it happen."

"A bigger boat would be nice if we're going to have a future in the reds," he agreed.

"I've got my eye on one already, but we need to have a good red season to make it happen."

"It'll come, boss. Have a great weekend."

"You too, Harvey. Tell Helen hello for me."

"Will do. She still expects you for dinner one night."

"Tell her I haven't forgotten. I'll take her up on her offer soon."

"Good night, then." He waved and left the wheelhouse.

†

Kendra closed her logbook and her eyes landed on a photograph of herself and her dad from several years ago. She was fresh out of high school and beginning her first year of working full time. She loved being out on the water, and working beside her father was an added bonus. Kevin had been more than a parent to her. He was her best friend and had always been supportive of her decisions, even when he didn't agree with her choices.

He had been there for the heartache when her first lover betrayed her. Jude, the woman she had given her heart to had cheated on her, while Kendra was working her tail off to provide them a good life. After the breakup, Kendra had moved back home and for two weeks had cried herself to sleep every night. Jude had been a difficult lesson for her and left Kendra determined never to be so vulnerable again.

✝

After a hot shower and a fantastic dinner, Kendra retired for the evening. She wanted to spend the next day working on the boat, providing that extra bit of cleaning to give it a good shine. She helped her dad clean the kitchen and then climbed the stairs to her room.

Their home, just a few blocks from the Gulf, built with a wrap-around balcony on the second floor, gave her a view of the harbor. She opened the doors, allowing the cool breeze to float into the room. She could hear the waves crash into the jetties outlining the harbor, and smell the scent of salt that was in the air as she climbed beneath fresh sheets. She listened carefully as her dad made his rounds through the house, locking doors and checking windows. He had followed this routine every night for as long as she could remember.

She and her father had lived alone in the house since her mother left, abandoning them when Kendra was twelve. Karen Drake yearned for a more exciting life and left town with a traveling salesman. Years later, Kevin received divorce papers from an address in New York, and they never heard from her again. Both were devastated in the beginning, but time and hard work helped them heal and formed a stronger bond between father and daughter.

Kevin excelled at being a single parent and Kendra grew into a strong, independent young woman. She graduated at the top of her class in high school and, when given the option to attend college, Kendra declined, choosing instead to continue working by Kevin's side learning about shrimping. She knew he was pleased that she wanted to remain with him to learn and eventually take over the business. He often told her he felt selfish for denying her the college experience, and the chance to enjoy her youth. Then she would remind him of her love for fishing and that she was where she wanted to be.

Chapter Two

Kendra always set her alarm clock, but as usual, her internal clock woke her five minutes before the alarm would sound at five. Years of waking before the sun rose had tuned her body for the early morning hours. Climbing from her bed, Kendra was eager to start her day. She looked forward to spending her Saturday morning alone on the boat, and then the rest of her weekend relaxing with her dad until their guest arrived.

After a hot shower, she dressed in cut-off blue-jean shorts, tank top, and her favorite pair of tennis shoes, before heading downstairs. She could smell the coffee brewing as she left her room and heard her dad puttering around the kitchen. Even in retirement, Kevin too was an early riser.

Kendra entered their small kitchen. "Good morning, Dad."

"Good morning. Pour a cup of coffee and have a seat. I'm cooking a full breakfast for us this morning."

"Need some help?"

"Nope, I've got this."

Kendra poured coffee, then stirred creamer into her favorite mug, and took a seat at the edge of the kitchen bar counter. She watched her dad place bacon on to fry and then reach for a carton of eggs.

"Fried or scrambled?"

"Fried sounds good."

"Grits or potatoes?"

"Thanks, but I'll pass on both and just have some toast. I want to get down to the harbor early this morning."

"Big plans for today?"

"Just some deeper cleaning. The boys are good on deck, but not so good in the galley or bunks. I want to take inventory of linens and supplies since we will be going out to deeper waters."

"Are you all set to have the freezer compartments installed next week?"

"Yes. I thought I'd surprise the crew with a long weekend and have them installed Friday. That way we can ensure everything's working properly before we head out for reds."

"That's a good decision."

Kendra sipped her coffee and browsed through the morning paper, paying close attention to the weather forecast. "Looks like we'll have fair weather next week."

"Perfect for shrimping," he said, with a lopsided grin.

Kevin finished cooking and brought plates of food to the table. She refreshed her coffee and poured one for her dad, before settling in beside him for the meal.

"Hey, Dad, are you planning on Lindsey staying here with us?"

"Yes, if you're okay with that. I thought she could use the guest room across from yours. She won't be on land long enough to justify renting an apartment, so I thought I'd charge her a small fee and let her stay with us."

"That makes good sense."

"Her dad says she's not big, but she's a scrapper," he added.

"You say the same about me, and I reckon I turned out fine."

"That you did. I couldn't be more proud of you."

"Thanks Dad. I hope she'll turn out fine too."

Kendra used the slice of toast to sop the egg yolk on her plate. "You sure I can't convince you to cook for us while we're out shrimping?"

"We'll see how things go, and if you think you really need me, I will. Otherwise, I'm thinking of taking up golf."

"I think that'd be great, Dad." She smiled as she slid back from her plate.

"I can see how you are anxious to go, so go, and I'll clean the kitchen. Is spaghetti good for supper?"

"Sounds great, Dad." Rising from her chair, she leaned over to kiss his cheek. "Call me if you need me to bring anything home."

"I will, honey, have a good day."

†

The sky was beginning to lighten as she walked the short distance to the harbor. Their boat, *Heaven Sent,* bobbed rhythmically in the water, the first sun rays gleaming on the freshly waxed hull. Her dad had taught her from an early age to take pride in their boat and to keep the equipment clean and in good repair at all times.

Storage compartments held the neatly folded nets, tucked safely beside the doors used to hold the nets open when in use. Kendra had purchased a spare set of larger nets for use with the reds, which were stored below deck. She had also purchased a heavier duty winch to install along with the freezer units, to handle the weight of the larger net capacity. The old winch, which had been adequate for years but could not haul the weight volume of the new nets when full, would be stored on board as a backup if needed.

Kendra had spent hours reviewing equipment and making plans to fish for reds, and she felt she was as ready as she could be. In anticipation for making their first run, she had ordered food and other supplies to be stored on board next weekend.

She stepped on board and unlocked the wheelhouse as the sun gleamed off the fresh paint. She loaded the stereo system with music and began cleaning the wheelhouse.

After several hours of cleaning, the wheelhouse and galley were sparkling. Kendra made notes of the first aid supplies and lighting she needed to add to her shopping list. The bunks were now equipped with satellite television, internet, and telephone service, so the crew could relax in comfort after long days at sea, and stay in contact with home.

She was washing the outside windows of the wheelhouse, but it was singing along with Jimmy Buffet that made her oblivious to the soft purr of a motorcycle filling the air.

†

Lindsey Bowen had ridden all night to reach the Gulf Coast. She and her father had visited once when she was a child, but her memory failed to remind her just how beautiful Northwest Florida was. The sun shone off the sugar-white sands of the beach and the water, the most beautiful emerald green she had ever seen. Very different from the deep blue of the Atlantic she was accustomed to seeing.

She parked her bike along the sidewalk next to the pier, the heated engine ticking from the long hours of riding. Lindsey pulled off her helmet and stepped off the bike. She heard music floating across the air and could not prevent the smile from growing on her face as she watched a woman washing the windows of the wheelhouse. The smile grew broader as she looked at the name of the boat. *Heaven Sent.* Her father had told her the name of the boat and she was delighted to see the gorgeous woman working on deck. The faded denim of the shorts, gave way to long tan legs, which seemed to go on forever as the woman continued working, unaware of her arrival.

She stretched her sore muscles and placed her helmet on the bike seat before striding toward the boat, her eyes never leaving the woman onboard. She stopped at the gangplank and waited for the woman to give her permission to come aboard.

Lindsey watched as the woman turned back toward the pier to find her standing there watching her closely. Clad in worn blue jeans, faded to show their age and thinning fabric, Lindsey sported a bandana tied around her head. She watched her glimpse toward the parking lot where the only vehicle was a sleek, black motorcycle. When her eyes trailed back to her, Lindsey smiled and cleared her throat.

"Captain Drake, I presume."

"That would be me."

"Permission to come on board, ma'am?"

"Granted and welcome aboard. Are you, Lindsey?" The woman was gazing at her with brilliant green eyes, the color of the Gulf water.

"Yes ma'am, I am," she replied with a quick smile. *Damn those eyes are gorgeous.*

"I'm Kendra." She walked toward her and reached out her hand. "Welcome aboard. I wasn't sure when you'd arrive."

"I decided to drive through the night. There's less traffic to deal with, and a cool breeze."

"You must be tired. Would you care for a cup of coffee?"

"I'd love one." Lindsey smiled.

The captain led her into the galley. "Have a seat and I'll put a pot on. What do you take in your coffee?"

"Just some cream, please."

Kendra walked to the counter to start the coffee maker, and when she turned back to the table, the woman had removed the bandana to reveal disheveled blond hair. A few freckles were dotted on her cheeks and her blue eyes sparkled when they met hers.

"So my dad says you want to work on my crew this summer." She leaned back against the counter, awaiting an answer.

"Yeah, I would really like to. I have experience working with my father. I was on his boat every chance I got. He's hoping I'll follow in his footsteps now that I have a captain's license so I can take over the family business when he retires in a few years."

Kendra was surprised by the deep voice and rich southern accent. "That sounds like a good plan." The coffee pot gurgled as the water finished running through the filter. Kendra turned around to pour two cups, stirring creamer into both, and carried them to the table.

"Thanks." Lindsey took the offered cup and moaned after she took a sip. "Pure heaven." She grinned.

"Nothing like a fresh cup of coffee," Kendra added.

"Dad thought it would be good for me to work for you this summer. He felt that I could learn much from you about leading a crew of men, but that's not the entire story."

"I know there was some issue, but I don't know any details. Dad left those up to you to share if you thought they were important."

Lindsey took another sip of coffee and set the cup on the table. "My dad thought it might be good for me to get out of town for a few months to let a situation calm down a bit."

Kendra could see the blush rising on the young woman's cheeks.

"I have to be honest with you and I'll understand if you don't want to take a chance with me. I was caught in a rather embarrassing position with the wife of a local preacher."

Unfortunately, Kendra had just taken a sip of coffee and the candor from the young woman caught her by surprise, sending the hot liquid down her windpipe. She broke into a fit of coughing, as she tried to clear her throat.

A distraught looking Lindsey tried to pat her on her back. "I'm sorry I didn't mean to make you choke."

Kendra raised her hand, her cheeks flushed red as she struggled to breathe. "It's okay," she finally managed to croak.

Several tense seconds passed before she could regain her composure. She eyed the coffee, fearful of taking another sip just yet.

Lindsey sat there.

"Sorry about that. You just caught me off guard."

"No need to apologize, I shouldn't have blurted it out like that."

"I appreciate your honesty."

Lindsey took a deep breath that she slowly released. "So, yes I'm a lesbian, and I fell for the flirtation of a married woman. Not my best decision ever, but I found out too late that she was just using me to get back at her husband. He came home early one day, and caught us together. As you can imagine, it wasn't pretty. Dad thought it best for me to leave to prevent a public scandal or lynching. I didn't waste any time disagreeing with him. When he called your dad and found out you might need an extra deckhand, I packed a bag and left town."

Kendra took a sip of coffee as she carefully selected her response. "I don't have any issue with your sexuality, but you'll have to prove yourself to the crew next week before I decide if you can join us. We've just received our license to fish for reds, so the money will be good if you work out."

Lindsey raised her head. Kendra noted the sparkle had returned to her eyes as she spoke. "I'll work my ass off for you given the chance."

"That's all I ask from any of my crew. My men are hard workers and won't cut you any slack because you're a cute female."

"I don't expect to be treated any different. Dad will tell you I can outwork most men."

"You'll be bunking with four men. Will that be an issue?"

"Not for me."

"I guess you have a try-out then. Do you have any questions?"

"When do we start?" she asked.

"We have one week to fish for browns and then we'll make our first trip for reds the following Monday."

"That sounds good to me. Can you point me in the direction of a boarding house or motel?"

Kendra chuckled for the first time since the woman came on board. "It's called the Drake Inn, straight up the street and second house on the right. Dad and I have agreed you won't be on land enough to justify an apartment, so he's going to hit you with a ridiculously low rent, and feed you like you've probably haven't eaten in a while."

"Are you okay with that?"

"Yes, I am. Dad and I discuss every decision when it comes to business. Go meet him for yourself and let him know I'll be home in a couple of hours."

Lindsey stood abruptly and reached out her hand. "Thank you, I promise I won't let you down. Is there anything I can help you with?"

"Thanks, but I've just got a few other things to handle. Go relax and take a nap if you want. You've got to be tired from the ride."

"I think I've gotten a second wind." Lindsey smiled.

"Fine then, you can finish washing those windows while I do some paperwork."

"Yes, ma'am." Lindsey grinned and left the galley.

Kendra watched her leave, admiring the view from the back side. "This ought to prove to be interesting," she said to the empty galley. She poured another cup of coffee, turned off the pot and walked to the wheelhouse. Her eyes kept drifting out the window as she felt her face smiling. *She's cute and not afraid of work.*

Kendra couldn't deny the young woman was very handsome but, on the verge of starting a season of fishing for reds, she couldn't afford to be distracted. Lindsey reached high to clean the top of the window and her shirt pulled free from her jeans to reveal an abdomen rippled with muscle. Kendra moaned as her eyes fell on the edge of a tattoo. *Good Lord, please stop tempting me.*

She softly chuckled and forced her eyes back to the computer screen. It had been two years since her failed relationship with Jude, and Kendra had buried her heartbreak deep in hard work. Her dad, always accepting of his daughter's sexuality and concerned with her lack of a social life, had encouraged her to date, but Kendra wasn't ready for more heartache. Her career was top priority and she doubted any woman would play second fiddle to a shrimp boat, even a very successful one.

As she washed the wheelhouse windows, Lindsey could see the captain tapping away at the computer. *Easy on the eyes and she has her act together.* She grinned as she sprayed cleaner on the glass. *She's exactly who I need to be learning from.* The cries of gulls drew her attention from the wheelhouse as they trailed a shrimper begging for a handout. She felt the smile grow on her face as they dove to retrieve scraps tossed overboard by the deckhands. *Life appears good here, and if I can stay out of trouble, this could be a good place for me to weather the storm.*

Lindsey finished with the windows and carried the spray bottle and rags into the wheelhouse. "The windows are clean, boss. What else can I do?"

"Store the cleaning stuff in the closet in the galley. I'm almost done here and I'll drop off a supply list at a local vendor and head for home."

"May I offer you a ride? I didn't see another vehicle in the lot."

"Thanks, but the shop is just a few blocks away."

"Would you mind if I walk with you then?"

"Not at all. Just let me print out this list and I'll be ready."

Lindsey walked into the galley to put away the cleaning supplies. When she returned to the wheelhouse, she asked, "Do we take turns cooking?"

"I haven't given much thought to that yet. I guess I should. I assumed I would do most of the cooking."

"I've cooked for Dad's crew for years. No one has abandoned ship or thrown me overboard, so I must be a pretty fair cook."

"You're pretty sure you'll make the cut."

"Or die trying." Lindsey grinned. "I know shrimping and I haven't killed anyone yet with my cooking. How can you resist that combination?"

Kendra chuckled. "We'll see how that goes next week, rookie," she replied as they walked from the wheelhouse. She locked the door behind her, then turned back to face Lindsey. "Let's go."

"Just waiting on you, boss." Lindsey grinned.

†

They walked the short distance to the general store, just a few blocks off the harbor, and Kendra dropped off her list of supplies with a request for delivery on Friday. Lindsey noticed that the shopkeeper seemed to be eyeing her closely.

"Hank, this is Lindsey, our new deckhand," Kendra said.

Lindsey stepped forward, her chest puffed out, and shook his hand. "Pleased to meet you, sir." The fact that the captain had just introduced her as the new deckhand didn't escape her, leaving her grinning at the man.

The older man chuckled. "Hank will do just fine. Welcome to Perdido."

"Thanks. I like what I've seen so far."

"I hope you're prepared for hard work. Captain Drake's a tyrant," he warned, and shot Kendra a wink.

"Now, Hank, don't go scaring off my help. We're going to be fishing for reds soon and I need good help."

"So I heard. Congrats. I hope you'll put a few batches back for me."

"I think I can fill that order." Kendra smiled. "I'll be by after the delivery Friday to pay the bill."

"See you then," Hank called. "Tell that old man of yours to stop in and see me."

"Will do. He's talking about taking up golf." Kendra grinned.

"That should be interesting," Hank added with a wave.

"Your dad's going to start playing golf?" Lindsey asked.

"That's what he claims. I think that just may be an excuse to drink beer."

"That sounds familiar," Lindsey remarked as they walked back to the boat.

When they reached Lindsey's bike, she again offered Kendra a ride.

"Thanks, but I'll pass. It's just a short walk."

"I'll see you there then." Lindsey pulled the helmet over her head and mounted the bike.

Chapter Three

"My goodness, you look like a miniature version of Paul," Kevin said when Kendra introduced him to Lindsey.

"He can't deny I'm his," she joked back.

"He was a few inches taller and about thirty pounds bigger than you when we first met in boot camp."

"He's only got about fifty pounds on me now," Lindsey answered. "He's stayed pretty lean."

"Hard work will do that for you." He eyed the green duffle bag sitting beside her. "Is that all the luggage you have?"

"I'm on a motorcycle, so I had to travel light. I figured if you decide to keep me on, I can always buy a few things."

He looked at Kendra. "Would you get her settled in the guest room upstairs and show her around?"

"Sure thing, Dad," she replied. "Let's go, rookie."

Kevin smiled as he watched the two young women climb the stairs chatting animatedly. It appeared that they were getting along pretty well which was a good sign of things to come.

†

"Come on, I'll give you a tour of the upstairs and you can unpack. After that you can join us for a cold drink." Kendra led her to the guest room.

"I'll be down in just a few then. Thanks for everything."

"You're welcome," Kendra replied and walked downstairs.

Kevin was puttering around the kitchen adding ingredients to his spaghetti sauce. "So what do you think?" he asked when she walked into the kitchen alone.

"She seems nice enough and is confident she will work her way onto the boat next week. With her experience, I doubt she will have any problems. I just hope she doesn't let her personal drama affect her work."

"Did she share her story with you?"

"Yeah she did. Sounds like the woman really screwed her over."

"I think you'll be a good influence on her," he added.

"Do ya now?"

"Yes, I do. You're in a position of authority, a hard worker, and a fair boss. You know what kind of worker a woman can be, where most captains wouldn't consider giving her a chance."

"That's true. She doesn't seem to shy away from work, so hopefully things will work out. Do you need any help with dinner?"

"Nope, I've got the sauce on simmering and was just about to crack open a couple of cold beers."

"I'm going to take a shower and freshen up then. Lindsey will be down once she gets settled into her room."

✝

Kendra stripped out of her clothes and walked into the bathroom to start the shower. She had managed to get everything done that morning that she had planned and would have Sunday to rest for the coming week. Maybe she would even see if her dad wanted to go fishing.

The water pelted off her skin as she leaned under the flow, relaxing her muscles. It had been a long, but productive week. The season had been a busy one so far and, if they had a good red season, she was thinking about giving the crew a couple of months off. They normally took December off and she could give them

January as well before going full strength again in February. That would allow *Heaven Sent* to go into dry dock for a fresh coat of paint and general maintenance before opening for the next season. Maybe, just maybe, she and her dad could take an overdue vacation. She smiled at that thought. Her dad had barely left Perdido in the last five years. Still, she could hope.

†

Lindsey heard the water running in the shower and a smile broke out on her face. "Stop it," she spoke to herself as she visualized Kendra in the shower. *I really can't screw this up.* She hung up the last pair of jeans and left the room. Maybe some distance would help take her mind off the wet, naked body of the woman who would be her boss for the next few months. *Yeah some distance, and a few of those cold beers Kendra had promised her.*

She headed down the stairs and went outside to where Kevin was.

"Make yourself at home and grab a cold beer from the fridge," Kevin offered when she emerged on the back porch.

"Thanks, can I bring you a fresh one?"

He raised the bottle and turned to her. "Sure, why not," he grinned.

When she returned with the beers, she handed him a new one.

"Thanks. Did you call your dad to let him know you arrived safely?"

"Not yet. I'll call him later. I sort of promised him I'd get a hotel last night and drive in later today. If I call now, he'll be suspicious."

"You drove all night to get here?"

"Yeah, the traffic was light and the weather was great." Lindsey smiled at him.

"I can't get over how much you look like Paul. You even have your dad's lopsided grin."

"I'm sure he would say the same if he saw you and Captain Drake together."

"I reckon we're two peas in a pod, too. How is your dad?"

"He's doing well. In spite of last year's storms, we had a good season."

"You had more than your fair share of storms last year. I hope we all get a break this year."

"Me too. I finally convinced him to let me ride out the last tropical storm with him on the boat. It was good experience, but nothing I'm in a hurry to do again."

"They're never fun, but it's safer to have the boats in open water."

"That's what Dad thinks too. He's seen too many vessels crushed against the piers or washed up on jetties."

"I'd take my chances on open water anytime." Kevin took a long drink.

†

Kendra dressed and stopped at the fridge to grab a beer before heading out to the porch to join her dad and Lindsey. She closed the door and a photograph caught her eye. She smiled at the image of her with her dad on the beach last summer. They had done some surf fishing and he had landed a large trout. She had asked someone to take the picture with her smart phone, and had the photograph printed, and he placed it on the refrigerator. The smile he wore was one of the most cherished memories of that day.

Lindsey was laughing when Kendra stepped out the door leading to the porch. The sound of her laughter was rich and much deeper than Kendra expected from the petite woman.

"Is Dad entertaining you with his humor?"

Lindsey wiped a tear from her eye. "He was just telling me about some of the antics he and my dad had shared when they were in Vietnam."

"I can only imagine what they got into together." Kendra slipped into her favorite rocking chair.

"We were scared as hell most of the time, but we found ways to keep our minds off the fighting, when we weren't knee deep in some river or belly-crawling through the jungle."

"I can't imagine what it was like being in the war. Dad doesn't talk about it much."

Kendra watched a change come over her father's face. The smile from his laughter faded and the wrinkles formed a scowl. She figured his thoughts had drifted back to the jungle.

"We saw a lot of bad shit go down, and most of it we try our damnedest to forget. Even the darkness didn't bring much respite from the constant fear of sniper fire or ambushes. Many of us drowned our thoughts in drugs or alcohol, but it was only temporary relief." She watched as he shook his head, and returned the memory to the back of his mind. "That was long ago in a land far away from here."

Lindsey seemed to sense he needed a diversion. "Your dad told me you might show me around town in the morning."

"That will take about thirty minutes," Kendra joked. "We can take a quick spin and then I thought maybe we could take the boat out for some fishing, if Dad's up for it. What do you say old man? Ten dollars for the biggest fish?"

"Make it twenty and you have a deal," he challenged, the bright smile returning to his face. He turned to Lindsey and asked, "You in?"

"You bet I am. I have to warn you though, fish fear me," she declared, her face deadpan serious.

"Oh you two are so going to owe me money tomorrow," Kendra promised.

"We'll see about that." Kevin chuckled. "I'm going to finish up dinner while you two figure out how you're going to pay up tomorrow." He grinned and walked inside the house.

"I love how the two of you interact," Lindsey commented. "Has it always been the two of you?"

"Pretty much. Mother walked out on us when I was twelve."

"That had to be hard on you."

"It was hard on both of us at first, but then we grew even closer, and with time we realized life would go on and we'd make each other happy."

"We lost mom two years ago to a massive stroke."

Kendra watched the pain fill Lindsey's face.

"I'm sorry for your loss."

"It hurt at first, but eventually the pain began to fade. We worked harder and longer hours, so by the time we got home, we were too exhausted to think about anything but food, a hot shower, and a comfortable bed."

A comfortable silence fell between them. The soft creaking of the cane bottom rocking chair filled the silence, relaxing Kendra until she felt her eyes grow heavy. "I'm going inside to check on Dad. Do you want another beer?"

"Thanks, but I'm good for now. I'm going to call Dad to let him know I arrived okay."

"I'll give you a few minutes of privacy then." Kendra nodded and went into the house. As she opened the door, she turned and watched as Lindsey pulled out her cell phone and stepped out into the yard, walking toward an old twisted oak.

"How's it coming in here?" Kendra asked when she stepped into the kitchen.

"The sauce is mighty tasty and I just put the bread in the oven. As soon as the noodles are ready, we can eat. I've got a cold salad in the fridge,"

"Do you want me to go ahead and set the table?"

"I'm a step ahead of you." He grinned nodding toward the table.

"That's nothing new." She walked to the sink and poured the last bit of warm beer down the drain. She looked out the window and saw Lindsey walking across the yard as she spoke to her dad. Kendra smiled as she watched Lindsey pace back and forth.

Kevin looked at his daughter when she stopped talking and glanced out the window to see what she was watching. He could feel the chemistry building between the two, even if they were still unaware of the growing attraction. Some fathers would be disturbed about their daughters being a lesbian, but he had always known that Kendra was different and would never be satisfied with a man. He was disappointed she would never be a mother, and he a grandfather, but his brother had several sons and grandsons to carry on the family name. All he wanted was to see her happy.

"You two seem to be hitting it off well."

Kendra jumped at the sound of his voice. She had been watching Lindsey more intently than she realized. When he spoke, his voice startled her. She battled to keep the flush from rising to her cheeks.

"She seems eager to learn and doesn't appear to shy away from work. I tried to send her up here earlier for a nap when I found she had driven all night, but she insisted on helping clean the boat." Kendra felt a smile forming on her lips as her thoughts returned to the T-shirt creeping up Lindsey's stomach as she stretched to wash the top of the windows.

"I would think it'd be nice for you to have another woman on the boat."

"I have to agree with you there. The men are great, but when it comes to cooking and cleaning, they sometimes fall short. Lindsey says she loves to cook, so that in itself will be a great help."

The timer on the oven sounded, and when Kevin turned to retrieve the garlic bread, Kendra glanced back out the kitchen window to find Lindsey walking toward the house. Even though she was slightly shorter than Kendra, the confident way Lindsey walked was really attractive. *I could definitely get used to watching her move.* Kendra watched closely as Lindsey stepped onto the back porch.

"Will you bring the salad from the fridge?" Kevin asked.

Kendra was so lost in her thoughts that she didn't acknowledge that she had heard him speak.

"Earth to Kendra."

"I'm sorry, Dad, did you say something?" Kendra was unable to hide her blush at being caught gawking at Lindsey, especially with the knowing smile her dad sported.

"Yes, darling. I asked if you'd bring the salad to the table."

"Sure thing, Dad." She rushed over to the fridge.

"Man, it sure smells good in here," Lindsey announced when she walked in.

Kevin beamed at her. "Come take a seat and we'll eat in just a few. What can I get you to drink? There's more beer, or if you'd like, I have a pitcher of sweet tea."

"Tea sounds great."

"You want some too, Dad?" Kendra asked.

"Please."

Kendra filled three glasses with iced tea and carried them to the table. "This looks great, Dad."

"Just a simple meal," he answered.

"Those are usually the best." Lindsey reached for the honey mustard dressing at the same time as Kendra.

When their hands met, Kendra smiled. "Go ahead, just save me some."

"Aye, aye, Captain."

Kendra took a piece of garlic bread and handed the plate to her dad.

"How's the fishing going for your dad?" he asked.

"He's been raking in the whites and rock shrimp. The water warmed quicker than usual this year."

"That's not a good sign," Kevin warned.

"Especially with hurricane season just a few weeks away," Lindsey agreed.

"Hopefully we'll be blessed with decent weather for the summer," Kendra said. "I'd love to get a full season of reds in."

"We can only hope, and pray," Kevin said.

Kendra cleaned the kitchen while her dad and Lindsey drank coffee at the table.

"Do you ladies have plans for the evening?" he asked.

"Not really, Dad. What did you have in mind?"

"I bought some fresh turkey necks at the market this morning. Those blue crabs you brought home last night were good, so I thought I'd go down to the docks and catch another batch to accompany the huge fish I'm going to reel in tomorrow."

"You're sounding pretty confident," Kendra said.

"I've no doubt that between the three of us tomorrow we'll catch a nice fish or two for dinner."

Kendra looked at Lindsey. "Are you exhausted yet?"

"Nope, I'm good. I haven't been crabbing in ages."

Kendra grinned at her dad. "It looks like we're going crabbing with you then. I'll do the netting, and you two can bring them up to the dock."

"Deal, I'll grab the lines and net, if you two will bring those buckets from the back porch and the turkey necks from the fridge."

"Let's do this. I'll get the buckets and meet y'all out front." Lindsey got up to leave.

†

The sun was well on its way to the horizon when the group met in the front yard. Kevin had a smile plastered across his face from ear to ear. Kendra loved seeing him so happy and her worries about his being bored with retirement were fading away.

Kendra slipped a flashlight into her back pocket and wrapped an arm around his shoulders as they walked down to the docks. Moored at the dock, *Heaven Sent* sat high in the water as soft waves lapped up against her hull in a relaxing rhythm.

Kendra extended the telescoping handle on the net and peered over the edge of the dock. She could see several large crabs scavenging around the pier posts. Deciding to get a jump on the harvest while her dad and Lindsey were preparing their lines, she knelt on the weathered wood and eased her net into the calm water. As she positioned the net behind a large crab she held her breath and then quickly scooped him into the net.

"Got ya." She lifted the net from the water. "I'm one up on y'all already," she called out as she lowered the net into a five-gallon bucket and shook the crab free from the webbing.

Kevin laughed. "She thinks she's gonna outdo us, but we have the ammunition," he grinned as he spoke. "Let's show her how it's done while she scoops up what she can around the posts."

"Bring 'em on," Kendra crowed, dipping her net into the water as she went for a second crab.

"Better get that net ready, Kendra." Kevin grinned and swung a turkey neck, sending it sailing across the water. He overturned a bucket, sat, and waited.

Lindsey moved a few feet away from him and mimicked his movements. The scent of the turkey necks would spread quickly through the warm water, and the crabs could not resist the lure of an easy meal.

Kendra netted two more crabs while she waited for crabs to approach the turkey necks. The light was quickly fading, but the darkness wouldn't stop them. The crabs would tug at their lines as they pinched tiny bits of flesh from the bait. When they felt the first tug, her dad and Lindsey would begin retracting their lines, drawing the crab toward the pier. She lowered her net into the water, and waited patiently for them to lure the crabs into her net. Kendra glanced down the pier at Lindsey who was concentrating intensely on her line. Her facial expressions led Kendra to believe she had a nibbler.

She watched as Lindsey slowly retracted her line. The lights from the pier illuminated the sandy bottom about ten feet out from the pier. Lindsey turned toward her when the crab came into view to make sure Kendra was ready with the net. Kendra walked next to her and extended the net in the direction of the crab. "Bring him on in," she whispered.

Kevin watched the two women as they worked together. Kendra was slightly taller, but Lindsey was just as lean and muscled as his daughter from hard days of working on a shrimp boat for most of her life. Both women were staring intently into the water as they followed the rapid approach of the hungry crab. He watched as Kendra scooped the crab in the net with a cry of excitement, and then he turned back to the tugging he felt on his line.

Kevin followed her movement as Kendra emptied the crab into the bucket while Lindsey cast out again. He returned his eyes to the line he was slowly bringing in.

"You got one on the way, Dad?" Kendra asked.

"Yep, so come on down so you can scoop him up."

Kendra lowered the net into the water as she walked toward her dad. They had caught crabs together ever since she could remember. Sure, it was easier when they were caught in the shrimp nets, but it was so much more fun and sporting to catch them together. She couldn't count the nights they had spent together, sitting side by side, as one would tease the crab close and the other would scoop them into a net. Some of their most important discussions had been made while they crabbed for dinner, the last being Kevin's decision to retire. He had been dropping hints for several months, but her heart still raced in her chest when he slipped an arm around her shoulders.

"The time has come for you to take the helm. You've worked hard and I've nothing left to teach you."

She remembered the tears in her eyes when she looked up at him and nodded. "I know I'm ready, but I don't want you to stop fishing with me."

"I'll still come aboard now and then, but she's all yours now. You've earned the right to be her captain."

"Are you going to get him or do I need to?" Kevin asked her now.

"Sorry, Dad, I was out there for a second," she carefully netted the crab.

"I noticed." He grinned. "Everything all right?"

"Yeah, just reliving a memory," she answered, and then lifted the net and carried the crab to the bucket.

For the next two hours, she moved between Lindsey and her dad, plucking the crabs they lured from the water until they had two of the large buckets full of crab.

"This should be plenty to accompany the fish and some hushpuppies," Kevin finally stated.

"I'll make some slaw to go along with them, too, if you'd like," Lindsey offered.

"That sounds good, but you'll have to stop at the market for cabbage during your tour," he told them.

"Not a problem, Dad," Kendra replied. "If you'll get the lines and net, we can carry the buckets."

"That's fine. Place them in the wet well to keep them fresh. We can clean them when we get back in tomorrow." Kevin tossed the extra turkey necks into the water to feed the remaining crab.

✝

The walk home was decidedly slower than the trip down and Kendra slowed her pace. She could see her dad's joints had stiffened while they were crabbing and she could tell he was in pain as they walked the short distance. When they reached the house, his limp was very evident.

"Let me have the net and lines and we'll meet you inside in a few."

Without giving him a chance to argue, she pushed him towards the door. She took the gear and watched him limp painfully up the walk before walking toward the garage.

"It's hard to see them slowing down, isn't it?" Lindsey asked.

"Yeah, he's always been my rock," Kendra answered, glad that Lindsey couldn't see the tears welling in her eyes.

"He will still be your rock. The pace will just be a little slower."

"I know, but I hate to see him in pain."

Lindsey placed a hand on Kendra's shoulder. "We'll just have to remind him to move around a bit more, so he doesn't stiffen up."

Comforted by the warmth of the hand on her shoulder, Kendra knew that Lindsey was probably experiencing the same thing with her father. "Time doesn't stop for any of us, does it?"

"Unfortunately no, we just have to make the best of what we have."

"Amen to that," Kendra said.

☦

They dumped the crab into the wet well, and then Kendra stored the gear as Lindsey rinsed out the buckets before turning them upside down to dry.

"Do you think you can sleep yet?"

"Like a rock. The day has finally caught up to me," Lindsey admitted as they walked to the house.

"There's no need to be up at the crack of dawn, so sleep in if you want to."

Lindsey chuckled. "I've forgotten how to do that."

"I understand that completely. Maybe I can get up before dad and cook breakfast for everyone. Do you like pancakes?"

"Is the Pope Catholic?"

"I'll take that as a yes." Kendra grinned as she held the door open for her. "You can hit the shower first and I'll rinse off after. Do you need anything?"

"Thanks, but I think I'm good."

☦

Kevin was in the kitchen preparing the coffee pot for the next morning.

"I've decided I'm cooking pancakes and bacon for breakfast in the morning, so don't jump up and start cooking, okay?"

"I won't be jumping up period. You may have to come pry me out of the bed," he warned.

"I'll believe that when I see it," Kendra replied.

"I'll see you in the morning," Lindsey told them and left the kitchen.

"Do you need some Ibuprofen, Dad?"

"I took two when I came in. I forget how fast these old joints stiffen up."

31

"I've been thinking about you taking up golf and I think it's a good idea. It might even help to limber your joints a bit."

"I'm thinking so, too." He replaced the lid on the coffee canister. "I'll look into buying some clubs this week."

"Awesome." Kendra leaned forward to kiss his cheek. "I love you, Dad."

"I love you too, baby girl. Thanks for crabbing with me tonight."

"I love it when we go crabbing."

They walked from the kitchen together and she hugged him before climbing the stairs. "See you in the morning, Dad."

"Sleep well," he replied and walked down the hall to his room.

Kendra started up the stairs and heard the shower running. She smiled to herself. *It is going to be nice having another woman in the house.* She pushed the door open to her room and pulled off her shoes. *No more running around up here naked though,* she reminded herself with a grin.

Chapter Four

Kendra woke with a start from a dream, her heart racing as she struggled to remember what she was dreaming. She sat up in the bed and brushed the hair from her eyes. The night was fading as she looked at her clock. It was nearly six, almost an hour later than she normally slept. *That must have been some dream to shut off my internal clock.*

She climbed from the bed and pulled on a pair of jeans and T-shirt before stepping into the bathroom to wash her face and brush her teeth.

When she emerged from the bathroom, she could hear movement downstairs and the aroma of bacon met her on the stairs. She wondered if her dad had awoken early and gotten hungry. She was surprised to see Lindsey standing at the stove, coffee mug in hand cooking bacon.

Lindsey turned her head, looked at Kendra with an amused smile, and arched her brow. "Good morning, I hope I didn't wake you."

"You didn't. I think I must have been dreaming about pancakes."

"I hope you don't mind me getting a head start on breakfast. I woke up and couldn't just stay in bed, so I thought I'd cook the bacon."

"That's fine with me. Do you need more coffee?"

"Yes, please." Lindsey handed Kendra her mug.

"Has Dad made an appearance yet?"

"I haven't seen him, but I heard a toilet flushing a few minutes ago."

"That may have been me." Kendra poured the coffee.

She handed Lindsey the mug and then walked to the pantry to gather ingredients to whip up pancake batter. "Do you like pecans?"

"I love them."

"Good, I'm feeling a little nutty this morning."

Lindsey chuckled at her comment. "I like nutty." Sparkling blue eyes turned in her direction.

Kendra felt her heart skip a beat from the intensity of Lindsey's eyes. She quickly averted her gaze, focusing on the contents of the pantry to give her time to collect her composure. She turned when she heard footsteps.

"I thought I smelled bacon," Kevin announced as he entered the kitchen. "Good morning, ladies."

"Good morning, Dad."

"Good morning, Captain Drake."

"I hope everyone slept as well as I did."

"I don't think I moved all night," Lindsey answered.

"Me either, until my stomach woke up growling," Kevin said with a smirk.

"Grab some coffee and have a seat. As soon as Lindsey finishes the bacon, I'll start on the pancakes." Kendra opened the fridge and took out a bottle of syrup, and placed it on the counter while she filled a pot halfway with water.

"I appreciate a cook that heats the syrup," Lindsey said.

Kendra placed the pot on a burner, and put the syrup in the pot, rewarding Lindsey with a smile. "You okay with pecans, Dad, or would you prefer blueberries?"

"Pecans sound great. Do you need me to chop them?"

"I've got this, Dad. You just sit and enjoy your coffee."

After finishing off a large platter of pancakes and bacon, the three of them worked together to clean the kitchen.

"I'll scoop out some baitfish while you two are out and meet you down at the boat," Kevin suggested as he emptied his mug into the sink.

"Is there anything else we need from the store?" Kendra asked.

"I think we're good on everything else," he answered. "Nature calls." He grinned and left the kitchen.

"I need to brush my teeth and then I'll be ready to go. I'll meet you in the driveway." Kendra nodded at Lindsey before climbing the stairs.

†

Kendra rolled back the top on her Jeep before backing it out of the garage. Country music blared to life on her radio and she reached to turn it down. The morning was blossoming into a beautiful sunny day. *This will be perfect for fishing.*

Lindsey walked out and climbed into the passenger seat. "Nice. I've always wanted a Jeep."

"I love it and it's perfect for the weather here." Kendra backed down the drive. She glanced back at the house to see her dad at his bedroom window watching as they drove off.

Lindsey realized that Kendra hadn't exaggerated when she claimed the tour wouldn't take long. The small island town was beautiful, but other than some stunning homes, a few shops, and restaurants, there wasn't a lot to it. The coastline was dotted with pleasure boats, shrimp boats, and fishing trawlers. The beach sand reminded her of cane sugar, and the water was a deep emerald green.

"I can't believe how green the water is here," she told Kendra.

"It's really beautiful and the whiteness of the sand really sets it off."

"Nothing at all like I'm used to," Lindsey replied as she gazed across the water.

"This is pretty much the grand tour. If we need special items, Pensacola is to the east and Mobile is west." Kendra pulled into the parking lot at the local market.

"I'll run in and grab the cabbage unless you want to come in," Lindsey offered.

"Nope, I'm going to enjoy this morning as much as I can."

"Be right back."

Kendra laid her head back against the headrest, enjoying the feel of the sun on her face, until a familiar sultry voice interrupted her relaxing moment. "Who's the new hottie?"

"Good morning to you, too, Jude," Kendra groaned. Jude, her ex, was the last person she wanted to run into today, or any other day for that matter. She opened her eyes to see Jude standing beside the Jeep. Their breakup happened two years before, after she saw Jude and another woman making out in her car when Jude thought Kendra was out of town on business. That pain had left scars on her heart that Kendra felt she would carry to her grave. Jude had taken great pleasure in saying that she had been seeing the other woman for months.

"Not going to introduce us? You have to admit, she's hot whoever she is."

"Has Deidra already kicked you to the curb?" Kendra growled.

"Not at all, dearie, she's at home cooking some lunch. Don't tell me you're still bitter over our breakup?"

"Quite the opposite, I couldn't be more relieved that I don't have to come home to you anymore."

"Ouch, that hurts," Jude chuckled. "You don't seem to be doing too bad, if that's your new girlfriend."

"I'm doing just fine, thanks. Don't you need to do some shopping or something?"

"Why are you being such a bitch?"

"Do I need to remind you that you were the one having an affair while we were a couple? So, it's not so much me being a bitch, it's more that I really don't want to talk to you."

"No, darling, you don't. Deidra does a much better job of taking care of my needs," she said sneering.

"Well don't let me keep you from returning to your little lap dog and having your *needs* taken care of."

Lindsey emerged from the store to see a handsome woman standing beside the Jeep. She continued walking, and when she saw and heard them having a heated exchange, her pace picked up.

"Is everything okay here?" she asked Kendra when she arrived at the vehicle.

"Yes. Jude is just leaving."

Lindsey felt the tension between the two women. She placed the bags of groceries behind her seat. "Well, I'm ready when you are, darling. Let's go home," she purred, completely ignoring Jude standing there. She could see the muscles of Kendra's jaw twitching as she turned to look at her and smiled.

"See you, Jude," Kendra replied. She started the Jeep and pulled out of the parking spot.

"I hope you didn't mind me putting it on a little thick back there," Lindsey asked Kendra when she pulled to a stop before entering the highway.

Kendra chuckled. "You couldn't have played that more perfectly. I loved the look on Jude's face."

"An ex, I take it?"

"Yeah, my last bad mistake," Kendra growled. "I was busting my ass to make a life for us and she was sleeping around."

"Stupid woman," Lindsey spoke without thinking.

Kendra frowned and then smiled. "Yeah, you could say that."

"I'm sorry she treated you badly."

"You live and you learn I guess." Kendra pulled out onto the highway to head for home.

Whoa, she just admitted she's a lesbian, too. Damn, I knew I was right. Lindsey couldn't help but smile as her heart thumped in her chest.

Kendra waited in the Jeep while Lindsey took the groceries inside. She smiled as she thought about the look on Jude's face when Lindsey climbed into the Jeep. It had felt good to get a little revenge, even if Lindsey was only putting on a show for Jude's benefit. She was still smiling when Lindsey returned and climbed inside.

"Do I have something on my face?"

"No, I'm sorry. I was just remembering the look on Jude's face. Thanks for giving her a nice shock."

"My pleasure, ma'am." Lindsey grinned.

Kendra returned her smile and they drove to the harbor to start their fishing adventure.

✝

Kevin had been busy, setting up rods and reels and placing buckets of baitfish next to each rod.

"You want to take us out, Dad?" Kendra asked as she worked to untie the mooring lines.

"Don't mind if I do." He grinned.

Kendra and Lindsey secured the last of the mooring lines on board and then walked to the wheelhouse.

"All set, Dad."

"I thought we'd go out a few miles and see if we can find some grouper," he suggested.

"That sounds great to me," Kendra replied. "Find us some fish, Dad."

She and Lindsey left the wheelhouse and took seats along a workbench to gaze out into the beautiful morning. The cloudless sky was a deep blue and a flock of gulls chased a fishing boat off to the west, their calls screaming for a handout of scraps. Large brown pelicans dove for fish or bobbed along the surface as they digested their meals.

Yeah, this is my kind of heaven, Kendra thought as she glanced over to find Lindsey seemingly engrossed in the beauty of the day too. Her spikey blond hair blew softly in the breeze as the sun kissed her tanned face. *She looks at peace on the water.*

"Relaxing, isn't it?" she asked Lindsey.

"I can understand why you love it here. It's one of the most beautiful places I've ever seen."

"I can't imagine heaven will be any prettier." Kendra sighed.

"You might just be right," Lindsey agreed with a smile.

Kendra knew they had just cleared the no-wake zone when she felt the boat speed up and the powerful engines roar to life. Her dad had fished the area his entire life and she could tell he was taking them to one of his favorite spots, about two miles off shore.

Kendra watched as he reached over to turn on the fish finder. Seeing the smile he sported, she knew they'd be stopping soon. She had pulled her sunglasses down to cover her eyes. The glare of the sun bouncing of the water reflected into her green eyes painfully as she gazed across the horizon. When she felt her dad backing off the engine, she knew he had found an area for good fishing.

"I think Dad's on the spot," she told Lindsey. "He'll cut the engines in a minute. You ready to lose some money?" she challenged.

"We'll see about that." Lindsey grinned and dropped dark glasses over her beautiful blue eyes.

What a shame to hide those eyes, Kendra thought as she stood and stretched.

Kevin killed the engine and checked the fish finder once more before leaving the wheelhouse. The waters were calm, so he felt no need to drop an anchor to remain over the spot he hoped would be on top of good fishing.

He picked up his hat to cover his head and stepped on deck. "Let's bait them up."

"First things first, Dad." Kendra grinned, pulled a twenty from her pocket and handed it to him. "Ante up, folks."

Lindsey smiled as she reached into her pocket and handed Kevin a bill. "Can we trust him to keep my money safe until I win it back?"

Kevin pulled out a twenty of his own and handed it to Kendra. "Go pin it up on the board in the galley for safekeeping," he instructed.

"Be right back."

Kevin looked at Lindsey. "Pick your spot and let's get this party started."

Kevin had definitely hit the jackpot and it only took a few minutes for them to begin reeling in brown grouper. *If this keeps up, we will restock our freezer in no time,* Kendra thought as she felt the tug on her line.

They pulled in eight to ten pounders with growing frequency, and the well was filling fast. She was baiting her hook when she heard the squeal of strain coming from her dad's reel.

"You got a good one on the line, Dad?"

"It feels like it. This one's got a lot of fight in him."

"Bring him on in," she said just as Lindsey let out a holler. "Damn, I've got a fighter, too."

"I better get my line back in the water quick," Kendra said and dropped her line into the water.

She and Lindsey both landed fish nearing fifteen pounds, but her dad was still fighting the fish he had hooked. "You okay, Dad?"

Kevin wiped the sweat from his face. "Yeah, he's got a lot of fight in him. Just when I think I'm making headway, he makes a run and I lose ground."

"Our money may be in danger if he lands this beast," she hollered to Lindsey.

"Get him, Captain," Lindsey yelled back.

Kendra watched as the heavy-duty rod bowed with strain as Kevin reeled the line. *That must be a helluva fish.* She reeled in her line and walked over to her dad. The strain was evident on his face and the sweat was running down his cheeks like tears. "Do you need me to give you a break?"

"Maybe in a few if he doesn't wear down. I hope I can bring him in, but I definitely will need you to gaff him to get him onboard."

"I'll be ready," she replied, and walked over to the rack where the long-handled gaff was stored. She would use the hook to grab the fish under his gills to haul him on board. If the fish was giving her dad this much fight on the line, there would be no way that, unassisted, he would be able to lift him onto the deck.

After ten more minutes passed, he still hadn't landed the fish. Lindsey had reeled in her line and walked over to them. "He must be a monster."

"Do you think it could be a Goliath, Dad?"

"Not this close to shore, but he's big. You still want to fight him?"

"Oh, hell yeah." Kendra could see the exhaustion and relief in her dad's face as she took the rod he offered. "Lindsey, will you bring Dad a bottle of water from the galley?"

"Sure thing." Lindsey rushed across the deck, returning with three bottles of water.

"Damn, he's got a good pull," Kendra commented as she cranked the reel. She watched the grin on her dad's face grow as he watched her fight the fish.

Lindsey handed him a bottle of water.

"Thanks." He downed half the bottle. "Man, that's good."

Lindsey twisted the top off another bottle and held it to Kendra's lips. "I think you're going to need this."

She took a long drink and looked at Lindsey. "Thank you."

"Welcome, now get that monster on board."

Kendra battled the fish for another ten minutes before she felt him begin to tire and she began to reel him closer to the boat. The muscles in her arms were starting to burn from the exertion and she knew her dad had to be exhausted from the fight. She glanced over at him and saw the smile on his face as he saw the glimmer of the fish's scales flash in the sun as she pulled him from the deep water.

"He's a monster of a fish," he cried. "Lindsey, can you handle the gaff?"

41

"Yes, sir." She picked up the long pole.

Just when Kendra thought she had him beat, the fish attempted to dive for deeper waters again. Kendra held firm and was relieved when the fight left him. She began frantically cranking the reel to take up the slack. If she couldn't keep the line tight and the fish got a burst of energy, he could snap the line with a frenzied attempt at freedom.

"Hot damn," Kevin hollered when the fish rose to the surface. "You've got him now, Kendra. Think you'll be able to bring him aboard without losing him?"

"I'll get him as close as I can, but you'll have to gaff him so we can get him on board," she told Lindsey.

"I'll be ready, just say when."

"Dad, you'll need to take the line and keep him tight. I think it'll take both of us to get him on board."

"No problem." She could feel the trembling in his hands as he took the rod from her.

"Now, Lindsey," she instructed as she released the rod to her dad.

It took two attempts, but Lindsey finally hooked his gills. "Got him," she cried out in what sounded like relief.

"We're going to have to work together to bring him in, Lindsey."

"Let's do it."

Together they began to pull the gaff pole up, inch by painful inch, until he broke the surface completely. With a final burst of strength, they lifted him over the rail onto the deck.

"Damn, he's big." Kevin whooped excitedly.

Kendra was breathless as she looked up to him. "At least 50, but could be 60 pounds," she gasped.

"Do you have a fish scale on board?" Lindsey asked.

"Yes, you two catch your breath and I'll go get it."

Kendra leaned back against the rail. "I can't believe he fought him that long. That fish is a monster." She grinned.

"We've definitely lost our money on this one, but seeing that smile on your Dad's face makes it worth a hundred times more."

"He's by far the biggest we've ever caught."

Lindsey leaned back next to her with their arms and thighs touching. Kendra could feel Lindsey's warmth against her bare skin. *Damn, it feels good to be this close to her.* She looked into Lindsey's eyes to find them sparkling with excitement.

When Kevin returned with the scale, Kendra hooked the fish and helped her dad lift it into his arms.

"Let me get a quick picture of this." Lindsey pulled out her phone. "Big smiles," she prompted, as she clicked off several frames. "Got it."

"Fifty-eight pounds and four ounces," Kendra announced. "You want to have this beast mounted or fileted?"

"He's way too ugly to mount, but he'll put a bunch of steaks into the freezer. We'll frame and mount one of Lindsey's photographs to remember this day."

"That sounds like a good plan. If you want, we can carry him to the sorting table, and when we dock, I'll bring out fileting knives and we can get to work."

Kevin grinned at her. "I brought some crab traps that are in the back of my truck. Maybe you can swap out your Jeep for my truck and bring them down. These carcasses will make good bait for them."

"No problem. I'll grab a couple of coolers, too, so we can put the filets on some ice."

"We will eat like royalty tonight," he replied with a broad grin on his face.

"That we will, Dad. Will you take us back in to the harbor?"

"With pleasure."

Lindsey winked at her. "Wait just a minute," she said, before disappearing into the galley. She returned seconds later carrying the three bills, handing them to him. "Congratulations on a hard fought victory."

Kevin attempted to refuse the money. "You two landed him, so I can't take your money."

"You hooked him and wore him out so we could bring him on board. You earned it, and a deal's a deal," Lindsey said.

Kendra smiled at him. "She's right, it's your win." Then she smiled at Lindsey. Her admiration for the younger woman was growing rapidly, and she appreciated the respect Lindsey showed her dad. *Too bad, you're only staying for the summer.*

They placed the fish on the sorting table while Kevin drove the boat back into the harbor. While waiting to process the fish, she and Lindsey took their seats back on the bench.

"What a great day to be out on the water." Kendra gazed across the Gulf.

"Good weather, good fishing, and good friends. What more could you ask for?" Lindsey agreed.

"Exactly. I don't think Dad will have any problems sleeping tonight after battling that beast."

"Me either, but watching him holding that fish made my day." Lindsey grinned and pulled out her phone and shared the photographs she'd taken.

"Those are good. I really would like to blow up one of them to hang in the house."

"This is my favorite." Lindsey pointed out a photo with both Drakes smiling widely at the camera.

"That is a good shot," Kendra agreed.

"I'll see about getting it blown up and printed this week."

"Just let me know how much."

"Are you kidding? It's the least I can do for you and your Dad."

✝

Kevin killed the engine and the boat floated beside the dock. Lindsey, along with Kendra, stepped onto the weathered wood to secure the mooring lines as Kevin secured the wheelhouse before joining them on deck.

"I'll be back in just a few with your truck," Kendra said.

"We'll get a head start on these fish," Kevin replied, and turned to Lindsey.

"Right behind you, sir." Lindsey smiled at him. "I'll come help with the traps and coolers when you return, Kendra."

"See you in a few then." Kendra strode off toward her Jeep.

Once Kendra left, Lindsey helped Kevin, who had picked up a fileting knife and begun working on the smaller fish. He dropped the severed heads and carcasses into a bucket for bait. It wasn't long before the filets started piling up on the sorting table.

"These will make for some delicious meals," he remarked, stacking another steak on the pile.

"We shouldn't go hungry for a while."

"That's for sure." Kevin dipped the tip of the knife into the body of the fish, the blade clicking against the backbone as he guided the knife the length of the fish. "That big boy alone will keep us fed through the summer. We may have to host a fish fry so the filets don't go to waste from freezer burn."

"That might be a fitting way to finish off the red season."

"Not a bad idea," he agreed with a grin.

When she heard the rattle of the crab traps as Kendra drove into the parking lot, Lindsey looked up.

"You two seem to be getting along well," Kevin said.

Lindsey smiled at him. "You've raised a good woman in your daughter. I really admire her strength and knowledge." *Not to mention she's drop dead gorgeous.*

"She can teach you a lot if you're willing to learn."

"I'm looking forward to that. I'm going to go help her with the equipment." Lindsey wiped her hands on a towel and walked off toward the truck.

Kendra parked the truck and stepped out to begin unloading the crab traps and coolers she had grabbed from the garage. She glanced up to see Lindsey approaching wearing an adorable smile. "You can take the coolers on board and I'll bring the traps." Kendra handed her a pair of coolers.

"You got it, boss." Lindsey grinned and picked up another cooler before walking back to the boat.

The soft sway of her hips was a sight to see and Kendra had to shake herself mentally to get back on task. *You're so doomed.*

She grinned as she picked up several traps and carried them to the boat before returning to the truck for the rest.

"You two have been busy," Kendra remarked as she stepped back onto the boat, nodding toward the growing pile of fileted fish.

"We haven't even touched the big boy yet," Kevin replied.

Kendra lifted a nearly full bucket and replaced it with an empty one. "I'll get started loading these traps unless you need my help."

"I think we've got this under control for now. We'll need your help on the big one though."

"Just give me a holler when you're ready." She carried the bucket onto the dock.

Kendra immersed herself in baiting the traps and tying lines to them from the spool of rope she'd brought from the house. She lowered the first of the traps into the water and tied it off to one of the pilings. The water was tinted pink from the bloody carcasses and she felt herself smiling, knowing the scent of the fresh blood would attract the crabs.

Lindsey swapped out buckets with her. The large head from her dad's catch filled up a bucket on its own.

"We're almost done with the smaller catches," Lindsey said as Kendra placed the large head in a trap. "If that doesn't catch a dozen crabs, I'd be surprised."

"I sure hope Dad has a plan for the all crab he's going to be catching with this many traps."

"I do," Kevin said from the boat. "Gene down at the market guaranteed he'd buy as many as I can catch. I thought it would be a good way to spend my mornings. He wants them live so I don't even have to clean them."

"The trash fish we catch in the nets should keep you set for bait," Kendra told her dad.

"That's what I'm hoping and if I need to, I can do a bit of surf fishing while you're out for reds or hook up with another of the shrimpers."

"You are going to retire one day, Dad, right?"

"I'll still be retired, but I can't sit at home all day, or play golf all the time. I'll do things at my pace though, so stop your worrying."

"I'm not worried." Kendra chuckled. "Let me drop this trap and I'll come help you two with the last one."

By the time they finished fileting the last fish, they had two large coolers filled with filets. "That's a lot of fish," Kendra groaned as she hefted one side of the cooler. "Lindsey, would you mind going to the truck to get the dolly? There's no need to break our backs if we can use equipment to do the hard work for us."

Lindsey nodded and rushed down the dock for the dolly.

"We talked about having a fish fry at the end of the red season," Kevin said as Kendra watched Lindsey striding to the truck.

"Good idea. I don't think we could eat all these by ourselves before they start to burn."

"Yep, that's the idea. I'll start planning once the time gets closer," he said. "I'll bait and hang the last two traps if you want to help her load the coolers."

"Deal, you've already got crabs creeping in toward the traps. Don't be surprised if you have a bunch caught by the morning."

"That's fine by me." He grinned. "I'll probably have to use everything I make on golf balls."

"Good point." She laughed and slapped him lightly on the shoulder. She stepped back on deck when Lindsey returned with the dolly.

†

"I'm going to shower and catch a nap if you ladies don't mind," Kevin said when they returned to the house.

"No problem, Dad. We'll get these fish bagged and in the freezer."

"I can go ahead and whip up some coleslaw, too," Lindsey chimed in. "I'll mix up the hushpuppy mix as well before we get

47

cleaned up. Then we'll all be fresh and ready to cook and eat dinner."

Chapter Five

Kendra stretched her legs out in front of her and took a long drink from her beer. Kevin and Lindsey sat across from her as a cool breeze blew across the porch.

"Thanks, ladies, for a wonderful meal, but I think this old man's going to call it a night."

"I won't be too far behind you, Dad. This is going to be a busy week."

"That it is, but an exciting one, too," he added with a sparkle in his eye. Turning to Lindsey, he warned. "I'd get a good night's sleep. She's going to work you like a dog to prove your worth to the crew."

"Yes sir," Lindsey answered. "I pretty much reckoned she would, so I'm right behind you." She stood to follow him into the house.

"You two go ahead. I'll lock up and set the coffee pot." Kendra watched them walk to the door.

"Goodnight, you two," Lindsey said and slipped past Kevin into the house.

"You want some breakfast in the morning?" He looked back at his daughter.

"Just some coffee and toast." Kendra stood and stretched.

"I'll have it ready when you come downstairs. Goodnight, honey."

"Night, Dad, sleep well."

"You too." He slipped inside the door.

Kendra watched as the light came on in his bedroom. It still felt strange for her to go out without her dad on the boat, but he deserved a chance to retire after all his years on the water. The long days of hard work had taken a toll on his body. She cringed whenever the arthritis in his joints made him limp painfully as he walked even short distances. She prayed that retirement would permit his body to heal enough to allow him some physical relief. Her heart felt heavy, weighted with concern for her father, as she entered the house and locked up for the evening.

✝

The sun crept above the horizon as the crew worked in unison to set the nets, and Kendra found herself smiling at the ease with which Lindsey had fallen into rhythm with the crew. She watched them work through the wheelhouse window until Harvey turned and gave her the signal that the nets were set. She was ready to begin the slow trawl through the smooth waters to gather shrimp in the nets. Kendra eased the boat forward as the crew disappeared into the galley for fresh coffee, while she started to trawl.

Kendra smiled when Harvey stepped inside and handed her a cup of steaming coffee.

"Thanks. We've been blessed with another beautiful morning." She nodded toward the golden orb rapidly filling the sky with light.

"Yes, we have. I hope this weather holds out all season."

She saw Lindsey step out of the galley and walk over to the railing sipping her coffee.

"How she doing?" she asked.

"Like she's been on this boat for years." He grinned. "She works well with the men, and gives their teasing right back at them. She's a good fit if that's what you're worried about."

50

Kendra nodded and took a sip of her coffee. "The last thing we need is drama, especially if we're going to be in tight quarters for days at a time."

"I don't think you have anything to worry about. I think she'll pose a challenge to the younger men to outwork her and that's good for the rest of us," he stated. "She knows her way around a shrimp boat and I don't think she'll tolerate them cutting any corners."

"Not that you would either." She smiled. "I know just how tight a crew you run, remember?"

"You still thinking we'll do four days this week?" he asked.

"Yeah. If we have a few good days I'll call it a week so we can get the new equipment installed and the boat ready for deeper waters. You and the boys can enjoy a long weekend and be well rested for next week."

"That sounds good. Everyone's excited to start the red season."

"Me too, Harvey."

"I'll give them a break for a few more minutes, and then we'll set up the sorting bins. Do you want us to keep any fish or crab caught in the nets?"

"Dad's going to need some bait for all those crab traps he bought, so keep any trash fish we get for them. You and the boys can take home any decent food fish or crab we catch. We filled our freezer with some nice grouper this weekend."

"Kevin was bragging this morning that he caught a sixty pounder."

"He did and it took both of us to hold that rascal up to the scales."

"I would have loved to see that smile on his face."

Kendra grinned, pulled her phone out of the holster, and handed it to him. She had saved the photo Lindsey had taken to use as her background. Both she and her dad were sporting huge smiles.

"That's a good shot." Harvey handed the phone back to her. "Definitely a keeper."

Kendra wondered if he was talking about the fish or the photograph as he turned and left the wheelhouse.

Outside she saw the crew milling around the deck and heard Harvey holler, "Let's get the sorting equipment ready to go," before he disappeared into the galley. She also watched Lindsey crossing the deck carrying what looked like an empty coffee mug. Kendra watched her move with a confident stride as she disappeared inside the galley. Then Kendra returned her gaze across the open water.

†

The groan of the winch promised full nets as Harvey began to bring them up from the floor of the Gulf.

"That's such a sweet sound." Kendra spoke aloud in the wheelhouse, knowing their first run of the morning would be a good one.

Kendra heard the cheers from the men as the nets broke the surface. That confirmed her thought. She watched them rush to place the bottom of the first full net into the mouth of a large cart and pull the tie releasing the bounty. The cart filled to its brink with healthy brown shrimp.

The activity continued as Lindsey and Charlie began pushing the filled cart to the sorting table to dump the contents, while the men worked on preparing the empty net for another run. Charlie moved the now empty cart under the remaining net, and the release of the tie filled it once again to the brim. He pushed the cart to the sorting table where he and Lindsey began sorting the different sizes of shrimp while the rest of the crew prepared and lowered the doors and nets into the water for a second run.

Kendra saw Harvey signal her that the nets were in position and moved the boat forward as the crew continued sorting the first run's catch.

A holler from the deck made her turn her head around in time to see Charlie picking up a large ray from the cart. He rushed to the side of the boat and hurled the angry creature back into the water. Happy to see that he completed the task without the barbed end of the ray's tail stabbing him, she watched as Charlie hurried back to the sorting table.

The first run had filled half of the containers with the large shrimp, and she knew if the next run was as good, their day would end earlier than normal. *The shrimp gods are smiling down on us.* She guided the boat forward as they started the next run. *Let's hope this lasts all summer.*

From the wheelhouse, Kendra watched her crew work with pride. Harvey and Lindsey had disappeared into the galley while the rest of the crew stored the full bins and placed the cart in position for the next haul. Charlie dumped two buckets of small shrimp off the back of the boat, so they could grow to a size large enough to harvest. She watched as the others stored several buckets of fish and crab in the cooler for the crew to take home.

They were halfway into the next run when Lindsey emerged from the galley with a plate stacked with sandwiches and chips, and carrying a tall glass of sweet tea. She brought them to Kendra. "Here you go, Captain," she said, placing the plate and glass down on a small workspace.

"Thanks, Lindsey."

"You're welcome. Give me a call in the galley if you need anything else," she said before leaving the wheelhouse.

Kendra picked up half a turkey sandwich and took a bite. *Dessert would be nice.* A wicked grin crossed her face. *Damn I need to stop thinking like this. She's only here for the summer, and when it ends, she'll be gone, and I'll be alone again.*

Once more, the groan of the winch signaled a heavy load in the net as it slowly pulled the harvest from the floor of the gulf. A smile grew wide on Kendra's face as she watched the crew, excited to see the bounty of shrimp hoisted on deck above the bins. Harvey, also wearing a huge grin, turned and gave her a thumbs up sign. This pass would fill their remaining bins and they could call it a day, and a good one at that.

Tim and Charlie busied themselves untying the nets, releasing the shrimp from the nets, and then they pushed the mounded carts and dumped them onto the sorting table. Harvey and Lindsey began sorting the catch as the others emptied the remaining net.

Harvey picked up a large shrimp that almost filled the span of his outstretched hand.

"Those are huge," Kendra said, over the loudspeaker.

"A good day's catch for sure," he hollered back at her.

The sun blazed down on them and the lack of a breeze on the Gulf had the crew dripping with sweat as they toiled. Kendra turned the boat for home and picked up speed, hoping to provide a cool breeze for the crew. Her eyes were drawn to the olive-green tank top Lindsey was wearing, and she saw the salt stains from her sweat covering the fabric with flower-shaped designs that stretched across her back. She watched as Lindsey wiped her brow with her forearm, the beads of sweat glistening on her golden skin.

"Damn," Kendra whispered, and tore her eyes from the handsome young woman to concentrate on guiding the boat home.

†

Kendra saw Kevin perched on the pier when she pulled alongside and the crew rushed to secure the boat. He whistled at the mounded bins of shrimp stacked neatly on deck, ready to transfer over to the seafood truck waiting at the end of the pier. He stepped on deck just as she emerged from the wheelhouse.

"You had a great haul today," he stated as he walked toward her.

She nodded. "Two good runs and we filled every bin we had, with shrimp left over."

"Should we cook up a batch for supper? We still have some slaw left over and I could fix some fries to go with."

"That sounds great, Dad. I'll bring a batch home when we're done here."

Harvey carried over a bucket filled with fish. "Captain Kendra told us you needed some bait for your crab traps. You want me to set this up on the pier for you?"

"That would be great, Harvey, thanks."

"Did you have a good harvest this morning, Captain Drake?" Lindsey asked.

Kendra watched her father beam with pride. "Four dozen of the prettiest blues I ever did see."

"Do we need to add some bait to your traps?" Kendra asked.

"Nope, they're good until tomorrow. I'll just hang the bucket off the pier for today. They will be good and ripe by tomorrow."

"That they will," Kendra agreed wrinkling her nose for effect.

Kevin chuckled. "I'll leave you to it then. See you back at the house."

Kendra saw her dad step onto the pier and pick up the bucket of fish, strolling slowly down the pier. Then she watched as the crew went into action. Harvey secured the nets while Lindsey slipped rubber boots over her shoes to begin rinsing off the equipment and deck. Tim and the others loaded the filled bins onto the waiting truck, returning with empty bins for tomorrow's run.

Kendra strolled back to the wheelhouse to record the day's catch and tidy up the boat. Once the crew was done for the day and on their way home, she'd take the boat to get it fueled and ready for tomorrow.

Lindsey watched her captain walk to the wheelhouse. With a deep sigh, she tugged at the thick hose and turned on the water to rinse off the equipment. She had just finished rinsing the sorting table when Charlie dropped the empty bins in the holder.

"You definitely win the wet T-shirt contest," he teased with a chuckle.

The cool water had splashed up from the table to soak the front of her shirt and she felt her nipples harden as he drew attention to them. She felt a devilish grin form on her face as she turned the hose on the unsuspecting young man with a laugh.

"Hey," he yelled, and ran out of reach of her hose.

Harvey broke into a laugh. "You're right, Charlie, Lindsey looks much better in a wet T-shirt than you."

The good-natured Charlie grinned at her. "I reckon I did deserve that soaking, but you better watch out when it's my turn to rinse off the deck," he warned.

"What was that? You want more?" she teased back, and threatened him with the squelched hose.

"Truce," he cried out, and raised his hands in surrender.

Kendra watched the exchange through the window of the wheelhouse and couldn't help but smile at the playful fun her crew was having. She prayed they would keep those high spirits for the weeks to come.

"All done for the day, Captain," Harvey reported as he leaned on the doorframe to the wheelhouse. "Is there anything you need help with?"

"You can toss me the lines as you take off. I'm going to fuel up before heading home."

"I'll tag along and help if you don't mind," Lindsey said. She was standing next to Harvey.

"That's fine with me. You can secure the lines and we'll get going."

"Aye, aye, Captain," Lindsey replied with a grin, before turning to follow Harvey.

When she saw the lines secured on deck, Kendra backed the boat from the slip and started toward the fueling dock.

"Mind if I join you?" Lindsey asked as she poked her head into the wheelhouse.

"Please do," Kendra answered, nodding toward the empty seat.

Lindsey slipped into the seat beside her. "We had a great day. didn't we?"

"Yeah we did," Kendra answered without looking at her. "Three more of those and we'll be set for the week."

"That sounds exciting. I bet you can't wait until the boat is outfitted for reds."

"I've waited all my life for that."

"Must feel really good to be so close to your goal."

"I don't think the entire impact has hit me, yet. It still feels like a dream."

"Soon to be a reality?"

Kendra finally turned to look at Lindsey with the sparkle of excitement in her green eyes.

"Thank you for allowing me to be a part of the experience," Lindsey said.

"You've more than earned your way on board. You've worked hard and are keeping the boys on their toes."

"I enjoy working with the guys." Lindsey shrugged.

"It's great having you on board." Kendra couldn't believe she had admitted that out loud. *Get a grip, you're still the Captain,* she thought. as she pulled into the fueling station, cut the engine and secured the lines.

"Fill her up please, Ben," she told the attendant.

"You got it, Captain Drake. You want to wait inside where it's cool?"

"No way, this is such a beautiful day."

He smiled at the two women. "Made even more so by you two ladies."

"Lindsey, this is Ben. Beware of the sweet talkin'," she warned.

"Aye, aye, Captain." Lindsey shot a wink to Ben.

Ben went about preparing the boat for fueling as the two women walked over to the railing to gaze across the open Gulf.

There was a flash of lightning many miles away. "I hope that brings us some rain," Kendra remarked.

"Has it been a drought season?"

"No, we've had some rain, but a good thunderstorm this time of year helps to keep the water temps down in the Gulf. Cooler water means less of a chance for something tropical to develop."

"Ah, I see. Let's hope for rain then." Lindsey leaned into the railing next to Kendra. "I could get used to this view. The water is so gorgeous here."

"Not at all like you're used to?"

Lindsey smiled. "The Outer Banks have their own type of beauty, but the water here is unbelievable, so clean, and clear. The color reminds me of your eyes."

Kendra felt the heat rise from her neck into her cheeks. She noticed the cringe on Lindsey's face.

"I'm sorry, I didn't mean to embarrass you. It was meant as a compliment."

"No problem." Kendra walked away to check on the progress of the refueling.

"You are a complete idiot," she heard Lindsey growl to herself.

Her heart was racing as she walked away from Lindsey. She needed to put some distance between them before she said something she would later regret. "How's it coming, Ben?

"Almost done here, Captain. Hey I heard you got your license to fish reds. Congratulations."

"Thanks, Ben, we head out Monday. I can't wait to get out there."

"I bet. I know you'll do well, but good luck." He removed the nozzle and replaced the fuel cap. "Add it to your account?"

"Yes, please. I'll see you later this week to top off the tank and fill up the reserve tanks."

"See you then, Captain." He grinned and stepped back onto the boardwalk.

She glanced back to find Lindsey still staring across the water as she slipped inside the wheelhouse and drove for home.

Lindsey tossed the lines onto the boardwalk when they reached the slip, and stepped from the boat to begin securing the lines.

She killed the engine, and locked the wheelhouse before picking up the bucket of shrimp to join Lindsey on the boardwalk.

Lindsey reached for the bucket, avoiding eye contact with Kendra. "I'll take care of these," she replied, and rushed ahead of Kendra.

"Hey," Kendra called out, and Lindsey stopped in her tracks.

"Thanks for the compliment. You can relax, okay, no harm, no foul."

A smile of relief crossed her face. "I'm going to clean these for dinner."

"Do you need help?"

"No, I've got this. You can check on your Dad, and I'll bring them in once I've finished cleaning."

"Okay, you know where everything's stored in the outbuilding. I'll check on Dad and get a shower in. Thanks."

"You're welcome," Lindsey replied, and slowed her pace to walk beside her in a comfortable silence.

✝

"Welcome home, honey," Kevin told her when she entered through the back door. He was at the kitchen sink, peeling the potatoes to cut into fries.

"Hey, Dad, you need some help?"

"Naw, honey, I'm good. Where's Lindsey?"

"Cleaning the shrimp for dinner. She didn't need help either, so I'm going to take a long hot shower before dinner."

"Take your time. I've got everything under control here. We'll eat at six if that's good for you."

"Sounds perfect, Dad. Holler if you need me," she replied, and left the kitchen.

✝

Lindsey peeled and deveined the shrimp, then cleaned up the workspace before carrying a large bowl of shrimp to the house. She entered the kitchen where Kevin was placing the sliced potatoes in the refrigerator to chill before cooking.

"Those look great," he said when she handed him the bowl. "Why don't you shower and relax until dinner's ready at six?"

"You sure you don't need some help?"

"No ma'am, I've got this."

"Okay then, I'll see you at six."

59

Kevin continued to toil in the kitchen preparing their dinner. He heard the shower running upstairs, a grin plastered on his face. He was pleased at how well the two women were getting along. Even though she wouldn't outright admit it, Kendra was enjoying the company of another woman in the house.

He always thought he'd make a great grandfather, and held out hopes that Kendra would someday be a mother. When she finally admitted to him that she was attracted to women, he took her in his arms and reassured her that, as long as she was happy, it didn't matter that she loved another woman. He would always support her decisions and hoped that she would find someone to share her life.

His grin widened as he heard the water stop running upstairs. *Lindsey would make a good partner. Too bad, she plans to return home at the end of the summer, but maybe they could at least become friends. Who am I kidding? I'm far too old to be playing matchmaker for my strong-willed daughter.* He couldn't stifle a chuckle as he placed a batch of fries in to cook.

†

The hot water worked wonders on her body, and Kendra found herself totally relaxed when she dried off and slipped into clean clothes. A glance at her clock let her know it was still early, so she did something uncharacteristic—she stretched out on the bed for an afternoon nap.

Her thoughts drifted back to the comment Lindsey had made about her eyes. It was just a friendly flirtation, and she had reacted badly to her remark. Maybe she was overreacting, or had Lindsey gotten under her skin more than she had expected?

†

Lindsey dressed and stepped into the hallway. She walked quietly past Kendra's closed door in case she was trying to nap. The shower had left her too wired to take a nap. She decided she would check to see if Kevin needed her help. She strolled into the kitchen as he was placing a batch of potatoes on to fry.

Kevin looked up and shot her a grin. "Feel better?"

"I most certainly smell better," she laughed. "Is there anything I can help with?"

"I've already set the table, but you can work on the fries if you're looking for something to do. The oil for the shrimp should be ready if you'll hand me the bowl from the fridge."

"Not a problem. I like to cook, and Dad says I find too much trouble to get into if I don't stay busy."

"That sounds like something he would say. So how are things going on the boat? Is the crew treating you fairly?"

"Oh yes, sir, they have been great to me. They are a lot of fun to work with, and Harvey has taught me so much already about running a crew."

"He's a good man and a great friend. We've worked together forever it seems. I think Kendra sees him as a second Dad."

Lindsey dropped a basket of fries into the bubbling oil. "I can tell she has great respect for his opinion."

"There's very little on a boat he hasn't seen or done." He dipped out the golden crisp shrimp. "You and Kendra seem to be getting along well."

Lindsey could feel a blush creep up her neck to her face, and she averted her eyes.

"Did I say something wrong?" he asked sounding confused.

"No, sir, I think your statement just caught me off guard." She lifted her face and looked him in the eyes. "Kendra is an amazing captain. I hope one day I can be half as good."

"I have no doubt you can be just as amazing. You work hard and seem to enjoy being out on a boat."

"I don't know what else I'd rather be doing."

Kevin's chuckle made her cock her head at him.

"My daughter told me the same thing when she graduated from high school. She could have attended college anywhere she wanted to go, but instead, she chose to hang with her old man and prepare to take over the business."

Ali Spooner

"So you think there's hope for me?"
"Without a doubt," he smiled.

Chapter Six

The next three days were just as successful as the beginning of the week, and when they finished unloading their haul on Thursday, the crew cheered when Kendra told them to enjoy a long weekend.

Friday morning, the work on installing the new equipment began, and Kendra found herself pacing as the men worked on board. She busied herself stocking the groceries with Lindsey's help, but she couldn't keep from walking out to check on the progress of the install.

Kevin arrived around eleven. "Is Lindsey here?" he asked as he approached her.

"Yes, she's finishing up the pantry," Kendra answered without taking her eyes off the workers. "Why? Do you need something, Dad?"

"Yes, ma'am, I do. I'm here to take the prettiest two women I know to lunch."

"I can't leave now, Dad. The men have barely begun the install."

"And your constant vigilance is only going to make them nervous and slow them down, so we're going to lunch."

Kendra finally turned to look at him. "Okay, Dad, I get your point. Let me go get Lindsey."

"I'll tell the men to call if they need you, okay?"

"Thanks," she replied, and went to collect Lindsey.

They nearly collided as Lindsey was leaving the galley when Kendra entered.

"Oh, hey, I was just coming to tell you I finished stocking the supplies. Is there anything else I can do?"

"As a matter of fact, yes. Dad has decided he's taking us to lunch."

"Lunch is always good," Lindsey replied.

"He thinks I'm slowing down the work with my constant vigilance."

"He's probably right, so let's get out of their hair and let them do their job."

"It's two against one, so I reckon I don't have much choice."

"That's right, Captain, so let's go." Lindsey grinned.

†

After a leisurely lunch, it was obvious to Lindsey that Kendra was eager to get back to the boat to check on the progress.

Kevin looked at Lindsey and shrugged.

She smiled back at him, gave him a slight nod and turned to Kendra. "I have an idea. Will you take a spin down the coast with me to show me around?"

"A spin," Kendra asked.

"Yeah on my bike. It's such a lovely day for a ride."

Kevin smiled and nodded.

"Unless you're scared to ride with me," Lindsey challenged.

"I'm not scared, but there's so much work going on at the boat."

"Work that will be completed as scheduled tomorrow if you'll let them do their work," Kevin reminded her. "I'll be at home if they need anything."

Lindsey watched as Kendra looked first at her, then at the smile on her dad's face. "I don't really have much of a choice, do I?"

"Nope," they replied in unison.

"Okay, but I want to be back in time to check on the workers before they leave for the day."

"Deal," Lindsey replied.

As they walked back toward the boat from the diner, Kendra started to enter the boardwalk to the boat.

"Oh no you don't," Kevin said. He hooked his arm through his daughter's.

"Just thought I'd try, Dad." She chuckled.

"Do you want to change into a pair of jeans before we go?" Lindsey asked.

"That's probably a good idea." Kendra began walking up the street to the house.

†

"I'll get the bike ready and wait for you out front," Lindsey said, heading off toward the garage.

Kendra began to enter the house and Kevin held the door for her. "After you, ma'am."

With a smirk on her face, Kendra replied, "Thanks, Dad. What are you going to do while we're away?"

"I'm going to take a nap." He grinned. "When y'all get back, I'm thinking we'll make this a beer and pizza night."

"It has been awhile since we've done that," Kendra said as she started for the stairs. "Enjoy your nap and I'll order the pizza when we get back."

"Have a good ride and be careful," he cautioned.

"Will do. See you soon, Dad."

Kendra watched her dad walk down the hall to his room, and then took the steps two at a time. She slipped into a worn pair of jeans and a light T-shirt before sliding her feet into her favorite boots. Her dad and Lindsey were right. The crew of workers making the install would do much better without her constantly looking over their shoulders. Getting her out of the way was probably the best thing they could hope for, so she might as well relax and enjoy the afternoon with Lindsey.

She picked up a pair of sunglasses on her way out the front door and smiled when she found Lindsey waiting for her.

"All set?" Lindsey asked, holding her hand out to Kendra to help her mount the bike.

"Yeah, thanks. So where do you want to ride?"

"Why don't we head west on 98. I've only been to the edge of town that way."

"Sounds like a plan." Kendra fastened the chinstrap of the helmet Lindsey handed her.

"Hold on tight." The motor roared to life and Lindsey eased the bike down the drive.

Kendra looked up to see her dad looking out the window, and thought she saw his smile growing as he watched them.

Kendra's hands rested on Lindsey's hips as the bike started down the drive. Kendra's smile grew as her hands circled Lindsey's waist while the bike raced down the street. Her body, sliding on the smooth leather seat, had her snuggled into Lindsey's back. It was a comfortable position. She was afraid to wiggle around on the back of the bike while it was moving, so she relaxed into Lindsey's body and enjoyed the ride.

†

The reflection of the sun glimmered across the water's surface as they rode parallel to the Gulf. It had blossomed into a beautiful day, and the bike cut through a cool, coastal breeze as they crossed into Alabama, and chased the sun as they rode west.

Traffic had come to a halt at one of the many drawbridges along the route, while the bridge rose to allow a ship to pass through on its way to the Gulf. Lindsey killed the motor and relaxed into the seat. She could feel the warmth of Kendra's body pressed into her back and her skin buzzed with excitement.

Her eyes scanned the water, watching the brown pelicans as they bobbed in the water, their eyes following the movement of the ship. Seagulls trailed the boat, their cries filling the air as they begged for handouts from the crew. She watched as the flock hovered over a pair of deckhands who were tossing scraps from their lunches to the diving birds. Angry cries echoed as the birds competed for the meager scraps of food.

Lindsey caught Kendra's eyes as she too watched the birds. "Isn't it odd? They will fight each other over scraps of food when all they have to do is to fly over the Gulf to hunt for all the fish they can stuff into their bellies?"

"They've been spoiled by human food for far too long," Kendra, commented. "Amazing what antics they will pull off for Fritos."

"I don't know, offer me a Twinkie and see what I'll do." Lindsey smirked.

"I'll have to stock up on Twinkies then."

Lindsey watched the heat rise to Kendra's cheeks. *She's so adorable when she blushes. I think it was her turn to have an 'oh shit' moment. Should I let that one pass, or make a remark?*

The blaring of a car horn broke Lindsey's concentration as an angry driver yelled out obscenities. "I guess he's getting overheated."

"The boat is almost through so we'll be moving again soon."

"Not soon enough for some of us." She grinned, nodding at the angry driver.

"He's got no choice but to wait it out with the rest of us."

They watched the mast of the ship pass through the opening, and when clear, the bridge began to lower.

Lindsey started the bike and eased forward as the traffic began to move.

The breeze was a welcome relief after sitting still on the bridge. Kendra was nestled into her back as they rode, her chin nearly resting on Lindsey's shoulder, and her hands were comfortably holding onto her hips.

"Take a left at the fork," Kendra instructed.

Lindsey followed the signs to Dauphin Island and pulled into an empty parking area.

"It's hard to believe this place isn't filled up with sunbathers with this beautiful weather."

"It's Friday. By tomorrow it will have wall-to-wall sunbathers. Until then, the beach is all ours." Kendra climbed off the bike. She pulled off the helmet and shook her hair free.

Lindsey removed hers and stepped off the bike, positioning the it on the seat and reaching for Kendra's.

"You up for a walk?" Kendra asked as she handed Lindsey the helmet.

"You bet I am." Lindsey laid it on the seat.

†

They walked side by side down the beach until they reached a secluded point where a large piece of driftwood made a perfect bench. They sat and gazed across the emerald water.

"This view is spectacular," Lindsey remarked. The breeze blew through her blond hair and she reached to move a rogue lock from her eyes.

"Thanks," Kendra told her as they sat perched on the driftwood. Their thighs touched as they sat close. The warmth from Lindsey leeched through the worn denim to curl around Kendra's heart. *What a perfect way to spend an afternoon off.*

Lindsey cocked her head. "For what?"

"For giving me such a pleasant distraction this afternoon."

A grin crept across Lindsey's face. "My pleasure, ma'am. Besides, your dad and I were worried you were going to wear out the deck with all your pacing."

"I'm sure the workers appreciate not having me looking over their shoulders all afternoon."

"I don't think anyone can blame you for being excited. You're about to begin a new adventure with your business."

"I can't believe it's only a few days away. I still feel like I'm dreaming."

Lindsey reached over and pinched her arm.

"Ouch! Okay, so I'm not dreaming this."

"No, Captain, it's very real. You're about to be hip deep in royal reds."

"I certainly hope you're right about that."

"Of course I am. Trust me."

"I do." Kendra waved her blowing hair out of her face.

They made small talk as they gazed across the emerald-green water until the sun started to sink toward the horizon.

"I think we should start back toward home," Kendra said, with a tinge of regret.

"Thanks for sharing this spot with me."

"You're welcome. It's a nice getaway and not far from home."

"Let's ride."

†

Lindsey wove the bike through traffic like an expert and they made it to Perdido in record time. She rolled up to the harbor and parked the bike, just as the sun was sinking to the horizon. "I thought you'd want a quick peek." She grinned as she killed the motor.

"Thanks."

Lindsey followed Kendra on board and was impressed by the amount of work the installers had done.

"I guess they do work faster if I'm not here." Kendra chuckled. "At this rate, they'll easily be finished by tomorrow."

"Do you think you can sleep tonight now?" Lindsey asked.

"Yeah, I'm pretty sure I can. I think I'll go ahead and order our supper. It's pizza and beer night. What do you like on your pizza?"

"Just about anything except anchovies."

"Good, we have a consensus on that." Kendra pulled out her cell, ordered two pizzas, and then looked back at Lindsey. "That's set. You ready to go home?"

"I'm ready for a cold beer."

"That does sound good. Let's go." With one last look at the completed work, Kendra followed Lindsey back to the bike.

†

"I was hoping you two would show up soon," Kevin greeted them as they walked toward the back porch. "I'm starving."

"The pizza is on the way, Dad. Are you ready for a cold beer?"

"I thought you'd never ask." He grinned.

"Sit tight, Captain, and I'll get them." Lindsey walked into the house.

"Did you have a good ride?"

"Yeah we did, and it looks like the guys got a lot done today."

"Tom says they should be finished by mid-afternoon if all goes as planned," Kevin replied.

"That's good. I want to take some clothes down Sunday and go top off the tanks and reservoirs."

"You'll have all day to do that. You could even sleep in a bit if you wanted."

"I'm not sure I'll ever be able to sleep in again."

Lindsey stepped back outside carrying three beers. "Here we go." She passed each of them a bottle.

They knocked out most of the pizza and a twelve pack of beer before retiring for the evening. When they paused at the stairway, Kevin grinned. "You two want to help me with the crabs in the morning."

"Love to," Lindsey answered.

"Goodnight, ladies," he told them as they climbed the stairs.

"See you in the morning, Captain."

"Sleep well," Kendra replied, with a smile growing on her face.

†

The weekend passed in a blur of activity, and when Kendra climbed the stairs for bed Sunday night, her stomach was churning with a case of rabid butterflies. She was worried she wouldn't be able to sleep, but after a hot shower, her body relaxed and sleep came easily. She dreamed of sailing deep into the emerald-green water, chasing the sun that raced across the sky.

Chapter Seven

Kevin had a full breakfast cooked when Kendra entered the kitchen. She started to protest, but her dad had put in a great deal of effort to send them off with full stomachs, so she said nothing.

"This looks and smells fantastic, Dad."

"You're going to have a long, busy day ahead, so you need to start it off right."

"Something smells heavenly." Lindsey walked into the room rubbing her hands together.

"Fill your plates and I'll bring juice and coffee."

"Thanks, Dad."

Once breakfast was done, Kendra got up from the table. "Time to go."

Kevin walked them to the door. "Good luck and call me tonight," Kevin requested.

"I will. Thanks again for a great breakfast."

"My pleasure, see you this weekend."

"Or sooner if all goes well," Lindsey chimed in.

"That would be fine, too."

†

Kendra tossed a small bag over her shoulder as they walked to the harbor. The horizon filled with golden sunlight as they stepped on board. Harvey had already made coffee and was passing out mugs to the rest of the crew.

"Good morning, guys," she called out. "Charlie, will you and Lindsey bring in our mooring lines? We've got a long ride ahead of us."

"We're on it, Captain." Charlie grinned as he punched Lindsey in the shoulder.

Kendra took a mug of coffee and headed to the wheelhouse to start the engine. She watched the crew secure the lines. "Let's do this," she spoke to the empty room before shifting into reverse to back out of the slip.

It would take most of the day to reach the deep waters where the reds lived. Harvey stepped inside the wheelhouse once they cleared the harbor.

"What would you have us do this morning, Captain?"

"Give the crew a run down on the new equipment and they can relax until lunch. After they eat, I'd like them to go ahead and prepare the new nets. I'm hoping we'll arrive in enough time to make a run late this afternoon."

"Yes, ma'am," he answered, wearing a huge grin.

Kendra settled in on her comfortable seat and watched as the boat passed the local fleets that were heading out for their morning runs for browns and pinks. Her radio rang with a chorus of well wishes. Captains she had fished with for her entire life wished her well on her hunt for reds. She was on her way to accomplishing a long-term dream, and nothing was going to stop her. Her heart, filled to bursting with the joy she was feeling.

Lindsey poked her head into the wheelhouse. "Mind if I join you?"

"Sure, come in. What are the rest of the crew doing?"

"Playing poker or watching television."

"I thought you'd be in the thick of a poker game, too."

Lindsey nodded toward the open water. "Not when I have a view this beautiful. Poker will wait until after dark. Oh yeah, Harvey sent you a thermos of coffee."

"Mind pouring me a fresh cup?"

"Not at all." She took the cup Kendra handed her and filled it with the steaming liquid.

"Thanks." Kendra took a sip and moaned. "He makes the best coffee."

The sound of the moan sent a shiver down Lindsey's spine. That something so innocent had such a profound effect on her made her realize she was in trouble. She knew she was a goner, and she would do anything to please the woman smiling at her.

"You look so serious, a penny for your thoughts?"

"I was just thinking how exciting it is to be with you on this adventure." *Whoa, I hope she buys that line. I don't think I can admit to her how I feel.*

"I'm glad you're a part of it."

Lindsey nodded. "You think we'll arrive in time to make a run before it's too dark to see?"

"I'm hoping so. I'm eager to get those new nets wet." Lindsey could see that Kendra's green eyes were alight with excitement. *Damn, I love it when her eyes light up like that.* Lindsey had to look away to keep the blush from rising to her face.

"Keep an eye on things for a few while I get rid of some coffee," Kendra said, and left the wheelhouse.

"With pleasure." She slipped into the captain's chair as Kendra left. There was nothing ahead of them but open water and the horizon in the distance. A glance at one of the monitors showed clear skies ahead. Even the clouds hesitated at ruining the perfect blue of the sky.

A half hour after returning, Kendra looked over to see Lindsey's head nodding as she sat in the co-pilots chair. "You've got time for a nap before lunch if you want."

"I'm just not used to sitting still this long. I think I'll go stretch my legs and see if Harvey needs help making lunch."

"I'm sure he'd love the help, see you soon."

Kendra watched Lindsey walk outside and lean over the railing, the wind ruffling her blond locks. *Why does the word*

73

adorable come to mind whenever I look at her? It's probably because she is adorable, and you're falling head over heels for her. "Maybe so, but it wouldn't work for us, and neither of us needs a heartache to deal with at the end of the summer. Better just to admire the view from afar, and keep my hands to myself." She spoke aloud. "Good grief, I'm talking to myself now."

Lindsey looked up at that moment, and she smiled and waved as she started for the galley.

After a leisurely lunch, the crew broke out the new nets and rigged them for shrimping. As the day grew long, Kendra glanced at the GPS system, and according to what she was reading, they would reach the boundaries of the red grid in another hour.

When they finished with the rigging, she stepped on deck. "We've got another hour or so and then we can drop our first nets. Relax, and I'll let you know when we arrive."

†

Lindsey stretched out on her bunk, the gentle rocking of the boat lulling her to sleep. She was having the sweetest of dreams when the loudspeaker crackled and Kendra's voice filled the room.

"We've hit our spot."

"Not quite, but I was getting close." Lindsey snickered to herself. In her dream, their bodies had locked in a passionate embrace as their mouths and hands were busily exploring one another. "I hope I can come back to that dream later." She grinned as she stood to return to the deck where everyone was moving into position.

Kendra gave the order to begin. It would take several minutes to lower and position the nets, and then she would begin the slow trawl forward, hopefully filling the larger nets with the cherished shrimp. The minutes ticked by slowly and when she felt the tension on the lines slacken, she knew they had reached the bottom. Her heart pounded in her chest as she opened the throttle and the boat inched forward.

"Now we wait."

She was used to feeling the drag of filled nets within an hour of trawling, but when the first hour passed, she felt no pull. She continued for another hour and then gave the order to bring the nets onboard. She heard and felt the whine of the winch as the nets lifted, and she held her breath for several seconds before she realized what she was doing. She let the breath out slowly in anticipation of her first catch.

The crew stared in disbelief as the first net rose to the surface and swung onto the deck. Kendra only had to look at their faces from the wheelhouse to know that their first net was nearly empty. Charlie pushed the bin beneath the net and Tim untied the rope. Several dozen reds dropped into the bin.

Her heart plummeted and she felt a wave of nausea lurch inside her. The crew moved to the opposite side of the boat to empty the second net, with an almost identical result. She cut the engine and joined the crew on deck.

Harvey was standing there with his head hung in what looked like disappointment for his captain.

"Well, that certainly isn't what I was expecting." She groaned when she looked at the meager catch in the bin. "Barely enough for dinner."

"I think we just seasoned the new nets, Captain," Harvey countered. "We know all new equipment needs to be broken in."

"I was hoping full nets would have broken them in." Kendra knew she had a worried expression.

"The shrimp will come, Captain," Lindsey said.

"I sure hope so." Kendra released a deep sigh.

"Do you want to make another run today, Captain?" Harvey asked.

"No, Harvey. I think I'll take us a bit farther out. We'll call it a night and start fresh in the morning. We can eat those tonight if you're up to boiling them."

"Will do, Captain. You heard the Captain, guys, let's get moving."

The crew went into motion, cleaning and storing the gear for the night while Kendra stalked back to the wheelhouse, shut the door, and started the engine. "Fuck," she growled as she opened the throttle to move the boat forward. She struggled to hold back the tears that filled her eyes.

Lindsey looked at the closed door and then glanced at Harvey.

Harvey shook his head. "Give her some time to deal with her disappointment." He handed her a bucket of shrimp. "She'll lick her wounded pride and be good to go in the morning. At least I hope she will."

"I'm sure you're right. Do you want me to get these ready to cook?"

"That would be great. We'll finish up here and I'll be in to help."

Kendra's eyes burned with hot tears as she stared out the window into the setting sun. "Where are you hiding?" she growled, her words echoing in the room. She prayed that she hadn't made a huge mistake bringing the crew to fish for reds when they were having a record brown season. With her confidence sinking to rock bottom, she did the one thing she knew would help her failing spirits. Kendra called home.

"Hey, honey, how was your day?"

"It was horrible, Dad. Have I made a mistake coming out here?"

"Absolutely not. Settle down and tell me what happened."

Kendra struggled to hold back her tears making her voice quiver with emotion. "We arrived in plenty of daylight to make a first run. I just knew we would bring up filled nets, Dad, but when they came up, they barely have enough to feed us tonight."

"You're probably still just too far north. Go deeper into the Gulf and start over in the morning. Most of all, stop worrying so much. They will come. You're much too good a captain not to find them."

"I pray you're right, Dad. I'd hate to have another repeat of today. I could see the disappointment on the crew's faces, and I never want to see that again."

"That's the spirit. Now you sound more like the daughter I know and love so much," Kevin soothed. "There will always be bad days in every season. Like a passing storm, you just have to ride them out."

"Thanks, Dad. I knew calling you would pick me up."

"You call me anytime. I always want to hear from you."

"I'll call again tomorrow, hopefully with better news."

"I'll be looking forward to hearing all about it. I love you, Kendra."

She felt her frown turn to a smile. "I love you, too."

"Get some rest. Tomorrow's a new day."

"Yes, it is. I want to take us another hour south and then I'll call it a night. Sleep well, Dad."

"You too, honey. Goodnight."

"Goodnight."

She hung up the phone and realized her dad was right. In her eagerness to start the season off well, she had erred in starting too far north. "Tomorrow will be much better," she promised herself and watched the last shimmering rays of sunlight disappear.

When she was satisfied that she had driven as far south as she dared, Kendra cut the engine and dropped anchor. She set the alarms to monitor their position. Confident they would sound if the boat drifted off course during the night in the Gulf currents, she recorded their position and closed her logbook. She turned off the overhead in the wheelhouse and smiled at the illumination of the control panels in the eerie darkness.

Kendra stepped into her private sleeping quarters, just off the wheelhouse. She washed her face in cool water to hide any remnants of her tears, and then joined her crew for dinner.

✝

"Something is smelling really good," Kendra announced when she entered the galley.

"The shrimp are almost done and Lindsey's working on some hushpuppies." Harvey handed her a cold beer. "You can join the others at the table and we'll be done in just a few."

She took a seat beside Charlie.

"Hey, Captain." He looked at her with a sheepish grin. "Are you up for some cards tonight?"

"I think I'll pass tonight, Charlie, but thanks for the invite. We're going to have a long day tomorrow, so I'm going to get some sleep."

"It'll be a good day tomorrow, Captain. I can feel it," Tim replied.

"I think I was just too overeager to get started, and we weren't far enough south to be on the shrimp."

"That's what we're thinking, too." Harvey placed a steaming pan of boiled shrimp in the middle of the table. "Tonight we get to sample what the next few months have to offer us."

"You have to admit these are beautiful shrimp," Kendra remarked.

"They taste like miniature lobsters." Lindsey brought a pan of hushpuppies to the table. "Anyone need a fresh beer?"

"Bring us all a round," Kendra requested.

†

Kendra left the crew to clean up from dinner before they started their poker game. She walked onto the deck to stretch her legs. She couldn't remember the last time she'd been on board after dark. The lines hanging from the outriggers swayed with the rocking of the boat as waves lapped at its sides. She was standing along the railing, gazing out at the reflection of the moon on the water when she felt a hand on her shoulder. She turned to find Lindsey beside her.

"Are you okay?"

"Yeah, today was a big disappointment, but tomorrow will be better."

The hand on her shoulder was warm and comforting. She was pleased that Lindsey didn't remove it right away.

"You're a good captain, and we all know that you'll find the shrimp, so go easy on yourself."

"Thanks, that means a lot."

"Is there anything I can get you?"

"Thanks, Lindsey, but I think I'm going to call it a night."

"Rest well, Captain, I'll have a big pot of coffee ready for you in the morning."

Kendra smiled lighting up her face. "Thanks. Goodnight, Lindsey."

Once in her quarters Kendra stripped out of her clothes and slipped into shorts and a T-shirt. The crisp sheets felt good against her skin as she stretched out in the comfortable bed. She felt the emotional drain on her body as she closed her eyes and let the movement of the boat rock her to sleep.

Lindsey stood for a while after watching as Kendra entered the wheelhouse and disappeared in the darkness. Finally she whispered, "Goodnight, my sweet Captain," into the breeze, and then walked back into the galley to join the card game.

After losing four hands in a row, she decided to retire for the night. She couldn't concentrate on the game and bid the crew goodnight. In spite of her best efforts, her thoughts kept drifting back to Kendra's smile when they talked earlier on deck. *If you only knew how that smile of yours affects me.* The grin grew on her face as she walked to her bunk.

Chapter Eight

The morning dawned brilliantly with the sun shining brightly and a cool breeze blowing across the deck. As Harvey predicted, Kendra chose to skip breakfast, so the crew set the nets and the trawl began while they cooked and ate breakfast.

Lindsey buttered two slices of toast and slathered apple jelly across them as Harvey filled a thermos of coffee. "I'll take it while you guys finish breakfast."

"Good luck getting her to eat that toast," Harvey replied with a chuckle.

"I can only try," she replied and left the galley.

"Mind if I join you?"

Kendra looked up to see Lindsey in the doorway. "Sure, come on in."

Lindsey placed the toast next to Kendra and unscrewed the lid on the thermos. "Hand me your cup, please."

Kendra reached for the near empty cup. "I told Harvey I didn't think I could eat breakfast."

"That's what he told me, but the acid from the gallon of coffee you'll be drinking this morning will only irritate your stomach, so please eat. I slaved over the hot toaster to make it for you and I put your favorite jelly on it, too." Lindsey smiled.

Her smile is too adorable to ignore, and she is trying to take care of me. Kendra reached for a slice of toast. "Just because you worked so hard," Kendra joked as she took a bite.

"Thank you."

Kendra could hear the tone of genuine concern in Lindsey's voice in spite of her teasing. "This does taste good."

"I'm glad you like it. Just give me a holler if you need anything else."

"Thanks again," she replied and watched Lindsey leave the wheelhouse.

✝

The crew positioned the bins to prepare for bringing in a haul. Kendra's smile grew when she heard and felt what she was waiting for. The boat gave an audible groan, signaling something of substance was filling the nets. She felt her heart lifting as the crew readied to bring up the nets.

Thank you, God.

She brought the boat to a crawl and lifted the microphone for the speaker system. "Crank them up, Harvey, and let's see what we've got."

He waved to her from the deck and pushed the switch to activate the winch.

She found she was holding her breath again, but blew it out with a sigh when the winch groaned with strain. Kendra cut the engine and walked out on deck just as Charlie and Tim guided the first net on board.

The net was ninety percent filled with the precious shrimp, and the crew cheered with excitement at the size of the catch.

"Now that's what I'm talking about," Harvey shouted.

A smile stretched across Kendra's face. "Let's get them processed," Kendra instructed and returned to the wheelhouse. A smile of relief crossed her face as she returned to her chair to watch the crew.

The catch filled up the bins. Lindsey and Charlie started bagging the shrimp for freezing while the rest of the crew brought up the second net, and prepared them for the next run. Each bag held ten pounds of shrimp when filled, a quart of water added before sealing each bag to speed the flash freezing process.

Tim and Charlie emptied the second net and reset it before lowering it overboard. They watched the net sink beneath the water, signaled Kendra that they were ready, and then joined the rest of the crew in processing the shrimp. Kendra began the trawl again.

Kendra watched as Harvey approached the wheelhouse sporting a large grin. When he opened the door, she heard Lindsey holler out, "Let's get cracking." She shook her head and chuckled at Lindsey's exuberance.

Kendra loved the smile on Harvey's face when he entered the wheelhouse. "How'd we do?"

Harvey grinned as he wiped the sweat from his brow. "I was given the honor of informing you we had a great first haul. We filled one hundred and ten bags. I knew you'd do it, you're definitely on the shrimp now."

"Hot damn." She grinned and lifted her hand for a high five.

Harvey slapped her hand. "I hope you bought enough bags."

Her face froze in doubt. "I bought a thousand."

"If this is going to be any indication of how our season is going to go you better go ahead and call in an order to double that for next week."

"That will be a call I'll gladly make, but let's see what the second run nets."

"This isn't a fluke, Captain. It's going to be great."

"Thanks for the vote of confidence, Harvey. It means a lot coming from you."

"My pleasure, Captain." He smiled. "With your permission I'd like to pull out some steaks for dinner tonight."

"Absolutely, Harvey, we need to celebrate."

"I'm on it."

Kendra watched him go, a spring in his step. She wished her dad could have been here to celebrate with them.

By sunset, they had managed four runs. Kendra would have been comfortable with ending the day at three, but the crew, stoked by their success asked her to make one more. That's all it took to convince her. At this rate, they would fill their shelves with the remaining bags in two more days and be ready to head home a day earlier than planned.

While making the last run, Kendra called home to tell her dad of their success and to ask him to double the order on bags. She could hear the pride in his voice as they talked, and she ended the call high on excitement.

"We can do this," she spoke aloud.

✝

While the rest of the crew finished processing the shrimp and handling the cleanup, Harvey and Kendra prepared a steak dinner. When everyone was seated around the table, Kendra raised her bottle of beer and looked in the eyes of each of her crew.

"Today we had a great day, and thanks to your hard work, we're well on our way to reaching this week's quota. Here's to the beginning of a great season. Thanks to each one of you."

"Cheers, Captain," Lindsey called out. They all brought their bottles to the middle of the table, touching simultaneously.

"To the reds," Charlie added.

"To the reds," Kendra repeated.

It was a long, but profitable day, and the crew showed signs that the exertion had taken its toll. With their stomachs filled, the crew left the dining area for showers and an early bedtime. They deserved a great night's rest after the hard work of the day.

Kendra was too excited to sleep. She showered and dressed in shorts and a T-shirt, then slipped back on deck. She saw a figure leaning on the railing and as she approached, Lindsey turned to face her.

The breeze was blowing through her hair and the peaceful look on her face made Kendra stop in her tracks. She slowly released the breath she was holding and willed her heart to drop back into her chest.

"Hey," she said as she leaned back on the railing next to Lindsey. "I thought y'all would be in bed already, as hard as you worked today."

"It was an exciting day." Lindsey took a drink of her beer. "Care to share this one?"

"Sure," Kendra reached for the beer. As their fingers brushed, she felt a rush of energy soar up her arm. She took a drink and handed the bottle back to Lindsey. "Thanks, that's nice and cold."

Lindsey grinned. "I cheated and snuck it into the freezer for a few minutes to get it super cold."

"Good idea."

"Why are you still up?"

"I just haven't wound down yet. I thought some fresh air might help."

"If we keep up this pace we'll be home early right?"

Kendra nodded. "Yeah we will. Did you have something you wanted to do?"

"That depends."

"On what?" Kendra asked taking the bait.

"Whether or not you're willing to share your dream and show me the boat you want to buy."

She grinned back into the deep blue eyes watching her. "I think that could be arranged."

"I'd like that."

"If he's in port Saturday we can go take a look. It's a bit of a drive to Biloxi."

"Ah, Biloxi, can we stop and blow a bit of my paycheck at the casinos?"

"I don't see why not. You've earned a break."

"Thanks, Captain." She grinned and offered her a last drink.

"I'm good, finish it," Kendra replied with a stretch. "I'm going to try to get some sleep."

"Goodnight, Captain," Lindsey said dropping the empty bottle into the galley trash before leaving for her bunk.

Kendra watched her go before disappearing into the darkened wheelhouse and then to her cabin.

†

Kendra surprised the crew the next morning by joining them for breakfast. Harvey had baked fresh biscuits and was finishing up sausage gravy when she arrived.

"That smells good," she remarked.

"Grab a plate and get some before the others get here. I'll bring you some coffee."

"Thanks. Will you join me?"

"Don't mind if I do, Captain." He poured two cups of coffee and joined Kendra at the table.

They were halfway through with the meal when Lindsey and the rest of the crew arrived.

"We've already got the nets in place, Captain," Lindsey reported as she poured a cup of coffee.

"I guess I better finish eating and get us moving." Kendra could feel her smile growing on her face.

"Take your time. We've got all day to fish," Harvey replied.

"That's true, but I'm eager to see what the day's catch brings." She took the last bite on her plate and sipped her coffee.

"Go ahead and I'll bring in your thermos, once the crew is eating," Harvey told her. "Leave the plate. I'll get that, too."

"Thanks, Harvey, I'll get us moving."

She slid into her chair and started the engine, allowing it to idle for several minutes as the nets lowered into the water, then she increased pressure on the throttle, urging the boat forward. The sun was beginning to crest the horizon as she gazed through the wheelhouse window. "Another beautiful day in heaven," she whispered as the boat eased forward.

†

The next two days proved just as bountiful, and Friday morning, Kendra announced at breakfast they were heading home after filling every bag she had available. There were several smaller bags they filled for the crew to take home to their families.

She even remembered her promise to Hank and froze a bag for him.

The trip back to the harbor took much longer with the boat loaded with shrimp. The crew took advantage of the opportunity to relax while Harvey took inventory of the galley and made a shopping list for supplies. Lindsey was restless and had talked the rest of the crew into cleaning the deck after lunch, so when they arrived at the harbor all they would need to do was unload and head for home.

Kendra watched with pride as they washed down the deck, then stored the nets and gear for the next week. As soon as land became visible on the horizon, Kendra called ahead to alert the delivery truck of their time of arrival and signaled the crew to begin loading the frozen bags into the bins for transport. The crew worked efficiently as a team and had the bins filled and stationed along the railing when she killed the engine. Charlie and Lindsey stepped onto the dock to secure the mooring lines.

Kevin was waiting at the dock with a beaming smile for his daughter. "What a haul," he said to Harvey as they started transferring the shrimp.

"Hey, Dad," Kendra called when she emerged from the wheelhouse.

"Great job, Captain." He smiled with pride.

"Could I talk you into a favor while we settle up here?"

"Anything you need."

"Drop a package of shrimp off to Hank for me?"

"I'd love to. That way I can brag about how well your first run has gone."

"Thanks, Dad. We'll meet you back at the house when you've finished," she said as Lindsey handed him the bag of shrimp.

"Beautiful. I hope you kept a bag for us?"

"We all have a package to celebrate with our families."

"I can taste them now." He licked his lips. "I'll see you soon."

†

Once the transfer was complete, Kendra called the crew into the galley. She passed out their traditional end of the week beer and delivered their paychecks. She calculated the checks based on the contracted price for the reds, and was pleased to pay her crew so handsomely.

"We had a great first week." She watched as the crew stared at the checks she had given them. "Don't spend it all in one place. I'll see you bright and early Monday, and we'll do it all over again."

Each of the crew hugged her before leaving, several with tears pooling in their eyes. The paychecks she was able to write were triple what a normal week would have netted them.

She and Lindsey were the last to leave the boat, carrying two bags of frozen shrimp. Lindsey placed a friendly arm around Kendra's shoulder. "I hope you'll allow me to buy you a nice dinner while we're in Biloxi."

"I have just the place in mind."

"So that's a yes?"

"Yes, ma'am, it is."

"Awesome," Lindsey replied as they walked up the hill.

Chapter Nine

Saturday morning blossomed into a beautiful day.

"Have a great time, you two," Kevin said when Kendra told him of their plans for the day. They invited him, but he declined their invitation. "Hank and I are going to the driving range to hit some golf balls."

"I'm glad to hear you're going to get out and have some fun, too," Kendra told him.

"I'll remind you of that when I call you to pull me out of the bed tomorrow." He chuckled.

"I've got plenty of muscle for backup." Kendra nodded toward Lindsey.

"I'll be sure to wear some pajamas to bed tonight then. I'd hate for Lindsey to see me in my boxers."

"No offense, Captain, but I've seen my dad in his boxers on many occasions, so I doubt you'd give me a scare."

"She'd probably be blinded by those white legs of yours though. I hope you're going to wear shorts so you can start getting some sun," Kendra teased.

"Ouch, that was a low blow." He grinned.

She chuckled. "We'll see you later tonight." Kendra kissed his cheek and turned to look at Lindsey. "You ready to roll?"

"Just waiting on you, Captain," she replied with a wink.

They worked together to remove the top, leaving the Jeep open to the sun and cool breeze as they drove down the coast. The beaches were dotted with sunbathers and families enjoying one of the last weekends of the summer season. Out on the water, boats of all shapes and sizes carried fishermen, and several commercial boats were heading out to the horizon.

Kendra glanced over to her shotgun seat. Lindsey was smiling, and her spiky blond hair blew in the wind as she sang to a country song on the radio. *Beautiful,* Kendra thought to herself before turning her eyes back to the road.

An hour and a half later, Kendra slowed the Jeep as they approached the harbor in Biloxi. The *Southern Star* was in port, and her eyes lit up when she saw the boat. She parked the Jeep and they approached the boat.

"You must be Kendra," a man stated. "You look just like your dad, only prettier."

Kendra chuckled and extended her hand. "You must be Captain Cole. This is Lindsey, one of my crew."

He shook their hands as Kendra introduced Lindsey. "Just Johnny to you, ladies. Your dad tells me you got your Reds license this year."

"I did and we've had a great first week. We filled up quickly and came in early, so I wanted to come take a look at the Star."

"Come along then and have a good look. I was just about to make some coffee. Would you ladies join me for a cup?"

"I never pass on a cup of coffee, and I haven't heard Lindsey say no either."

"Make yourselves at home while I brew a pot. Go anywhere you like," he added.

"Thanks, Captain."

Johnny disappeared into the galley as Kendra and Lindsey inspected the equipment on the deck. The freezers, bins, and other equipment were in immaculate condition. Pleased with what they saw on deck, they went below to check out the sleeping quarters and engine room, finding them in great condition as well. When they returned to the galley, Johnny was pouring the coffee.

"Have a seat at the table and I'll bring the coffee over."

They took their seats and when he brought mugs of steaming coffee they settled into a friendly banter.

"So what did you think of the old girl?"

"She's just as beautiful as I imagined. The photographs don't begin to do her justice," Kendra praised. "Are you still planning to sell at the end of the year?"

"I am. I've got a commitment to the crew to finish out this season, and then I'm going to start enjoying retirement."

"Dad's actually taking up golf," Kendra told him.

"I hope to do that as well so I can spend some time outside. The wife wants to travel, so I'll need something to do while she shops." He chuckled.

"I wish I could talk Dad into doing some traveling. It's hard to get him away from the water though."

"I can understand that. We've spent so many years out in the Gulf, she feels like another spouse. She treats you grand on some days and leaves you frustrated on others. Kinda like a wife," he joked.

"That's one way of explaining it," Lindsey replied. "I think my Dad would agree with you on that. He fishes off the Outer Banks."

"Ah, the mean Atlantic. I'll stick with my Gulf any day."

"It is beautiful here," Lindsey agreed.

"The fishing is much more reliable here. Even in slim years the profits are still good. We can sell anything we catch to the local markets and restaurants."

"That is a plus, having the local restaurants open all year long. After Labor Day, in the Outer Banks, some of the bigger places start shutting down for the season."

"Open all year round here, so you can always have fresh seafood."

"You may think me crazy, but it tastes different here too," Lindsey commented.

Kendra found herself smiling as she agreed with the assessment.

"Not as briny as the Atlantic," Johnny remarked. "It's still good seafood on the East Coast, but not as good as here, except for the lobster. We just don't have great ones here."

"That's true. Nothing like a good Maine lobstah," Lindsey spoke in her best Maine accent.

Kendra took a sip of coffee and steadied her voice before speaking. She sent up a silent prayer that Johnny didn't have a contract on the boat yet.

"Have you had any offers on the Star, yet?"

"I've had several interested parties, but nothing solid yet. Are you seriously interested?"

Kendra grinned. "Yes sir, I want this boat. Will you take a down payment today?"

"I'd love to feel like she's being kept in the family. I'll take whatever you can afford to put down, and I'll have my lawyer draw up a contract."

Kendra took a check out of her pocket and handed it to him. She watched as his eyes lit up when he saw the amount of the check.

"Are you sure you can afford this now?"

"I've been saving up for years," Kendra assured him.

Johnny extended his hand. "We have a deal, young lady. Let me go write up a receipt and I'll be right back."

When she turned back to the table, Lindsey was watching her. "You certainly made his day."

"No, he made mine, by accepting the offer."

"Congratulations, my friend, she's a beauty and will be perfect for fishing reds."

"Yes, she will. I can't wait."

Johnny returned with the receipt and got contact information from Kendra. "I'll let you know when the lawyer has the sales contract written up."

"Sounds great. I'll look forward to hearing from you and thanks for the coffee."

"My pleasure, ladies. Have a great rest of your weekend."

91

"Let's go celebrate," Lindsey told her as they stepped back onto the pier.

"Pinch me first, so I know I'm not dreaming."

Lindsey reached over and pinched her arm. "You just bought a boat."

"Yeah, I did," Kendra answered, grinning wide.

†

They arrived at one of the casinos and settled in at two slot machines. Lindsey ordered two beers, and when they arrived, she held out her bottle. "To the new owner of the *Southern Star*," she toasted, and Kendra tapped her bottle.

"How does it feel to own two shrimp boats?"

"Amazing. I still can't believe all this is happening."

"You've worked hard for years and it's paying off. What do you plan to do with *Heaven Sent*?"

"I'm still working on that plan. She'll definitely stay in the family and will fish for the smaller shrimp. That I do know."

"Will Harvey take her over?"

"No, he's got no ambition to be a captain. Besides, he's too good a first mate to lose, and he'll be needed on the bigger boat."

"You'll work it all out."

Kendra's good luck continued when she hit a jackpot of four hundred dollars only two hours after they arrived.

"I think I'll quit while I'm ahead. Go ahead and play as long as you like, I'm going to walk around for a bit."

"I won't be here much longer. This baby is getting ready to hit," Lindsey predicted.

"Good, because I'm getting hungry and you promised me dinner."

"We forgot all about lunch, so you have a right to be hungry. You sure you don't want to eat now?"

"No, we're good. The restaurant doesn't open for another hour."

"Cool. I'll track you down in just a little while then."

Kendra cashed in her winnings and strolled around the casino. She found herself in the dollar slot section and, even though she had decided not to play more, she found herself taking a seat and inserting a five-dollar bill. On her third pass, the machine lights started flashing and the dollars began adding up. She sat and stared at the machine as a five-hundred dollar win showed up on the screen. She hit the payout button and walked to the cashier.

"You're back already?" the woman asked.

"I guess this is just my lucky day," Kendra grinned, and handed her the slip.

"I'd say so," the woman replied as she looked at the slip. "How would you like the bills?"

"Hundreds, please." Kendra smiled as she watched the woman count five bills.

"Congratulations. Will I see you again?"

"No, ma'am, I'm not going to press my luck."

"Smart move. Too many times I see folks get greedy and play it all back, hoping for another big pot."

"Not me," Kendra replied. "Thanks."

She placed the bills in her wallet and turned around to see Lindsey smiling at her.

"Did you hit another jackpot?"

Kendra smiled. "I put a five in a dollar machine and won a five hundred dollar pot. How'd you do?"

Lindsey held up her ticket. "Four hundred for me. I think we'd better take our money and run."

"Agreed,. Come on, you have a dinner to buy."

"Lead the way, boss." Lindsey grinned and followed her from the casino.

†

Kendra parked the Jeep in front of Mary Mahoney's and climbed out.

"I know it doesn't look like much from the outside, but the food is to die for. Back in the day it was a bordello, and today it's one of Biloxi's premier eateries," Kendra said.

"I trust you to pick out the best spot."

"Good, and I'm glad you hit a jackpot. I'm really hungry now."

"You can eat to your heart's desire ma'am. I've always got plastic if I run out of cash."

Once seated, a tuxedo-clad server approached them. "Good evening, ladies, what may I offer you to drink?"

"Would you like a bottle of wine?"

"That's good with me," Kendra replied.

"What would you recommend?" Lindsey asked the server.

"We have an excellent Riesling."

Lindsey nodded.

"I'll give you ladies a moment to peruse the menu while I prepare your wine."

"So, Kendra, what do we want for appetizers?"

"Definitely some fried crab claws."

"Sounds good. Would you also like to share a shrimp cocktail?"

"That would be awesome."

"Do you have any recommendations for entrées?"

"You can't go wrong with anything on this menu. I'm going to have the filet and fried shrimp."

"I was thinking the filet and the fish of the day, especially if it's grouper," Lindsey said.

"Just be sure to save room for dessert. They have excellent bread pudding."

"Maybe we can share one then."

"There will be no sharing of dessert, if you want one, order your own," Kendra warned.

"Yes, boss." Lindsey suppressed a grin.

The meal was as terrific as Kendra had promised and they ordered coffee and desserts to end their meal.

"I have to admit, this was one of my all-time best meals," Lindsey said.

"I've got no complaints either. Thank you for a lovely meal."

"It's been my pleasure." Lindsey paid the bill.

Dark had descended when they emerged from the restaurant. "Wow, I didn't realize how long we'd been inside. Are you okay to drive?" Lindsey asked.

"Yes, I backed off the wine to let you finish the bottle, and I've had plenty food to soak up what I did drink."

"I did have more than my share of the wine, didn't I? It was too good to waste." Lindsey chuckled.

"I'm glad you enjoyed it as much as I did. We may have to stock the boat with a few bottles."

"You won't get an argument from me."

Kendra took the Interstate for a faster route home. When they pulled in the driveway and into the garage, she left the top down on the Jeep.

Lindsey stepped out and stretched. "Thanks for a great day."

"I had fun too."

"Do we need to restock the boat tomorrow?"

"Yes. I have groceries being delivered at ten so sleep in, if you want."

Lindsey grinned. "There's little chance of that happening."

†

Kevin was still awake and watching football when they entered the house. "Welcome back, girls."

"Thanks, Dad. Did you have a good day?"

"I did, and so far I haven't broken or pulled anything. I do think I'll be feeling some muscles that haven't worked in a while in the morning, though. How was your day?"

"It was great. I put a down payment on the boat, we both won pots at the casino, and dinner at Mary Mahoney's was fantastic as usual."

"Oh that does sound good. Hank and I boiled up a mess of your reds for dinner. They sure were good."

Lindsey yawned. "I'm going to call it a night. I'll see y'all in the morning."

"Goodnight, thanks again for a great day."

"Thank you for letting me invite myself along. I had a blast."

"Sleep well," Kevin told her. "Are you going to sit up with your old man for a bit?"

"Sure, Dad."

"Before you sit down, will you grab us a beer then?"

"Absolutely."

"Thanks," Kevin replied when she handed him a beer and sat beside him. "Now that you're going to be the owner of two boats, have you considered what you're going to do?"

"About a second captain you mean?"

"Yes. You can't be in two places at once, and I'm sure you'll want to keep a boat running the local waters."

"I talked with Harvey several weeks ago, and he's not interested in getting a captain's license. I've got a few months yet to come up with a plan."

"I think an option just went up the stairs." He grinned.

Kendra looked at him in surprise. "Do you mean Lindsey?"

"Well I didn't see anybody else go upstairs."

"Smart ass."

"She has a younger brother who can take over her Dad's boat when he chooses to retire, and I think she's really enjoying her time here. At least give it some thought."

"I will, Dad," she promised. "To be honest, I thought she'd be chomping at the bit to go back to the Outer Banks."

"Maybe so, but I doubt it."

"What makes you think differently?" Kendra asked curiously.

Kevin turned to fully face his daughter. "I know we don't talk about much personal things, but the woman is in love with you."

Kendra nearly choked on the drink of beer she had just taken. "What are you talking about?"

"Well, you obviously have blinders on, but when she looks at you, you can see it in her eyes."

"You're serious aren't you?"

"Kendra, I love you like no other, but you can be dense as hell at times. She looks at you the way I looked at your mother. She loves you and I think she'd be good for you."

"When did you become a matchmaker?"

"Just recently, when my bullheaded daughter refused to see what's right in front of her. I've never seen you as happy since she got here."

Kendra was quiet for several minutes while she pondered her dad's revelations.

Kevin finished his beer. "Now, I'm going to bed. Lock up and I'll see you in the morning."

"Goodnight, Dad. Love you."

"I love you too, Kendra."

Kendra turned the television off and picked up their empty bottles. She carried them into the kitchen to dispose of them and prepared the coffee pot for the morning. When she climbed the stairs, she saw the light coming underneath Lindsey's door, and a smile grew on her face. *Is he right? Does she really love me?*

She undressed and climbed into bed still pondering those questions.

Chapter Ten

Kendra woke the next morning, her face sore from smiling during her sleep. She had fallen asleep thinking about Lindsey, and her thoughts had turned into the most beautiful of dreams. She made her way into the shower and, when she emerged from her room, the smell of coffee and the sound of bacon frying met her on the staircase. Walking into the kitchen, she expected to find her dad cooking breakfast, but Lindsey was in front of the stove whipping up batter for pancakes. Lindsey turned when she entered.

"Good morning, boss, I hope you're hungry. Your dad wanted pancakes today."

"Pancakes always work for me. Anything I can do to help?"

"Grab a cup of coffee and join your dad at the table. I'll have the first batch ready in a few."

Kendra poured a cup of coffee and walked to the table. "Do you need a refill, Dad?"

"I'd love one, darling," he replied, barely taking his eyes off the newspaper he was reading.

She picked up his mug and walked over to the pot. Kendra caught Lindsey not watching and snagged a slice of bacon.

"Don't think I didn't see that."

"It smells too good. I had to have a bite." Kendra smirked and stuffed the slice in her mouth.

They had finished breakfast, and she and Lindsey were washing the dishes, when the phone rang. "Hang tight, I'll get it," Kevin said.

Kendra heard him answer the phone and turned to look at him.

"Hey, Betty," he said.

She watched as her dad's face blanched white as he listened to the caller. He sat down in a chair, seemingly stunned speechless by what he was hearing.

"Dad, is everything all right?" she asked.

He looked up at her, and she could see the panic in his eyes. He held up a finger for her to wait for a second. "Of course I'll be there. Tell Henry I'll be on my way today and I'll see you soon. Thank you for letting me know. Goodbye, Betty."

"Dad, what's wrong?" she asked.

Lindsey turned around and looked at Kevin.

"It's your Uncle Henry," he said to Kendra. "They rushed him to the hospital this morning. He's had a heart attack and needs open heart surgery."

"Oh no, Dad. Are you okay?"

"Yeah, I just didn't expect that from Henry. He's an avid fitness buff, even at his age."

"That will work to his advantage in surgery. I'll call and make flight reservations for you if you want to pack a bag."

He nodded and walked over to Kendra who hugged him tightly. "He's going to be okay, Dad, so don't worry."

"We're not young men anymore," he said, with tears in his eyes.

"Do you want me to go with you?"

"No, stay and keep the business going. Thanks for offering, but I don't know anything you can do. Hell, I don't know what I can do, but be there for Henry and Betty."

"I can be there for you."

Kevin looked at her and forced a smile. "You're worse than me about hospitals."

"You've got a point there. I'd probably get us both kicked out," she replied. "Go pack and I'll get on the computer."

"Is there anything I can do to help?" Lindsey asked.

"Go up to my room and grab my wallet off the dresser while I boot up the computer please."

Kendra watched her fingers shake as she reached to turn on the computer on her desk. Henry was her dad's only sibling, and was his senior by four years. He and his wife Betty had retired to Phoenix, Arizona, several years ago. She heard Lindsey racing back down the stairs, and took the wallet from her. "Thanks."

"I'll take care of the groceries, while you help your Dad," Lindsey offered. "Just call if you need anything, okay?"

"I'll take him to the airport and get back as soon as I can."

"Just take care of him and don't worry. I've got this under control." Lindsey turned to leave.

"Lindsey," Kendra called after her.

Lindsey stopped and turned back to her.

"Thanks for being here and helping."

Lindsey smiled back at her. "There's no place I'd rather be. See you later."

Kendra nodded and turned back to the computer as she heard the front door close. She could hear her dad moving around in his room as he packed his bag. She logged on to check airfare to Phoenix. There was a seat left on a flight from Mobile, but they would need to leave soon for the airport if he was going to be able to make the flight. Kendra booked it and then made a reservation for a car at the Phoenix airport. Then she went to check on her dad.

He had finished packing his bag and was sitting on the edge of the bed, fighting back tears. She walked over to him and wrapped her arms around him.

"He's going to be fine. Uncle Henry is in the best place he can be right now, so be strong for him and Betty."

"I don't know what I'll do if he doesn't pull through."

"Then don't even dwell on it. Think positive thoughts. Are you sure you don't need me to come?"

"No, darling. I'll get it together and be all right. Did you get me a ticket?"

"Yes, but we need to go soon to make it on time."

"I need to stop at an ATM, along the way."

"No you don't." She pulled out her wallet and handed him eight hundred-dollar bills. "I hit a couple jackpots yesterday," she grinned.

Kevin shook his head and placed the bills in his wallet. "Take the money out of the account to replace this."

"Don't worry about it." She picked up his bag. "You okay to ride in the Jeep?"

"Sure, I could use the fresh air to clear my head."

"Let's go."

†

Kevin was unusually silent on the ride to Mobile, worrying Kendra. "Will you call me when you arrive, and let me know you got there safely?"

"Yes, but I'll wait until I get to the hospital and have an update on Henry."

"That's a good idea. Please keep me posted this week. I programmed the number of the satellite phone into your cell, so call whenever you can."

"I'll call you every day. Is morning or night better for you?"

"Both are better for me, Dad." She smiled.

"Both it is then."

She pulled up to the curb at the airport. "I've already checked you in, so all you need to do is clear security, and then gate-check your bag. You didn't bring any weapons did you?"

"No, I left the machine gun at home," he teased, and opened the door.

Kendra jogged around to the back of the Jeep and took out his bag. She hugged her dad tightly. "I miss you already. Tell Uncle Henry and Aunt Betty hello from me, and please call anytime you want to. Deal?"

"Yes, yes, I will. I promise."

"Be safe and I'll see you soon."

"You, too, be careful driving back, and have a great week."

Kendra nodded and watched as he grabbed the handle of his bag and rolled it toward the entrance of the airport. The emotional weight riding on his shoulders made him look older as he turned and waved goodbye. She smiled, returned his wave, and turned to wipe away tears as he disappeared inside.

She pulled into the cell lot and waited until his plane took off, and then headed for home.

Kendra groaned as traffic slowed to a crawl just outside the tunnel in Mobile. "Damn, not today," she growled as she drove ten feet then stopped. It would be another mile before she could detour through downtown, bypassing the heavy traffic. She jacked up her radio and sang along with the tune to pass the time. Even the upbeat country song did little to lift her spirits. When she was close enough to see the exit, she turned onto the shoulder and left the Interstate.

†

Lindsey turned at the sound of the Jeep and watched Kendra drive away with her dad. She sent up a silent prayer that all would work out well, then looked back toward the harbor. She stepped on board and walked over to unlock the galley. The delivery would arrive shortly, but she took a few minutes to explore the boat. As she stepped into the wheelhouse, her heart felt heavy. Kendra had barely pulled away, but Lindsey was missing her already. Lindsey sat in the captain's seat and looked out at the view Kendra saw every time she left the harbor. A glance down to a small desk revealed a notepad, and she smiled at the thought of Kendra doodling on the pad as she spent endless hours behind the wheel. She was even more surprised to see her name written on the pad with a large question mark beside it. She wondered what was the question Kendra needed to answer about her. She left the wheelhouse to enter the small cabin set aside for the captain.

She couldn't resist picking up the pillow and lifting it to her face. She took a deep breath, inhaling the scent of Kendra's shampoo and the alluring scent of her perfume. She chuckled at her behavior. "This is really weird," she spoke aloud. "I'm pining over a woman I can never have."

She placed the pillow back on the bed as she heard the back-up alarm of the delivery truck. The groceries had arrived. She stepped back out on deck to supervise the unloading, and after signing for the order, began storing the supplies.

Lindsey finished stocking the groceries and closed the galley. She had decided to walk to a local shop to check out the wine selection, intending to purchase several bottles of the Riesling they had shared the previous night as a surprise for Kendra. *Here I go again, being a romantic.* She smiled and headed for downtown.

Surprised by the extensive selection of wine, Lindsey decided to rely on the expertise of the shop owner to make selections for her and she smiled as she left the shop with six bottles of his finest Riesling. It drained her wallet of the last of her winnings, but it was for Kendra, who was damned well worth the cost. Lindsey walked back to the boat, entered the captain's suite, and opened the small refrigerator. Lindsey smiled as she spied a wine rack, which would allow two bottles to chill at a time. She slipped the bottles into the cradle, and then carried the rest of the crate to the small pantry, storing it for future use.

She stopped by her own berth before leaving the ship, checking her supply of clothing and hygiene products. As she was about to step onto the deck, she looked up to find Kendra coming on board.

"Welcome back," Lindsey said.

"Thanks. Did you get everything stocked and stored?"

"Yes, ma'am, I did."

"I appreciate you taking care of the order while I got Dad settled."

"No problem. I was happy to help. How's he holding up?"

"I think he's still in shock, but he'll get himself together before he makes it to the hospital."

"He's a strong man and he'll be ready to deal with whatever comes his way."

Kendra smiled. "Yes, he is."

"Is there anything else we need to do here?"

"Nope, everything else should be set. I need to do some laundry for this week."

"I've got some to do as well. We can do it together and I'll cook dinner later," Lindsey suggested. "Does chicken Alfredo sound good to you?"

"Sounds delicious, but I'm not sure we have the supplies for that," Kendra said.

"Okay, so here's the deal. We go home, I'll make a list while you bring your laundry down, and you can go to the grocery while I start laundry."

"That sounds like I got the better end of the deal."

Lindsey chuckled. "I don't care that much for grocery shopping."

"All right, hop in," she instructed as they reached the Jeep.

†

Kendra exchanged a laundry basket for a grocery list. "I'll be back shortly."

"Take your time. I'll get the laundry started."

"See you in a bit then."

She watched as Lindsey carried the basket and began sorting the clothing.

Kendra drove to the grocery for her supplies and then pulled into the local wine shop. A glass or three of the Riesling they had shared last night would go well with the dinner Lindsey had planned. She parked and went inside.

"I'd like a bottle of your best Riesling," she told the man working behind the counter.

"That's a very popular request today. Another young lady came and bought six bottles earlier today. I may need to take a bottle home to the wife." He grinned as he led her to the selection of wines.

"This is the best." He pulled out a bottle.

"Do you have any already chilled?"

"Let me check and see," he answered, and walked back to a cooler.

104

His smile matched Kendra's when he returned carrying a bottle.

"You're in luck."

Kendra paid for her purchase and drove home. She parked the Jeep in the garage and walked into the kitchen, handing Lindsey the bags of groceries as she walked to the refrigerator.

"What's that?" she asked as Kendra placed the bottle in the refrigerator.

"I stopped off for a bottle of that Riesling that was so good last night. I thought it'd be good with dinner."

"Good idea." Lindsey smiled and busied herself with the groceries.

When they finished the laundry, Lindsey returned to the kitchen to begin dinner.

"Is there anything I can do to help?" Kendra asked.

"Yes, you can pour us a glass of wine and keep me company."

"At least let me make the salad."

"Okay, you can make the salad after you pour us a glass of wine." Lindsey grinned as she filled a pot with water.

"What time was your Dad arriving in Phoenix?" Lindsey asked as they were drinking the last of the wine.

Kendra checked her watch. "He should be there and on his way to the hospital by now. I expect him to call within the hour with an update on his brother."

"I hope it's good news."

"Me too," she answered.

"I was thinking I'd take our clean clothes down to the boat," Lindsey said.

"Do you want some help with that?"

"No, stay in case your Dad calls. I can handle the laundry on my own."

"Fine then, I'll pick up the kitchen, while you're gone."

"Okay by me." Lindsey agreed and left for the boat.

Kendra was cleaning the kitchen when her dad called. "Hey, how is Uncle Henry?"

"He's resting now, but he looks pretty haggard."

"How are you?"

"Tired from the travel, but glad to finally be here. Henry's scheduled for surgery at five tomorrow morning. He made me promise to take Betty home for a few hours of sleep. She's been here all day and looks worse than Henry."

"You both need a good night's rest. Tomorrow will be a long day of waiting."

"Yes, I know. I'll try to get her to eat something and get some sleep. The hospital is close so we can leave at four and be here to sit with him in pre-op until they take him for surgery."

"I'll be on the boat by five so call me there. Please try to get some rest."

"I will. We're going to leave in just a few minutes."

"Okay, goodnight, and I'll be waiting for your call in the morning."

"Have a good night and a great week."

"I will, Dad. I love you."

"Love you, too."

When she ended the call, Kendra broke down in tears, her body leaning against the kitchen counter for support. That is how Lindsey found her.

Lindsey rushed across the room when she heard Kendra crying and took her in her arms, holding her close. "Easy now," she whispered. Her hands stroked the back of Kendra's head.

Kendra's sobs seemed to leave her speechless as she fought to regain her breath.

"It's okay, you're going to be fine." Lindsey whispered calming words of reassurance to her friend.

After several long minutes of torture, Lindsey felt Kendra begin to relax and catch her breath. When she finally looked into Lindsey's eyes, they were red rimmed and filled with tears.

"Are you ready to talk?" Lindsey whispered.

To Lindsey's regret, Kendra stepped back away from her and wiped her eyes. "I'm sorry for being such a mess."

"You have nothing to apologize for. It's been a bitch of a day for your family."

"Yeah it has," she agreed. "Dad finally called."

"Is everything okay?"

"It's as good as can be expected, I guess. Uncle Henry goes in for open-heart surgery at five in the morning. Dad sounded very tired and worried."

"He's not used to traveling and that kind of stress. He'll bounce back once he knows his brother has come through surgery tomorrow," Lindsey soothed.

"I sure hope so. I wish I'd gone now."

"There's nothing you could do there and you'd be someone else for your Dad to worry about." She saw Kendra cringe at her remark and smacked her forehead. "That sounded horrible, didn't it?"

Kendra nodded. "I get your meaning though, so thanks, even if it did sound terrible."

Lindsey wiped the hair out her eyes. "I never promised to be good with words."

Kendra managed a weak smile. "No, you didn't. Thanks for being here though."

"That's what friends are for. Now go take a shower and hit the sack. I'll set the coffee and lock up."

"I'm too drained emotionally to argue. I'll see you at four."

"I'll be ready, boss."

Finished with her shower, Lindsey was walking past Kendra's room when she heard her crying. She knocked on the door and then stepped inside the room. Kendra was sitting on the edge of her bed with her hands covering her face. Lindsey knelt in front of her and took her hands, moving them from her face. "What's wrong?"

107

Kendra sniffled as she fought her tears. "I'm just worried about Dad. Uncle Henry's heart attack has me worried about losing Dad."

Still holding her hands, Lindsey lifted them to her lips and kissed them. "That's not surprising that you're worrying about your dad. Believe it or not, you're not a superhuman captain," she said. "Even captains are allowed to cry." Lindsey's eyes were filled with tears witnessing Kendra's heartache.

Kendra leaned forward and kissed Lindsey, her lips lingering.

Lindsey felt her heart pounding when Kendra's soft lips touched hers, catching her completely off guard. Thankfully, her body reacted and her lips parted to invite Kendra into a deeper kiss.

Kendra took her hands and softly stroked Lindsey's face when she ended the kiss, her eyes searching the depth of Lindsey's eyes for a reaction. She leaned her face into her caress.

"Will you stay with me tonight?"

"Yes," Lindsey whispered. She stood and took Kendra in her arms, feeling her body trembling as she stroked her hair. "Everything's going to be all right."

Kendra nodded. "Are you ready for bed?"

Lindsey answered by walking around the bed and pulling the bed covers back for them. She waited until Kendra turned off the light, and climbed into the bed and then crept in beside her. "Roll onto your side and I'll hold you until you go to sleep."

Kendra turned onto her side as Lindsey snuggled into her body and wrapped an arm around her waist. The warmth of Lindsey's body was comforting and she could feel Lindsey's heart beating against her back. She reached down, taking Lindsey's hand in hers and tucked it beneath her chin.

Lindsey held her until Kendra stopped trembling and relaxed as she drifted off to sleep. She could feel the smile stretching her cheeks as she thought of the tender kiss they had shared and silently prayed it wouldn't be their last.

Chapter Eleven

Kendra was surprised that she had slept the night through when she woke, and she found she had turned in Lindsey's arms and was now facing her. Lindsey was awake, her blue eyes sparkling.

"Good morning. How long have you been awake?"

"Not long. Did you sleep well?" Lindsey asked.

"Yes I did. Thank you for staying with me."

"You don't need to thank me. I was here because you needed me, and I wanted to be here."

Kendra felt a blush rise to her face. "I wanted you beside me." She reached up to stroke Lindsey's face. "I can't deny any longer that I'm falling for you."

"You don't know how happy that makes me." Lindsey smiled. She leaned in and kissed her sweetly.

"This will be complicated, you know. I'm still your captain on the boat."

"I'll be content to have you at home if you want me."

"I want you." Kendra smiled and rolled on top of her. "Damn, how I want you."

Lindsey pulled her face down for a passionate kiss. "I want to make love with you, but now is not the time. We have to meet the crew soon, and I don't want to rush our first time together."

"It will be worth the wait," Kendra promised.

They separated to prepare for the day and met in the kitchen. Kendra was eating a slice of toast when Lindsey arrived. "Do you want some breakfast?"

"I'll have what you're having, but I'll fix it, so sit tight. You need a refill on your coffee?"

"Sure, thanks."

Lindsey dropped two slices of bread in the toaster and poured a cup of coffee before taking the pot to refill Kendra's cup. "Do we have apple jelly? I'm thinking it's an apple jelly kind of day."

"In the door of the fridge," Kendra informed her as she stirred her coffee.

Lindsey prepared her toast and joined Kendra at the table. "Have you heard from your dad yet?"

"No, not yet, he'll probably wait until Henry goes in the operating room to call. There's a three-hour time difference."

"You're probably right, and that does make sense to wait," Lindsey replied as she took a bite of toast.

†

When they reached the boat, Harvey was already on board, brewing a pot of coffee. "Morning, ladies," he called out when they entered the galley.

Over a cup of coffee, Kendra brought him current on the events with her dad and uncle.

He put an arm around Kendra. "Are you sure you need to be here this week?"

"Dad didn't want me to miss the week of fishing. I should have insisted on going with him, but you know how he is."

"Yeah, I do. Please keep me posted. I don't know Henry well, but I know how your dad worships his big brother."

"That he does. I'm going to get the engine warmed up while we're waiting on the rest of the crew."

Harvey waited for her to enter the wheelhouse then turned to Lindsey. "How's she really doing?"

"She had a rough night so I'm going to try to get her to nap later."

"That's a good idea. We're lucky to have you with us. It's nice having a second captain on board for times like these."

"I just thought you liked my cooking." Lindsey grinned.

"Well, that too," he added with a smirk.

"Good morning, sunshine," Charlie declared when he stepped on board the boat. "I hope everyone had a great weekend like me."

"I'll leave you to fill him and the rest of the crew in on what's going on." Lindsey poured another cup of coffee and walked out on deck.

✝

Kendra took a sip of her coffee and looked up to see Lindsey sitting at the rail staring out across the water. She was glad that Lindsey was there for support and had proven herself invaluable to the boat, but there was more. She loved the way the sun kissed her blond hair and the tanned skin of her neck as the wind blew her short hair. Kendra smiled thinking of the night they had shared. She was falling in love and it felt wonderful.

Lindsey loved the way the gulls soared on the currents, diving and squawking at each other as they hunted for breakfast, or argued over scraps from a passing boat. It was hard to keep from laughing at their antics as they begged for more, swooping close to the boat hoping for a handout.

"You're out of luck this morning," she called to them, and they flew off in search of a different boat.

She drained her cup and turned back toward the galley. She noticed Kendra watching her from the wheelhouse, so she lifted her mug and pointed. Kendra nodded and raised her mug, indicating she'd like a refill. Smiling at their unspoken communication, Lindsey stepped inside the wheelhouse to retrieve the empty mug.

"I'll bring it right back."

†

After they left port and had been underway for hours, Kendra's dad called to say that Henry had finally gone into surgery. It would be at least six hours before they were done. Kevin promised to call once Henry reached recovery and they got an update from the surgeon. Kendra filled in Harvey and Lindsey who were in the wheelhouse with her.

"Now will you take Lindsey's advice and go get some rest?" Harvey asked.

"Yes, I'll take a nap, but don't let me sleep all day, and Lindsey, don't run us ashore anywhere."

"I'll try my best. Other than another boat or an oil rig, I'd say we're pretty safe."

"Wake me for lunch then."

As Kendra slipped inside her quarters she heard Lindsey say, "Finally, I get to drive this boat."

"See you at lunch," Harvey replied.

†

The morning burned on, and besides two other shrimp boats, they encountered nothing but sparkling water and clear skies. A light tap on the door alerted Lindsey to Harvey's entrance as he brought her a tray of food.

"Grilled cheese, tomato soup, chips, and sweet tea," he announced, setting the tray beside her on the table.

"That smells terrific."

"A favorite from the captain's childhood," he shared. "I thought it would give her some comfort today."

"That's sweet and kind of you, Harvey."

"She's like the daughter I never had."

"And she thinks of you as her second dad."

112

"Now you flatter me."

"You have to know it's true. She values your opinion over any other on the boat, and says you're the best first mate she's ever worked with."

"I should be. Her dad taught me everything I know about shrimping, as he's done with her."

"Are you going to wake her or let her sleep, Harvey?"

"I'm going to do just as she asked and wake her for some lunch. If she chooses to get more sleep, I'm fine with that."

"Tell her we have everything under control if she needs more rest."

"I will, and thanks again for being here."

"My pleasure, Harvey."

Lindsey started her meal and several minutes later, she heard a tap of the door to the captain's quarters, as Harvey took lunch to Kendra. She was just finishing her soup and munching on the chips when she heard Kendra enter.

"Mind if I join you?"

"Not at all." She made a movement to forfeit the captain's chair, but Kendra stopped her.

"Sit still." Kendra took the extra seat, setting her tray on the table. "Harvey made us a treat today. A good one, too, very tasty, reminds me of being a little girl."

"It was one of my favorites, too. Still is," replied Lindsey.

"What do you plan on doing this afternoon?"

"I was thinking I'd bake us a cake unless you wanted more sleep."

"If I sleep any longer, I won't sleep tonight."

"Yellow cake with chocolate icing okay with you?"

"That sounds perfect to me."

"I think Harvey's planning to fry chicken, and make rice and gravy to go with it."

"Between the two of you, you're hitting all my favorites."

"Good to know, boss, good to know."

"Are you ready to take over?" Lindsey asked when they finished lunch.

"Yes, I am, thanks for taking over for me."

"You're welcome." Lindsey stood and picked up their trays. "Time for me to go see a man about a cake."

Lindsey left the wheelhouse with the sound of Kendra's laughter ringing in her ears. *That's a good sound.* She smiled as she walked to the galley.

✝

Lindsey placed the cake in the oven and then joined the men at the table. "Okay, who's ready to lose some money?"

"Hopefully you are," Charlie replied. "I'm on a roll."

"Time to change that. Deal me in, boys." She sat, rubbing her hands together, ready for battle.

It took two hands for her to warm up and begin winning pots. The smell of the baking cake filled the room. She won another hand and Charlie playfully tossed his cards on the pile.

"That's not fair, she's cheating," he cried.

"How exactly is she cheating?" Harvey asked.

"By distracting us with the smell of that cake." He grinned. "I can't focus on anything but how good it's going to taste later tonight."

The table broke out in laughter right on cue as the timer sounded.

"You're saved by the bell." Lindsey laughed, and walked to the oven to take the cake out to cool. "Go ahead without me. I'll play catch up later tonight."

She poured two glasses of tea. "I'm going to check on the captain. Harvey, do you think you can keep them away from the cake?"

"I've got your back," he grinned, as he shuffled the cards.

✝

Kendra was on the phone when Lindsey entered the wheelhouse and the look on her face was one of relief. "That's great news, Dad. Do you think you can relax now?"

Lindsey placed the glass of tea in Kendra's free hand.

"So when do they think he'll be out of the woods? Really? Wow that's amazing," Kendra said into the phone.

Lindsey took a seat and waited for the call to end.

"Okay, call me later when you get back to Uncle Henry's. Love you, too." Kendra ended the call and let out a deep breath.

"Good news I take it," Lindsey said.

"The surgery was a success. They had to unblock three chambers, but everything went well. He's already back in his room on the cardiac floor, and Dad told me they planned to get him up and walking tomorrow afternoon."

"That's amazing."

"He'll still be in the hospital for about a week on IV antibiotics to prevent infection, but everything so far has gone like planned."

Lindsey was about to say something, but was interrupted by an alarm on the console. She watched as the computer screen came online.

"That can't be good." Lindsey frowned as they watched a weather alert came on-screen.

A tropical depression was highlighted on the screen just south of Puerto Rico, and the ticker tape report projected the depression to strengthen quickly, turning into a tropical storm within the next twenty-four hours. The next screen showed the projected path, a high probability of the storm turning east and heading back out into the eastern Atlantic. Two other paths, however, with lower probability, showed the storm heading up toward the Outer Banks, or turning west and heading into the Gulf.

"Give your dad a call to make sure he's seen this alert." Kendra handed Lindsey the phone before turning back to the computer screen. "When you're done, round up the crew and bring them here, please."

"Will do, boss." Lindsey heard the clicking of the phone as the satellite picked up the signal and then the phone began to ring. She breathed a sigh of relief when her dad answered the phone.

"Hello."

"Hey, Dad, it's me, Lindsey."

"Hey there, sweetie, is everything okay? I didn't recognize the number."

"I'm on the boat's satellite phone. We're out in the Gulf, going out for reds, but Captain Drake just got a weather alert and wanted to make sure you got it as well. There's a storm brewing that has the potential of making it to the Outer Banks by next weekend."

"I'm booting up the system now, but tell her thanks for the heads up. How have you been doing?"

"I'm great. Kendra's dad had to fly to Phoenix yesterday. His brother suffered a massive heart attack and needed surgery today."

"Have you heard from him? Is his brother going to be okay?"

"Yes, she had just talked to him before the weather alert came up. Things went very well, and he should be in the hospital about a week."

"That's good news. Damn, I see the storm track now. Hopefully, it will head back out to sea or die off completely."

"I hope so, too, but please keep an eye on the storm, Dad."

"I will. You said you're out in the Gulf fishing reds, is that right?"

"Yes, sir, we'll hit our grid tonight unless the captain turns us around to head for home."

"That probably won't be necessary for at least a couple more days. Maybe you can get a few passes in before heading back."

"Hopefully so. I'll keep in touch. Stay safe, Dad."

"You too, honey. I'll call this number if anything changes here."

"Thanks, Dad. Love you."

"Love you, too, baby girl."

†

Lindsey walked into the galley. "Wrap it up, boys, the captain wants to meet with us in the wheelhouse. We've got weather issues."

The men groaned at ending the game, but followed her into the wheelhouse.

"I just wanted to give you a heads up on a weather alert we just received. The National Weather Center is tracking a depression. The scientists feel it has a strong chance of becoming at least a tropical storm, but more likely a hurricane," Kendra told them.

"Aw man," Charlie groaned.

"What about the track?" Harvey asked.

"Still early in the game, but one of the tracks does send it potentially our way, in four to five days. The best case scenario is that the Gulf Stream flow takes it back out to sea in the eastern Atlantic."

"That's good to hear." Harvey relaxed a bit.

"I'll keep a close eye on the track, and if we need to high tail it home we will. What I need to hear from you is whether or not you want to bust it for the next three days, and hopefully get our quotas and head in early, just in case."

Lindsey noticed several heads nodding as Kendra spoke and looked into the faces of the crew. "I think we'd all be in agreement to push a little harder to make the quota and head for home."

"I'm certainly on board with it," Harvey agreed. "If we put in just before sunrise, and bust it until the sun goes down, we can probably get in four, maybe five runs."

"I think that's doable, but it's going to be long days," Kendra warned.

"Hell yeah, let's do this," Charlie said. "I don't know about y'all, but I enjoyed the hell out of last week's paycheck, and I want another, even better."

"If we fill all the bags I ordered for this week, we can double your check, but I will not put the crew or the boat in any danger."

"Thanks, Captain," Tim replied. "We'll make it happen."

"We should arrive at the edge of the grid in about an hour, and I'll drop anchor for the night. I'd suggest we have a hearty meal and get a good night's sleep."

"You heard the Captain, let's get to fixing supper," Harvey instructed, ushering them out of the wheelhouse.

"I've got a cake to frost. Do you need anything?" Lindsey asked.

"A strong westerly wind to blow the storm away from us."

"I wish I could get that for you." Lindsey shrugged, and followed the crew to the galley.

†

Kevin kept his word and called Kendra just as the sun was going down and she was preparing to drop anchor.

"Henry's doing remarkably well. I think he's even excited about starting to walk tomorrow."

"That sounds good. I just hope he stays positive once the pain medications start wearing off. We know he's a fighter, but don't let him overdo things," Kendra warned.

"I don't think we have to worry about that. His personal nurse has to be kin to Nurse Ratched. She could probably bench press more than I could in my youth."

"That's good to hear. How are you holding up?"

"Tired, but relieved that the surgery went well. I know the tough part is just beginning, but I feel good about his rehab."

"I love you, Dad."

"I love you too, baby girl. Did you make it out to the grid yet?"

"We just arrived and I'm about to close her down for the night. Harvey's frying chicken for dinner."

"That sounds so good. Rice and gravy, too?" he asked.

"Don't you know it. Lindsey's made a cake, too, yellow with chocolate frosting."

"Aw man, you're killing me." Kendra could almost see his smile across the phone lines. "Go ahead and get her tucked in for the night and enjoy a good meal. Just know how jealous I am at this moment."

"I will, Dad. Will you call again tomorrow?"

"Yes, but if there are no changes, I'll wait until he walks to let you know how it went."

"Sounds good. Have a good night, Dad, and get some food and rest yourself."

She ended the call and fought a momentary pang of guilt about not telling her dad about the potential weather problem—*he has enough on his mind.* Hopefully, the television in Phoenix wouldn't be broadcasting about the storm just yet. They could get a full boat and on their way home before he found out. She could at least hope for that luck.

Kendra dropped anchor, and once she felt the tug of it planting in the floor, she killed the engine and closed out her logbook for the night. She turned up the volume on the weather alert system, and followed the smell of frying chicken to the galley.

†

After the meal, Lindsey finished cleaning the galley before walking onto the deck for some fresh air. The breeze had picked up and felt good on her face as she looked up at the brilliant stars. Movement to her left alerted her to Kendra's presence, sitting on a small bench next to the wheelhouse.

"Hey, boss, you okay?"

"Yes, just too wired to sleep just yet. I had a long nap today thanks to you."

Lindsey grinned at her. "Would a nice glass of wine help you relax?"

"That would definitely help."

"I'll be right back then." She disappeared into the captain's suite.

Lindsey smiled as she pulled open a small drawer and pulled out the corkscrew she had picked up at the store as an afterthought. It would have been horrible to have such lovely wine but no way to open the bottle. She held her breath as she began the process of uncorking the bottle, working it free from the bottleneck, breathing again only when she heard the pop of the cork. She had to chuckle when her search failed to locate wine glasses, so she took a pair of mason jars down from the cupboard. She poured the wine into the jars, re-corked it, and returned the bottle to the fridge. She picked up the jars and walked back on deck.

"Not exactly a wine glass, but these will do in a pinch." She handed Kendra a jar.

"I will add some to my next shopping list. Where did you come up with the wine?"

"I stopped off at the wine shop and picked up six bottles of Riesling. I'm not certain it's the same as we both liked, but the shopkeeper declared it his finest."

Kendra smiled. "So it was you. The shopkeeper told me a young woman had been in earlier and bought six bottles."

"Yes, it was me." Lindsey grinned and made a bow.

"Good job." Kendra lifted her mason jar to Lindsey. "Care to share my bench?"

"I'd love to." Lindsey took a seat beside her. "Gorgeous out here isn't it?"

"Yeah, you'd never know there's a storm brewing out there."

"Stupid question, but have you checked the weather report lately?"

Kendra smiled at her and Lindsey felt her heart melt a little more. "Still strengthening, and slowing down. That's never good."

"How much longer until you think they'll have a better idea of the track?"

"Two, three days tops."

"We better work hard these next few days then."

"We can do this, if the shrimp are still as plentiful as last week."

"You'll find them, just like you did before, Captain."

Kendra took a sip of the wine and she turned to face Lindsey. "Thanks for having faith in me."

"That's so easy. You're a great captain." Distracted by the shine of the wine on Kendra's lips, Lindsey found herself thinking how much sweeter her lips would taste. She cleared her thoughts when she realized Kendra had spoken.

"It helps to have a great crew to back me up." Kendra had a tremor in her voice.

Twenty minutes later, they had finished the wine. "Would you care for another glass?"

"No, I think that was enough to relax me."

"Let me have your fine china and I'll go wash them," Lindsey said. "I'll bring them back to you tomorrow."

"Thanks, Lindsey. That was just what I needed. Have a great night."

"You too, Captain. Goodnight." Lindsey fought the temptation to kiss Kendra. She would wait to allow the captain to make the first move on the boat.

Kendra stopped in the wheelhouse to check the weather before retiring for the evening. Not much had changed from the earlier report.

"Just give us a few more days," she whispered into the darkened room. She double-checked the volume on the system and retired to her cabin.

Stretched out in her bed she felt the gentle rocking of the boat and let the wine relax her into a restful sleep.

Chapter Twelve

Harvey woke earlier than planned from the rocking of the boat. The wind and waves had increased significantly overnight. He climbed out of his berth to dress and walk on deck. The skies were still dark, but he could see ominous clouds racing in front of the moon. There was a drop in the temperature that, while noticeable, might not be enough to affect the approaching storm. He returned to the galley, started the coffee, and picked out items for breakfast. It would be a long day ahead and he wanted the crew to start it with a robust breakfast.

Lindsey heard Harvey head up on deck and slipped from her berth. He would probably start breakfast before the crew woke, and she planned to offer him her help.

He looked up when she arrived in the galley. "Good morning."

"I hope so. Those clouds look a bit ominous today."

"I just pray we can get two or three long days in before we have to head for home."

"Amen to that. What can I do to help?"

"Cube up some ham and cheese, then chop a few of those green onions. I thought we'd have some good scrambled eggs, fried potatoes, and toast to get us started. I don't imagine we'll have time for a leisurely lunch today."

She pulled out a knife and began chopping the onions. "In between runs, I can come in and prepare sandwiches. I'll put chips in a bowl so when we can take a short break everything will be ready to eat."

"That's a good idea. I can help to make things go quicker."

The outside door opened and Kendra entered the galley. "Good morning."

"Morning, Captain, did you rest well?" Harvey asked.

"Not bad, Harvey, and you?"

"Slept like a rock." He grinned. "Grab a couple of mugs of coffee for you and Lindsey if you will."

"Will do. What can I do to help? You two look like you're whipping up a feast."

"You can make a pile of toast," Harvey said.

Kendra passed a mug of coffee to Lindsey and went to work on making toast.

"What's the latest on the storm?" Lindsey asked.

Kendra dropped six slices in the toaster and pushed the lever. "It's still growing, unfortunately, but no clear path yet. She's got a name now, too."

"Dare I ask?" Harvey replied.

"Tropical storm Dani."

"Damn, I hate four letter storms. They almost always come into the Gulf," he groaned.

"Is that true or you pulling my leg?" Lindsey asked.

"Oh, it's true," Kendra, agreed. "Erin, Opal, Ivan, Kate, all have paid us a visit."

"Damn," Lindsey echoed Harvey's concern.

The door opened again and Charlie came through.

"Go ahead and get the rest of the crew moving, breakfast will be ready in just a few," Harvey instructed as he whipped up two dozen eggs. He turned to Lindsey, "Drop your ingredients in the bowl and let's get this party started."

"You want me to do the eggs while you finish the potatoes?" she asked.

"Be my guest." He handed Lindsey a spatula. "Captain, will you pull out jelly, juice, and ketchup?"

"You got it." She buttered the last of the toast to pop up, and put out what Harvey had asked for.

Lindsey watched as Kendra scooted back her chair and stood. "I'm going to get the engine warmed up," Kendra announced. "As soon as you can, get the nets in the water and the doors set so we can start a pass. You can clean up once we start to trawl."

"Yes, ma'am," Harvey answered. "You heard the captain. Eat up boys."

"Thanks for a great breakfast," she told them, and left the galley.

†

When the nets were in place, Kendra began their first pass of the day. The lights on the front of the boat lit the water as the sun had yet to rise. The crew prepared the deck for the first haul while Lindsey cleaned the galley.

The sun was beginning to creep above the horizon as the crew finished the setup. Beautiful hues of red, orange, and gold filled the eastern sky. Lindsey felt Kendra back down the power on the engine and she looked up to see her give Harvey a thumbs-up sign to start the winches. The crew held their collective breaths until the first full net rose above the railing, guided onto the deck above the bins.

Charlie was the first to let out a yell. "Now that's what I'm talking about!"

Lindsey turned to see Kendra smiling as they untied the first net and the bins overflowed.

"Let's get them emptied and back in the water as fast as we can," Kendra instructed over the intercom.

Kendra watched as the crew carried out their tasks, two men retying the emptied net while the other two brought in the second net. Harvey and Lindsey began the process of bagging the shrimp.

The first pass netted a great first haul with full nets. Charlie and the other crew took the filled bags to store in the freezer. The nets also brought in several nice grouper that they placed in a live well for a future meal. Harvey walked to the wheelhouse to report the catch.

"One hundred and fifty, and a half-dozen nice grouper," he reported.

"A good start, but we have a long way to go."

"We'll get there, Captain."

"Yes, we will," Kendra agreed.

Two more passes brought in three hundred and ten more filled bags. When they finished storing the shrimp, Lindsey and Harvey went to the galley to prepare lunch. They had a nice stack of sandwiches ready. Harvey handed her a plate of sandwiches and chips for the captain.

"Do you care to do the honors?" he asked.

"I'd love to."

"Send the rest of the crew in as you go. We might as well eat while we can."

Lindsey picked up a glass of tea and left the galley. "Lunch is ready," she called out on deck.

"I'm starving," she heard Charlie say as she entered the wheelhouse.

"Lunch is served, Captain. I brought tea, but do you want a refill on your coffee thermos?"

"That would be great, but eat your lunch first. Thanks for bringing it to me."

"My pleasure. I'll bring your coffee in just a bit then." She picked up the thermos and returned to the galley.

They managed to get in four passes before darkness overtook them. Kendra called it a day and the crew began cleaning the decks and preparing the nets for the next day.

"Once you are done, why don't you guys get cleaned up while I start cooking some spaghetti? Y'all did a great job today, and it's time for the captain's special," Kendra said.

"You won't get any argument from me," Harvey replied. "A hot shower and a cold beer might make me feel human again."

"Charlie, will you take a case of beer into the freezer to get good and cold while y'all are getting cleaned up?" Kendra asked.

"Yes, ma'am, I'm on it."

Kendra turned to look at Lindsey. "Would you like to use my shower so everyone can shower quickly?"

"I would love to, thanks."

"Let me get started then." Kendra entered the galley wearing a huge smile.

✝

"That was a great meal, Captain," Charlie said.

"I'm glad you enjoyed it. Y'all deserved a steak after the hard work you put in today, but we didn't have time for that." She looked at her tired crew. "I don't think anyone will have trouble sleeping tonight."

"Definitely not me." Harvey stretched.

"I think Tim's already on his way," Charlie teased.

Tim had finished eating and was starting to nod off. Charlie nudged him awake. "Go hit the bunks, man."

"I think I will. Goodnight, everyone."

"I'll clean up here and then hit the sack," Lindsey said.

"I can get this. All I did today was drive."

"You cooked, so I'll clean," Lindsey insisted.

"We're going to leave you two to hash it out," Harvey chuckled, and ushered the tired crew from the galley.

"Seriously, you can keep me company and have a beer if you want, but I'll clean up here."

"Very well," Kendra relented and twisted the top off a fresh beer. "You want one?"

"I will in just a minute, when I get these dishes in the washer."

Lindsey filled the dishwasher and placed the few leftovers in the refrigerator. "We had a good day today, didn't we?"

"Yes, we did. If we can repeat it tomorrow, and the next, we'll head home Thursday."

"I forgot to ask if you heard from your dad today."

"He called twice. Uncle Henry's doing well. Already complaining about the hospital food." She chuckled.

"That's a good sign." Lindsey took the beer Kendra handed her and sank into a chair.

Kendra noticed a grimace on her face. "I think the crew will all be sore tomorrow."

"That is a very good possibility. I know I will be. I can only imagine how Harvey's feeling right about now."

"I'm planning to come out of the wheelhouse to help out tomorrow and hopefully give him a bit of a rest."

Lindsey looked at her with bright blue eyes. "No offense, Captain, but have you heard the expression 'too many cooks in the kitchen'?"

"Of course I have. What's your point?"

"We have a system in place that works well. While I appreciate your intention, having another body on deck may be counter-productive."

Kendra appreciated her candor. "I understand. I just don't want you guys getting hurt from being overly tired."

"We'll be fine. Just keep finding us good shrimp."

"That I can do." Kendra lifted her bottle to Lindsey. "To finding good shrimp."

"Cheers." Lindsey took a long drink. "That freezer makes the beer perfect."

Kendra smiled. "Another plus of having a freezer on board."

Lindsey yawned. "I'm toast. See you in the morning."

Kendra reached over to push a strand of hair back from Lindsey's face and let her fingers caress down her cheek. "Get some sleep. Tomorrow will be another long day," Kendra warned.

"You too, goodnight." Lindsey dropped her bottle in the trash bin and left the galley.

Kendra smiled. "You have a wonderful crew, Captain Drake. Cherish them," she reminded herself.

✝

Kendra felt like she had barely fallen asleep when she heard an alarm sounding from the wheelhouse, jarring her awake. She leapt from the bed and rushed into the room to find the computer screen flashing an update from the Hurricane Center. She clicked on the screen and read the alert. Dani was now a Category One hurricane and was drifting further west toward the Gulf. The torrential rains she dumped on Puerto Rico and Cuba had left mudslides and flooding in her wake. Kendra winced when she clicked on the storm path projections, which revealed the percentage was increasing of the storm coming their way. She checked wind speed and the rate at which the storm was moving. Still relatively slow moving, the storm wouldn't reach south Florida for another day. She and the crew could safely work two more days at this speed and still have time to race the storm back to land.

The crew would have ample time to go home and batten down the hatches to ride out the storm or collect their families to evacuate to the north. She would apprise them of the situation when they met for breakfast in a few more hours.

Kendra expected her dad to learn about the storm sooner or later, but she hoped for later. She would have the crew safely returned to their homes, have the shutters closed on the house, and be fully prepared to face the storm as she took the boat deep inland into the protected waters of the bay. She doubted Lindsey would choose to evacuate, and honestly, she would appreciate the extra pair of hands and the company as she rode out the storm on board.

Kendra had weathered two storms on the boat with her dad and felt confident she could keep the boat safe from the storm.

She climbed back in bed, eager to fill their quota and head back home.

†

Over breakfast, Kendra gave them the news. "I think we need to decide what we want to do later today. We can work one more day or head for home. I'll keep an eye on the reports so we have the most current data."

"I think we all want to work another day, if we can do so safely," Harvey said.

"Does anyone plan to evacuate? If so, we need to head in sooner."

"You are the only one close to shore. I think the rest of us have heeded your dad's advice and bought stand-by generators for our homes, so we should be in good shape," Charlie stated.

The rest of the crew nodded in agreement.

"Will you need help securing the boat?" Harvey asked.

"Not if Lindsey will join me. I've taken the boat deep in the bay with Dad twice, so that's what I'll do again. Stay with your family and if you can, keep an eye on our house. I'll make sure that the shutters are closed and the generator is ready. It'll run the house as long as the natural gas isn't interrupted. My main worry will be the storm surge and trees."

"I think we can keep an eye out on it. You know Charlie's going to be out in the storm until his wife locks him in the house," Harvey added.

Kendra looked at Lindsey. "Are you up for a few days on the bay?"

"That beats being cooped inside a house any day."

"Okay, so now we just figure out the timing, and we're set."

†

The nets were filled to their maximum each time they arrived on deck, and the crew worked quickly to empty them and get them back in the water. They opted to work through lunch to get another run in and get that much closer to their quota.

Kendra returned to the galley, took packages of steaks out of the freezer to thaw, then again to soak them in marinade, and put potatoes in the oven to bake. She would grill the steaks while the crew cleaned up and relaxed.

As the sun raced to the horizon, the crew brought up the final nets of the day. The extra run helped as they harvested nine hundred bags, placing them three quarters into their quota.

Kendra silenced the engine and dropped anchor for the night before going to set up the grill.

Charlie looked at what she was doing. "I hope that means we're getting a steak tonight."

"Absolutely, Charlie, y'all have more than earned it these last two days."

"All right. I call dibs on the first shower," he called out.

"Would you mind if I use your shower again so I can come back and help?" Lindsey asked.

"Sure, will you put the beer in the freezer before you go?"

"Absolutely, boss." She grinned, went into the pantry for a case of beer, and placed it in the freezer. "What else do you want to go with the steaks?"

"I've got potatoes baking. Would you mind putting a salad together and a couple bags of corn on to boil when you get back?"

"No problem," Lindsey answered and went to shower.

"I'll go ahead and get the water for the corn boiling," Harvey offered.

"Thanks, Harvey," Lindsey called and kept walking.

"We did well today, huh, Captain?" he asked.

"Yeah, we did excellent. I think we can head for home around lunch tomorrow, and make it most of the way home, even loaded down."

"That sounds like a good plan. Do you need anything before I head down?"

"Nope, just put the water on to boil. Once the grill is heated, I'll start on the steaks."

"I can taste the steak already." He grinned.

Kendra was proud of the effort the crew had put in and was happy to crank up the grill to prepare steaks for their dinner. She smiled even more broadly when Harvey reminded her that there was half the cake left, too, for dessert, if anyone wanted something sweet.

He handed her a cold beer. "Those look and smell delicious."

"They do smell good, don't they?"

"My mouth's watering. The water was boiling so I went ahead and dropped the corn in to boil."

"Thanks, Harvey. Lindsey will make a salad when she returns. Do you think that will be enough?" she asked.

"Looking at the size of those steaks? I'd say that will be plenty. Poor Tim may fall asleep mid-chew they are so big."

Kendra laughed at his comment. "He did look worn out."

"He's having trouble adjusting to sleeping on the boat. I think I'll recommend some Melatonin to him for our next trip out. It'll help him sleep, but not leave him groggy."

"That's a good idea, Harvey. Thanks."

†

Lindsey found herself smiling as she stepped into Kendra's shower. She couldn't resist the urge to open the bottle of shampoo to get a whiff of the fragrance. Her stomach flipped with excitement at the visual that flashed before her eyes. Locked in an embrace, she had her face buried in Kendra's hair. "Down girl," she whispered, and finished bathing.

She returned to the galley and dropped half a dozen eggs in the boiling water to add to the salad. The aroma of the steaks cooking had her stomach growling as she prepared the remainder of the salad.

Charlie walked into the galley, handed her a beer, and asked, "Anything I can help with?"

"Go ahead and set the table for us. Check to make sure we have plenty of tea for supper, too."

He opened the refrigerator. "Two gallons," he reported.

"That should be plenty, with beer for those who want it. Thanks for the beer."

"You're welcome." He started setting the table.

"Can you also pull another of the big bowls down for me for the corn?"

"Sure thing, short stuff." He chuckled and reached over her head to pull down the bowl she requested.

She pulled out a large pan, lined it with aluminum foil, and handed it to Charlie. "You want to run this out to the captain? She may have some steaks ready to come off the grill. I'll cover them and keep them warm until they're all done."

✝

Lindsey pushed her plate away and groaned. "I can't eat another bite."

"It looks like we can have steak and eggs for breakfast in the morning," Harvey announced.

"You're always looking ahead, aren't you, Harvey?" Kendra asked.

"This steak was way too good to let it go to waste. I'll cut up the leftovers and we'll have a feast to get us started in the morning."

"Sorry, boss." Charlie grinned as he held up a bone stripped of every morsel of meat.

Kendra grinned at him. "Did you get enough to eat?"

"Yes, ma'am, but that's not gonna keep me from having a slice of cake and a glass of milk."

Lindsey groaned at the mention of more food. "You go right ahead. I can't even watch."

"Go ahead and relax. Tim and I are cleaning up tonight."

"You won't get an argument from me."

✝

Lindsey took her beer, and walked outside. She eased down onto the bench and lifted her face to the breeze. The winds were picking up and felt good against her skin.

"Do you mind some company?" Kendra asked.

"Never, especially when it's you. That was a great meal."

"Thanks, I'm glad everyone enjoyed it."

"So you think two more runs will fill us tomorrow?"

"Even it if doesn't we're heading in. I won't risk us being caught out here."

"What's the storm doing?"

"Waffling east to west, but I don't trust she won't make a strong turn our way. I want to be protected before she arrives."

"Is there anything we need to pick up in town before we take her into the bay?"

"I'll need to top off the fuel. I'll ask you and the crew to stow away everything possible inside, or get it tied down as soon as we head home. That'll save us some time."

"What do we need to do at the house?"

"Secure the shutters over the windows, unplug anything not necessary to run the house, put chairs, and other outdoor items in the garage. Then pray."

"How long will it take us to get safely tucked in the bay?"

"Usually about an hour and a half, but it depends on the traffic on the water. Most of the smaller boats and pleasure craft go into storage for the storms. Some captains prefer to ride out the storm on the open water, but Dad and I have always preferred the bay."

"That has to provide you more protection, especially from rogue waves."

"Yes, there's that, and it's less far to swim or paddle if something goes amiss," she answered with a serious face. "I prefer the comfort of seeing land in bad weather."

Lindsey gazed out to the south at the clear skies and brilliant sprinkle of stars. "It's hard to believe that just a few hundred miles south, mayhem is on its way. It seems so peaceful out tonight."

A comfortable silence had fallen between them. They relaxed against the bench and Kendra's hand was resting on Lindsey's thigh. The warmth of their bodies pressed close together brought her a sense of contentment. Her eyes were growing heavy and she felt Kendra stand and stretch. "I'm going to call it a night. Sleep well, my friend."

"You too, Captain."

Lindsey enjoyed the cool night for several more minutes before retiring to her berth for the night. The gentle swaying of the boat rocked her to sleep within minutes.

†

Kendra looked up when Harvey came into the wheelhouse the following morning. She had the engine idling low as it warmed and was studying the weather maps. He was looking as worried as she felt.

"She's growing, isn't she?" he asked.

"Yes. She's up to a Category Two this morning."

"Last night, as I was smoking a cigar on the deck, something just didn't feel right in my bones. She's small now, but I've seen too many storms increase in size quickly once they hit the Gulf. I'm worried that a big storm is brewing."

"Me, too. How would you feel about getting the crew up and dropping the nets so I can trawl while you cook breakfast? I think it's time for us to finish our work here and get back home."

"I'll get them up and moving." He exited the wheelhouse.

Kendra pressed a few switches and felt the anchor winch engage as it began the ascent from the floor of the Gulf. "If that noise didn't wake the crew, Harvey certainly will."

†

Lindsey was surfacing from a dream when she heard the groan of the anchor winch. She sat up in the bunk just as Harvey walked in. "Is everything okay?"

"So far. The captain wants to get a jump and get the nets wet so she can fish while we cook and have breakfast. She's anxious to get us home."

"I'll get the rest of them up if you want to start working on breakfast," she told him.

"Good luck getting them moving," he replied, and went topside.

Lindsey walked from berth to berth, gently shaking each occupant awake. "Wake up you guys. The captain wants nets in the water before we have breakfast."

Charlie groaned. "I was having the nicest of dreams." He wiped the sleep from his eyes.

"You can get back to it later. We've work to do before we can head home," she explained. "I'll meet you all on deck." She left them to get ready and walked out to prepare for work.

✝

When the wind hit Lindsey in the face, she knew what was making Kendra anxious. It had picked up noticeably from last night's gentle breeze, and was coming up from the southeast. She didn't need a weather report to know Dani was on her way.

Twenty minutes later, the nets were in the water and Kendra began the trawl as the crew headed to the galley for breakfast.

Lindsey carried a tray into the wheelhouse for Kendra. The plate, full of scrambled eggs, slices of leftover steak, hash browns, toast, juice, and a thermos of coffee, had her mouthwatering as she placed it on the small table beside the captain.

"Enjoy, and give me a shout if you need anything."

"Thanks. Eat a hearty breakfast. It's going to be a busy day," Kendra warned.

"Will do, Captain."

served Lindsey a plate when she returned to the galley.

"Thanks, you going to join me?"

"I'll be right behind you."

"What's the plan this morning?" Tim asked her.

135

"Two quick runs, then we'll head for home. When we start north, we need to load the frozen bags into the bins to prepare for unloading once we reach the harbor. Then we need to prepare the boat for the storm, securing anything we can below and making sure things are tied down on deck."

"Will we make it in tonight, Harvey?" Charlie asked.

"No, probably not, loaded down as we are, but we'll be damned close. Maybe an hour or two from home at most. I'd advise each of you to call home sometime today to get your family started making preparations for the storm, if you haven't already done so."

"I almost hate to ask, but do you think we'll get paid when we get home tomorrow?" Charlie asked. "I'm not sure if we'll evacuate, but if we decide to, some extra money would be helpful."

"The captain plans to write paychecks later tonight. They won't be exact, based on this week's run, but they'll be identical to last week's check. She said she'd adjust them next week once she gets the final total on this week's haul."

"That's awesome," Charlie shoveled the last bit of food into his mouth. He noticed Tim and the other men where already finished eating. "We'll get the bins in place and the bags ready to go, while y'all finish eating. Thanks for another great meal, Harvey."

"You're welcome, and thanks for getting us set for the first run. We won't be long," he promised.

"Take your time. We've got this handled," Charlie answered, winking at Lindsey.

Lindsey watched the crew leave and then turned back to Harvey, smiling. "You're really good with the crew."

"I learned a long time ago, if you treat your crew good, they'll run through walls to get the work done. Even Charlie, though still young and inexperienced, he's falling into stride with the rest of the crew."

Lindsey stabbed the last morsel of steak and popped it into her mouth. "That really was a good breakfast. Do you want me to start cleaning up in here?"

"That would be great. I'll go check on the captain, and be right back to help."

✝

Kendra was on the phone with her father when she saw Harvey walk into the wheelhouse.

She looked at Harvey, smiled, and shrugged. Her dad had finally seen the weather report and was giving her an earful, never pausing for a breath, for not keeping him informed.

When he did finally pause, Kendra said, "We will be headed home before lunch today, and I'll have the crew safely delivered home, and the boat tucked away in the bay by nightfall tomorrow."

Kendra shook her head. "No, Dad, you're right where you're needed. Uncle Henry and Aunt Betty need you there with them. Trust me, I've got things under control here. Besides, you probably can't get a flight back in until after the storm moves through."

"I do trust you, Kendra, I just worry about you."

"I've got the best crew a captain could ask for, and Lindsey is going to help me with the boat, so stop worrying." She winked at Harvey.

"Do you need anything?" Harvey whispered.

She shook her head, mouthed thanks, and watched Harvey leave.

"Well, you had better call me every few hours once you get the boat in the bay. We should be able to stay in touch with the satellite phone at least," he grumbled.

"I promise, Dad."

"All right. Call me tonight so I'll know how close you are to home, and keep an eye on the reports."

"Yes, I will." It was her turn to groan. "You taught me well, remember?"

"Yes, I did, and I'm very proud of you."

"Thanks, Dad. I love you, and we'll talk again tonight."

"Stay safe, Kendra," her dad said before ending the call.

☦

When the final nets of the trip were hauled onboard, the crew worked quickly to empty them into the bins. Then they began securing the riggings, and storing the doors below deck. Lindsey and Harvey continued to bag shrimp and when done, set them up in the freezer. Tim and Charlie had already stacked the frozen bags in the storage bins, leaving plenty of room for the new bags to freeze.

It was well past lunchtime when they had the boat in order. "What would you guys like for supper?" Harvey asked.

"What are our options?" Tim asked.

"We can have chicken Alfredo, or we can process those grouper we netted and fry them up with some hushpuppies and coleslaw."

"I vote for the grouper," Charlie piped in. "I'll even volunteer Tim and me to clean them."

"Done deal. Lindsey and I'll start preparing the rest of the meal." He turned to Lindsey. "Will you check on the captain to see if she needs anything, and run the supper menu past her?"

☦

Kendra's timing was perfect. She turned off the engine and set the anchor, just as Harvey was removing the last filet from the fryer. She shut down the wheelhouse and walked to the galley in search of her crew and a cold beer.

"Just in time," Harvey told her when she entered. "Charlie, get your captain a cold one."

"This looks delicious." She joined them at the table filled with food and accepted the icy beer from Charlie.

"Just wait 'til you taste Lindsey's hushpuppies."

"Have you already been sampling, Charlie?" Kendra asked.

138

"I couldn't help myself, Captain, they looked too good not to try."

She looked at the massive pile of hushpuppies. "There's enough there to feed a small army, so no harm done. Thanks for another great week." She lifted her bottle to the cheers of the crew. "Now, let's eat before it gets cold."

They finished the meal and shared another beer while discussing the next day's plans before retiring for the night.

"I hope to have us in port by eight in the morning and have the truck there ready to offload the haul. If all goes well, you'll be back home by nine," she told them, and handed out the week's paychecks. "They aren't exact, but I'll make up the difference next week once we've tallied this week's haul."

"Thanks, Captain. Can I ask one more favor?"

"Sure, Charlie, what is it?"

"Can you give me the satellite phone number so I can call you to check to make sure everything's going well in the bay?"

Kendra smiled warmly at the young man. "Of course I can. I'll give each of you the number before you leave tomorrow."

"I hope you know you can contact any of us, if you need anything," Harvey reminded her.

"That means a lot to me, and I'll call if there is anything I need. I'm just praying everyone will weather the storm safely, and we can get back on the water soon."

"Amen to that," Tim replied.

The men started to filter out of the galley after it was cleaned, leaving Kendra, Harvey, and Lindsey to finish their beer.

"What time do you want to be underway in the morning?" he asked.

"Just as soon as it's light enough to see," she answered. "Dani is picking up speed, and is hell bent on paying us a visit. She's still a Cat Two, but she's predicted to strengthen further."

"Do they have an estimate on landfall yet?" he asked.

"Two days tops at this point, and anywhere between Panama City and Mobile."

"That gives us plenty of time to prepare. Are you sure you don't need one of us to help with the boat?"

139

She looked at Lindsey. "I don't think there's anything else we haven't prepared for. I'll call and let you know when we're safely tucked away in the bay."

"I'd appreciate that," Harvey replied. "For goodness sakes, please don't forget to call your Dad. I can just see him renting a car to drive back in the storm."

"I'll do my best to keep him safely in Arizona." She grinned.

Harvey stood. "I'm going to call it a night, ladies. See you in the morning."

"Goodnight, Harvey. Rest well." Kendra turned to Lindsey. "I think we should call it a night, too."

"You won't get any argument from me," Lindsey answered. "I'm toast."

"Thanks for all your hard work this week."

"Just doing my job, ma'am." Lindsey grinned, her eyes sparkling with mischief.

Kendra chuckled. "Goodnight then."

As they started to leave, Kendra called out, "Lindsey."

Lindsey turned and Kendra reached for her and leaned in close. She kissed her softly on the lips. "Thanks for all of your support." She left Lindsey staring after her, speechless, and walked to her cabin, wearing a huge grin.

Lindsey lifted her fingers to her lips. The kiss was so soft, she wondered if she had dreamed it but she could taste the lip balm that Kendra used. "Damn," she whispered and retired to her bunk, her cheeks filled with a smile.

Chapter Thirteen

The next morning dawned with cloudy skies and a brisk wind blowing across the deck. Kendra was thankful that the crew had finished preparing the boat for the storm the day before, and they could remain inside for the rest of the trip. Once they got into port, they'd unload the shrimp and depart for home. Kendra was focusing on staying the course when the door opened and Lindsey entered with a thermos of coffee.

"Good morning, Captain." Lindsey placed the thermos on the table. "Harvey is going to make pancakes and sausage for breakfast."

"That sounds good. I'm actually hungry this morning."

"Do you want me to take over here so you can go share a meal with the crew? I think they'd appreciate it if you did."

Kendra looked at her curiously, but nodded. "Just keep on this course and I'll be back soon."

"Got it." Lindsey took the seat Kendra vacated. "Wow, look at how much bigger the waves have grown overnight. The water is slapping the side of the boat and sea spray is covering the deck."

"Keep her steady," Kendra said before leaving the wheelhouse.

†

Harvey took a plate of food and glass of juice to the wheelhouse for Lindsey.

"Thanks, I was afraid Charlie would eat all the pancakes," she teased.

"He's giving it a good try, but I think I've finally managed to fill him up. Thanks for giving Kendra a chance to do some bonding with the guys."

"My pleasure. I get to work with them on deck, but she spends most of her time alone in here behind the wheel. She needed a break."

"I understand. Most people assume the captain has the easiest job on board, but I'd rather deal with the physical work all day long than have the responsibility that rests on her shoulders,"

"I agree with you, but sometimes it's good to get behind the wheel." She grinned.

"I'm sure she appreciates having you on board. It takes some pressure off her, knowing there's another licensed captain on the crew."

"It's good experience for me, too. You and the boys have taught me a lot already."

"You're a hard worker and it's been a pleasure having you with us."

"Thanks, Harvey, that means a lot coming from you."

"Enjoy your breakfast and give me a holler if you need something else."

"I'll be doing good to finish all this," she answered, motioning to the plate.

Harvey had been gone only a few minutes when the next weather alert came across the system. Lindsey watched the video from the hurricane hunter's report and whistled when she saw the size of the storm. More importantly, the storm was picking up speed and heading northwest. There was no doubt that Dani, or at least the effects of her outer bands, would be in the area much earlier than planned. She picked up the microphone and radioed the galley.

"Captain Drake, will you return to the wheelhouse?"

Kendra looked at Harvey. "This can't be good. Let's go see what's going on."

"Can you boys clean up here?" he asked.

"No problem, Harvey. Thanks for a great meal."

"You're welcome, Charlie. Let's go, Captain."

"What's up?" Kendra asked as she and Harvey walked into the wheelhouse.

"A new weather report." Lindsey pointed to the monitor and clicked the mouse on the video.

"Damn, she's getting big. Faster too," Kendra groaned.

"Looks like we're getting company sooner than planned," Harvey pointed out.

Lindsey looked at the notepad. "As close as I can calculate, we'll begin to feel her effects by midday tomorrow. If she keeps the same speed."

Kendra looked at the clock. "We should be in port in a half hour. Let the boys know the update and get them ready to unload us quickly, so we can all make for home," she told Harvey.

"Is it too risky to go ahead and move the bins to the deck?" Harvey asked.

"I'd rather not risk anyone getting hurt from the bins shifting unexpectedly, Harvey. Just tell them to move quickly once we approach the dock."

"Yes ma'am," he answered, and left to return to the galley.

Lindsey could see the worry on Kendra's face. "Do you want to top off the tanks while I shut down the house when we get in?" she asked.

"That would save us some time. Do you know what all needs to be done?"

"I think so. I was paying attention." She grinned. "Unplug all the unnecessary electrical items, secure the shutters on the windows, check the connections on the generator, and lock up behind me."

"Impressive," Kendra said. "The shutters are self-locking once you've pulled them shut. You'll have to pop the screens from the inside on the second floor to shutter the bedroom windows."

"I can handle that. Is there anything you need from the house?"

"Nothing that I can think of that we don't already have on board."

†

The boat begin to slow as Kendra positioned her for entry into the slip. She looked out the wheelhouse window and saw the crew pulling the bins out of the freezer.

"Let's hoof it, guys," Harvey was telling them as they went into action.

Kendra's eyes then tracked to the dock where the truck was already in place, waiting to take the shrimp to the market, She let out an audible sigh of relief. Once the truck was loaded, she signed over the paperwork on nineteen hundred and twenty bags of shrimp, pleased that they had nearly reached the quota for a full week.

Proud of what they had accomplished, the crew's celebration was short since they were eager to leave the boat to go to their families and prepare their homes for the storm. She hugged each one and wished them luck as they left.

"I'll see you soon." Lindsey waved and hurried up the dock toward the house.

She entered the house and climbed the stairs to close the second story shutters and unplug clocks and lights. The house was eerily quiet as she moved from room to room. The shutters locked with ease, and when she moved downstairs, the ticking of the grandfather clock welcomed her. With the interior secured, Lindsey closed the downstairs shutters, and checked the generator. Everything was set, so she locked the house and started back to the harbor.

✝

Kendra returned to the wheelhouse and left the slip to top off the fuel tanks.

"Are you heading up to the bay?" the man at the fueling station asked Kendra.

"Yeah, I still think that's a safer bet than being out on the open water."

"You'll have some company up there. Captain Lucas left about an hour ago."

"That's good to know. Hopefully, the storm will turn or at least pass quickly."

"Let's hope. Stay safe, Captain."

"Will do."

The fueling finished, Kendra drove the boat back to the slip where Lindsey was already waiting. She jumped on board and Kendra kept moving.

Lindsey walked into the wheelhouse. "All set at home," she said.

"Thanks, you probably saved us an hour or so."

"Would you like some coffee?" Lindsey asked as Kendra began to guide the boat through the channels that would take them inland to Perdido Bay.

"That sounds great." Kendra kept her eyes fixed out the front window as they approached the narrow pass.

"I'll brew a fresh pot and make us some sandwiches for an early lunch."

"Sounds good," Kendra said, focusing on the route until the boat reached the open waters of the bay. She was confident of her abilities to guide the boat to safety, but there were several spots in the channel where the depth to support a boat her size narrowed. The last thing she wanted to do was to run up on one of the sandbars crowding the sides of the boat. "Just ten more minutes," she added as she passed a familiar buoy.

✝

Lindsey didn't want to distract Kendra so she took her time in the galley. She scouted the pantry and freezer, looking for something to cook for dinner, and smiled when she found a package of frozen chicken Alfredo. She checked the instructions and found that she had plenty of time to cook, once the boat settled in for the night. She made a crisp salad and placed it in the refrigerator to chill. When she felt the boat pick up speed, she knew Kendra had cleared the channel. She picked up the tray of coffee and sandwiches and started for the wheelhouse.

†

"Phew, I'm glad to be through that," Kendra breathed a sigh of relief when Lindsey entered.

"I figured you were headed into a tight spot, so I took my time."

Kendra sat back in her seat and poured a cup of coffee. "Thanks. You always seem to know just what I need."

"I try to do my best." Lindsey grinned. "How long will it be until we reach a safe spot?"

Kendra looked at the clock. "In about another half hour at most."

"What do we need to do when you drop anchor?"

"Double check everything that is still on deck to make sure it's secure. Once that's done, we sit back and wait to see what Mother Nature has in store for us."

"I can start checking the deck now."

"Eat lunch first," Kendra told her, picking up a sandwich. "We still have plenty of time, and daylight."

Lindsey took a seat and bit into a sandwich. "I need to make a confession," she admitted.

Kendra cocked her head. "What is it?"

"I've never ridden out a hurricane on a boat, so I don't know what to expect."

Kendra returned her sandwich to the plate and turned to look at her directly. "The winds and rain will reach us first, so the swells will have us rocking pretty good." She grinned at her. "I hope you don't get seasick."

"I haven't yet, and I hope that continues."

"Me too, there's nothing more miserable."

"Do we have to worry about the rains?"

"Other than getting soaked, no, I wouldn't think so. As long as we don't spring a leak, we're good."

"Will there be obstacles that put us in danger of a hull breach in the bay?"

"Not as deep as we'll be, unless we collide with another boat. There will be at least one other shrimper in the bay and let's hope that's all. Sometimes owners of larger pleasure craft will bring their boats in, anchor them, and leave them unattended. If one of those breaks free, we may have troubles."

"What other hazards should we expect?"

"Tornados on land and water spouts in the bay could be our biggest danger. There's nothing we can do about those, but pray." Kendra watched as Lindsey swallowed hard. "Try not to worry. We will be as protected as we can be."

Lindsey was about to ask another question when the phone rang.

"Hello, Dad. Caller ID is a wonderful thing." Kendra chuckled. "Yes, we're almost to the center of the bay. No, no bad weather yet. How's Uncle Henry?"

Lindsey picked up her coffee, another sandwich, and then stepped outside.

Kendra watched Lindsay go as she listened to her dad's report. She realized how thankful she was that Lindsey was here with her, especially with her dad so far away. "Yes, Lindsey is here helping me, and we should be dropping anchor in a half hour. We'll have an early dinner and keep an eye on the weather. Yes, I'll call you when the weather starts to pick up, but have faith we'll be safe, Dad. You taught me well."

Lindsey had left the wheelhouse to give Kendra some privacy. While outside she couldn't keep her eyes from drifting back to the south. The sky was beginning to fill with heavy dark clouds, and she knew they would have heavy rains during the night. The sound of an engine brought her attention back to the boat and she looked to see another shrimp boat several hundred yards ahead of them. It looked smaller, but from this distance it was hard to tell. She finished her sandwich and returned to the wheelhouse.

"Dad asked me to tell you hello, and to keep me out of trouble." She grinned.

"He must have a lot of faith in me."

"If you haven't noticed, he thinks a lot of you, and so do I," Kendra added.

"Thanks, boss. I've really enjoyed being here and have learned a lot from you."

"He actually has a great idea that I'd like to discuss with you once we're settled tonight."

"Maybe we can discuss it over dinner. I've got a salad made and I thought I'd put some Alfredo in to bake while we secure the boat."

Kendra chuckled and shook her head. "See, you're already ahead of me."

Lindsey shrugged. "You know I've got to make sure we eat."

✝

Two hours later, with the boat secured for the night, they sat down to a meal. "This looks delicious," Kendra said, smacking her lips.

"It didn't take much to pop it into the oven, but I admit it does taste good." Lindsey was about to take another bite when she dropped her fork. "Damn, I forgot something." She jumped up from the table.

Kendra wondered what she was up to when she left the galley, but she returned moments later with the opened bottle of wine and two wine glasses. "Where did those come from?" she asked with a laugh.

"I swiped them from the house when I was there." Lindsey grinned and placed the glasses on the table and began working on the cork.

"Damn, you really do think of everything."

"Like I said, I try my best, ma'am." She poured their wine, handing a glass to Kendra. "To weathering the storm." She lifted her glass to the toast.

Kendra took a deep breath. "When we got home Saturday night, Dad asked me to join him for a beer when you went upstairs. He wanted to talk to me about you."

Lindsey placed her glass on the table, and couldn't help swallowing hard. "Have I done something wrong?"

"Oh, no, I'm sorry to make you think that. Actually, it's quite the opposite. You've done everything right. Once I take ownership of the *Southern Star*, I'll be in need of a captain to take over this boat for the local fishing. Dad suggested that captain be you."

Lindsey was glad she wasn't holding her glass. Surely, she would have dropped it when Kendra made the offer.

"Do you think that would be something you'd be interested in considering?"

"I hadn't any clue that was what you were going to ask, but yes, I'll give it some thought. Of course, I need to talk this over with my dad, before I can give you an answer. I need to know he'll be on board with this." Lindsey picked up her glass and took a drink.

"I would expect nothing less and there's no need for a decision right away. I won't get the *Star* until the new year."

"Wow, I really had no idea you'd be asking that question."

"Both dad and I are confident that you'd make an excellent addition to our fleet."

"I'll definitely give it some thought," Lindsey answered, just as the first bands of rain arrived, pelting the windows.

†

The rain brought full darkness and it was impossible to see anything through the windows of the galley. Before the rains, they had been able to see the beacon flashing atop the other shrimp boat anchored five hundred yards away, but now even that light was impossible to see.

They decided to settle into the den area off the galley to watch the weather news while they still had a television signal. The Weather Channel was running continuous coverage of the storm, and they were relieved that Dani hadn't grown in strength.

"She's still a big storm," Kendra warned, as they listened to the forecaster.

When the video loop began to play, the air filled with the howling of the wind as the feeder bands were indeed arriving in full force. Kendra looked at Lindsey's wide eyes. "Those will come and go all night, so don't be alarmed."

"I'm used to the sound, but I'd never believed it would be so much more intense on the water," Lindsey admitted.

"You'll get used to it soon enough. Are you up for a stroll outside? I'd like to check the deck, to make sure everything's in good shape."

"Sure." Lindsey took the slicker Kendra offered her.

"Just don't get too close to the rails. I'd hate to have to fish you out of this mess."

"I'll be right behind you, so don't stop suddenly." Lindsey followed her outside.

†

The winds had subsided when they stepped outside, but the rain continued to fall. Kendra switched on a flashlight as they walked toward the freezer. The gear they had strapped to the walls of the unit was still firmly in place, and everything on deck looked to be in good shape. Kendra lifted her hand to shield the water from her eyes as she looked across the bay, searching for the other boat. For a brief second, she caught a glimpse of their beacon in the distance.

"We both appear to be fully anchored and not drifting," she shouted to Lindsey. The winds were beginning to increase again. "Let's head back in." She led Lindsey back to the galley.

"That wasn't too bad." Lindsey hung up their slickers.

"This is just the beginning," Kendra warned.

"So what do we do now? It's only eight."

"Are you up for a movie and popcorn? Kendra asked.

"Fine with me, I'll make the popcorn and you can set up the movie."

"What kind of movies do you like?" Kendra called after her.

"Anything but blood and gore. What's your favorite?"

"My all-time favorite is 'Fried Green Tomatoes.'"

"Silly question, but do you have a copy onboard?"

Kendra chuckled. "That was a silly question. I love that movie, too, and could watch it over and over, but I promise not to make you watch it more than once."

"Deal," Lindsey replied as she began popping the popcorn.

Halfway through the movie, the winds increased and the boat began rocking with significantly more force.

"Should we check the weather report?" Lindsey asked.

"Probably not a bad idea," Kendra reached for the remote to switch back to the television.

"Whoa," she cried out when the video came on the screen. Dani had dramatically increased the speed of her movement and would reach them before dawn.

"She's moving quickly, huh?"

"Yeah, but that can be good, if she blows through quickly. She's still a Cat Three storm though, so she'll be packing big winds."

"Like now?"

"Even worse, I'm afraid. I think I'll take a look around the deck."

"Want me to go with you?"

"No need for both of us to get soaked. I'll be back in just a few." Kendra slipped on a slicker and picked up a flashlight.

151

†

The wind assaulted her as soon as Kendra stepped out the door. She braced herself against it and switched on the flashlight. Over the din of the storm, she heard metal striking metal and started across the deck. She pushed forward and sea spray showered her as the waves crashed into the side of the boat.

The salty spray stung her eyes as she pressed forward. Squinting to keep it out of her eyes, she failed to see the flicker of bright metal when it hit the beam of her flashlight. She felt the searing pain on her right cheek and fell to her knees.

Kendra felt the sting of salt burning her cheek and the rush of hot blood as it poured from the cut just below her eye. She lifted her hand instinctively to her wound, and when she saw her fingers coated with blood, she cried out.

"Damn, that's gonna hurt." She turned her head at the sound of the door slamming and saw Lindsey rushing toward her. She lifted her hand to slow her friend and shouted out a warning. "Be careful, there's a loose strap flying around."

Lindsey heeded her warning and stopped several feet away from her. Kendra picked up the flashlight and crawled toward her.

"I see blood, are you okay?"

"The buckle of that strap cut my cheek, but I'm going to be okay."

Lindsey took the flashlight from her. "Close your eyes," she warned and then lifted the beam of light. "Your cheek is sliced open and it's bleeding profusely. Another inch higher and you could have lost your eye. Can you make it inside okay?"

"Yes, it's just a cut."

"Go inside and clean your cheek, and see if you can stop the bleeding. Can you do that?"

"Yes."

"Good. I'll secure the equipment and make sure the strap's secure."

"Please be careful."

"I will," Lindsey promised.

Lindsey watched until Kendra entered the galley before turning back to search for the loose strap. As Kendra had warned, it was flying wildly through the air, and she understood how the injury had occurred. If she hadn't known to look for it, the strap could have injured her as well.

She timed the flight of the strap and lunged for it as the wind slowed. She pulled the fallen equipment back into place, and buckled the strap, pulling it tight and tying the loose end to secure it further. Then, she rushed inside to check on Kendra.

Kendra was leaning over the kitchen sink, a bottle of betadine in her hand, letting loose a string of obscenities. She finished cleaning out the wound with sterile pads as Lindsey came inside. If the wound hadn't been so serious, Lindsey would have considered smiling at the colorful language her friend was spewing.

"Let me take a look." She stood next to Kendra.

Kendra pulled the blood soaked pad from her cheek and Lindsey winced. The buckle had sliced the meaty part of her cheek down to the bone.

"That bad huh," Kendra remarked, when she saw Lindsey's expression.

"You could probably use some stitches, but that's not possible tonight."

"No, it's not in this weather, but I've got something that will work. Bring me the first aid kit from the table, please."

Lindsey rushed back to the table, returning with the kit. "What do we need?"

"There's a tube of surgical glue and a package of steri-strips. You'll need to use the glue to seal the wound and secure it using the steri-strips to hold the tissue in place while the glue sets. Do you think you can do that?"

Lindsey had blanched white at the sight of the wound, but nodded her head in answer.

"Try to seal the tissue as close as possible to reduce the scarring, please," Kendra instructed as Lindsey opened the steri-strips. "Do you have enough light here?"

"Yes, I think we're good." Lindsey felt her hands shaking as she twisted the cap off the glue. *I've got to do this right, for Kendra's sake, so suck it up.* "Are you ready?"

"Yes. Place the glue as quickly as you can and I'll hand you the steri-strips."

"On second thought, could we move to the couch where you can put your head in my lap?" Lindsey asked.

"Good idea."

Lindsey carefully used the glue to seal the wound. Kendra handed her the small strips that would hold the tissue in place. "You're going to have one helluva shiner. Do you think you could stand some ice to prevent your cheek from swelling?"

"I can only try. Bring me a bag of frozen veggies from the freezer."

"First, let's get you out of this slicker. Are you dry underneath?"

"Pretty much," Kendra answered as Lindsey helped her out of the slicker. "Unlike you, you're soaked to the bone."

"I'll go change once I get you settled."

"Why don't we move into my cabin? It will be more comfortable in there."

Lindsey looked at her. "You realize I need to keep an eye on you tonight, right?"

"I was hoping you would."

"Okay. Do you have anything for pain or inflammation?"

"Just some extra strength Ibuprofen. They're in my medicine cabinet. I can take a couple while you change out of those wet clothes before you catch a chill."

They left the galley to enter the crew berths. Kendra walked to a door Lindsey had not realized was the entrance to the captain's cabin, but she was glad it was there.

"Come in when you're ready. I'll set the alarm on the console for any weather alerts. I can hear those from my cabin."

Lindsey nodded and waited for her to leave before stripping out of her wet clothes. She had begun to shiver, and used a towel to wipe the water from her skin. She then pulled out a pair of sweats, a T-shirt, and a pair of socks. Her hair was still damp, but she felt the chill leaving her body as she brushed her hair and teeth.

✝

Kendra could feel her cheek swelling as she rested on her bed. Glad the glue seemed to be holding, she hoped with the support of the steri-strips, the swelling wouldn't open the wound again. She winced when she lifted the bag of frozen peas to her face.

"Damn that hurts," Kendra said aloud.

The ice and Ibuprofen should reduce the swelling. She hadn't actually received a blow to her head, so a concussion was not a danger, but she was pleased that Lindsey would be keeping her company. She grinned when she felt the frozen peas shift in the bag as her body heat warmed the bag. *I've got to remember to buy some real ice packs.*

Lindsey knocked on her door.

"Come in," Kendra called out.

Lindsey entered, carrying two cans of soda. "I wasn't sure if you were thirsty."

"Thanks." She took a can from Lindsey. Holding the homemade ice pack with one hand, she began to struggle to pop the top on the can.

"Hang on, let me get that for you." Lindsey opened the drink.

"Thanks again."

Lindsey nodded and took a seat in a recliner next to the bed.

Kendra took a drink and smiled at Lindsey. "You know, I didn't take a blow to my head, so there's no need for concussion protocols to be followed."

"I'll leave if you want me to." Lindsey began to stand.

"That's not what I meant. I just don't want you worrying about a concussion needlessly."

"I agree. Your pupils are fine, and your cheek took the blow, so I don't think there's a problem with you sleeping if you want."

"I'm glad you're here to keep me company. It gets lonely in here sometimes and the storm doesn't make it any easier."

She watched Lindsey relax into the chair. The bag of peas was beginning to drip, getting her shirt wet. "I think this bag has done its job. Would you mind tossing them back in the freezer?"

"Not at all, would you like another bag? Maybe some carrots this time."

"Sounds good."

"I think I'll make us something sweet. Do you have any preferences?"

"Surprise me."

"Relax and I'll be back soon. Do you want the television on?"

"Sure. Hand me the remote if you will. Oh, will you toss me a dry shirt? My peas got this one wet." She pulled the shirt over her head. "Shirts are in the second drawer,"

Lindsey felt her mouth go dry, and her cheeks flush, as she watched Kendra hand her the shirt. She took it and quickly looked away, searching for a hamper as she walked to the drawers that held Kendra's clothing.

Lindsey opened the drawer, pulled out a shirt, and turned to hand it to Kendra. "Will this one work?"

"That's perfect."

Lindsey watched as she raised the shirt over her head. Kendra's skin was flawless and the muscles of her lean form were evident as she stretched the shirt over her body.

"All set?"

"Yes, thanks."

"I'll be back soon. Call out for me if you need anything."

"I'm just going to relax and watch some television," Kendra replied taking the remote in hand.

Lindsey saw Kendra's eyes getting heavy as the medication began to relax her. Kendra was already asleep before she could leave the room.

Lindsey walked into the galley and turned the oven on to preheat. She had brownies on her mind and mixed up the batter while the oven heated. She checked the freezer and smiled when she saw a carton of vanilla ice cream. "Brownie sundaes here we come," she whispered.

The winds had calmed, so Lindsey decided to take a look around outside during what she knew would be a short break in the weather. After placing the brownies in the oven, she cracked the galley door open to find that even the rain was taking a break, and she slipped outside closing the door quietly. The dense darkness made it impossible to see much beyond the deck, but on board, everything looked to be in good condition.

Back in the galley, Lindsey checked the timer on the stove, and then walked back to the captain's cabin to check on Kendra. She was sleeping peacefully with her hand still clutching the remote. Kendra was wearing a smile and Lindsey wondered what she was dreaming to bring about the smile. Her cheek was beginning to turn an ugly, deep purple as the bruising began. It had terrified her when Kendra had looked up at her with blood streaming down her face.

Now she felt relief that the wound wasn't any more serious than it was. Kendra had been lucky, she could have just as easily have lost her eye. She would have a scar to carry with her for a long time, and it promised to be painful to smile for a few days, but she would heal. Lindsey watched as Kendra released a deep breath with a sigh and shifted on the bed. Satisfied that Kendra was okay, she returned to the kitchen.

The timer was flashing a five-second warning as she reached down to shut it off. She removed the fragrant brownies to cool on the counter for several minutes. Her mouth was watering as she filled two glasses with ice, poured milk into them, and then placed them on a tray with napkins and spoons. Losing patience to allow them to fully cool, she cut the pan of brownies in quarters and used a spatula to place the slabs into bowls. She felt the smile growing on her face as she scooped two portions of ice cream over the brownies and drizzled chocolate syrup to finish the dessert.

She carried the tray full of the sumptuous treats into Kendra's cabin and placed it on a bedside table. Kendra was still sleeping peacefully and, for a moment, Lindsey contemplated not waking her. As she sat down on the edge of the bed, Kendra's eyes began to flutter and then opened.

She smiled up at Lindsey and then winced. "I was having a terrific dream about brownies."

Lindsey returned her smile. "You must have smelled them cooking while you slept." She reached over for a bowl.

Kendra pushed herself up on the bed when she saw the bowl Lindsey had in her hand. "That looks sinfully good."

"I hope you enjoy it. Be careful, the brownie may still be hot. I couldn't wait any longer. They just smelled too good to wait."

"I agree with you, let's try it," Kendra replied.

"This one's yours." Lindsey grinned and handed her the bowl.

"All mine?"

"All yours, I promise."

Kendra took a bite of the luscious dessert. "Oh my goodness, you've outdone yourself with this one," she cried. "Oh, and iced milk too? Are you sure you weren't peeking into my dream?"

Chuckling, Lindsey shook her head. "No, I just thought it'd be a good combo."

"This is so good," Kendra groaned.

"I'm glad you're enjoying it."

The flickering of the television screen caught her attention. "Damn, that's one big storm."

Lindsey turned her head to look at the screen. "She almost fills up the Gulf."

The colorful projection cone flashed on the screen. "Looks like she'll make landfall east of us," Kendra predicted. "That's a relief, but we'll still get her rains and winds."

Lindsey picked up the tray with the emptied dishes. "Do you need anything else while I'm in the kitchen?"

"I couldn't even dream of eating another bite." Kendra grinned.

"I'll be right back."

Kendra fluffed the pillows on the bed as Lindsey left the room.

Kendra was channel surfing when Lindsey returned to the cabin and took a seat in the recliner. "Is there anything you'd like to watch?"

"Something with action."

"Oh yeah, here we go," Kendra cheered as a car chase filled the screen.

"Perfect."

"Not quite."

Lindsey looked at her with curiosity. "What else do you need?"

Kendra patted the bed. "For you to get comfortable."

Lindsey kicked off her shoes and eased onto the bed.

"There. Now this is perfect. Thanks."

"My pleasure," Lindsey managed to say. Her heart was racing as she tried to relax, her body so close to the woman who had stolen her heart. She could feel the warmth of Kendra's thigh next to hers, as she struggled to concentrate on the movie. Their bodies were so close, she feared moving. She wasn't sure how she could conceal her excitement if more of their bodies were touching.

Kendra's hand drifted over to her thigh as they pretended to watch the movie. Lindsey trembled under her touch. She looked over and locked eyes with Kendra.

"Are you cold? You had quite a chill earlier." Lindsey could hear the genuine concern in her voice.

Lindsey closed her eyes, to prevent Kendra seeing the excitement in them. "No, I'm not cold," she answered between gritted teeth.

Kendra's face blossomed into a mischievous grin before what looked like a pain-filled grimace filled her face.

"Stretch out with me then," Kendra said.

Lindsey was afraid her heart would pound its way out of her chest, but she scooted down on the bed, flat on her back, with her left arm tucked under her head. She looked over at Kendra to find she had turned onto her side and was smiling at her.

Kendra gently placed a hand on her shoulder and Lindsey could feel her body trembling beneath the touch.

"Lindsey?"

Lindsey feared her teeth would chatter since she was trembling so uncontrollably. "I'm listening." She fought her body for control.

"I want us to make love tonight." Kendra waited a few seconds and then reached up with her right hand and let her fingertips trail down Lindsey's jaw.

Lindsey skin burned with excitement beneath Kendra's caress. "There's not a fiber in my body that doesn't want you right now," she admitted.

"That's all I need to know." Kendra leaned down to brush her lips across Lindsey's jaw up to her lips.

Their first kiss was soft, as Kendra's lips and tongue explored Lindsey. She nibbled on her lower lip and Lindsey let out a soft moan. "There's not a fiber in your body, I don't want right now," Kendra whispered.

"Oh, Kendra, I'm about to explode just from a kiss. I'm all yours," Lindsey whispered back.

Chapter Fourteen

Kendra reached over and turned off the lamp, leaving the cabin illuminated by only the muted television. Her hand had crept under Lindsey's shirt as they kissed, and the soft, warmth of her skin beckoned her. "I need to be naked with you," she breathed against her skin.

"Undress me," Lindsey requested, and then sat up in the bed.

Kendra lifted the shirt over her head and tossed it onto the chair. "You are so beautiful," she whispered against Lindsey's skin as her lips kissed across her shoulder to her neck. The fingertips of her left hand traced down Lindsey's spine, causing her to shudder with desire. "We really must get you some relief," she teased as she lowered Lindsey back onto the bed. "Lift your hips for me."

Lindsey was beginning to doubt she had any control left over her body, but managed to lift her hips to allow Kendra to push her sweats down her body. With Kendra's help, the pants ended up in the chair, leaving her naked, vulnerable to the hungry look in Kendra's eyes.

Kendra's face lit up with a smile as her eyes landed on the tattoo several inches below her navel, which spelled "Heaven." She chuckled as her fingertips traced the black letters inked into the soft skin. "What's this all about? I've been wondering what the ink was since I first caught a glimpse of it."

"Being too drunk and stupid to resist a dare on our senior trip to Daytona Beach," Lindsey admitted.

Kendra's eyes devoured every inch of Lindsey's body. Her breasts were small, but beautifully rounded, her nipples erect, begging for attention. Her stomach rippled with muscles, and her mound of carefully trimmed blond curl glistened with moisture. She felt her tongue run over her lips as she ached to kiss and taste every inch of what she saw.

"Well I have to say, the tattoo is very fitting. Your body is like a piece of heaven dropped to earth."

Lindsey blushed and tugged at the hem of Kendra's shirt, and was pleased when she reached behind her head and pulled it off. Then Kendra laid back on the bed and removed her shorts before turning back on her side. When she looked into Lindsey's face, the look of tenderness took away her breath.

Kendra placed a knee between Lindsey's legs to spread them as she draped her leg over her. She felt her hand trembling as she reached out to caress the supple mound of Lindsey's breast, and her breath caught in her throat when her fingers touched the erect nipples.

Lindsey could feel the wetness of Kendra's excitement on her leg. She reached over to guide Kendra on top of her and thought she would faint with the pleasure that roared through her. She carefully buried her hand in Kendra's hair, and softly drew her face down for a kiss.

Kendra moved her hips slightly as their kiss grew more passionate, and she was delighted that their bodies molded together so perfectly. She could feel the vibration of Lindsey's moan in her mouth from the slight movement, so she began to slowly roll her hips. Lindsey's response was immediate, as she reached down to cup her ass, as her hips gently rolled, bringing them both pleasure.

Lindsey broke the kiss and her excited body was near erupting. "Just a little firmer," she whispered into Kendra's ear as she buried her face in her neck.

The sound of her voice trembling with need was all the encouragement Kendra needed as she began grinding her hips into Lindsey.

"Oh hell yes, Kendra," Lindsey cried as she convulsed with pleasure, sending Kendra tumbling over the edge with her, their bodies moving together in unison as they climaxed together.

Kendra lifted herself up on her arms and looked into Lindsey's eyes. "Now I'm going to have my way with you."

"Anything you wish, my captain," Lindsey teased as she struggled to calm her breathing.

"I think it's time for me to have a taste south of heaven," she suggested.

Lindsey moaned with anticipation.

Kendra planted soft kisses over her eyes and face before moving down to her neck. She took her time, breathing in the scent of Lindsey as she explored her lover's body with tenderness and curiosity. She made mental notes of how Lindsey reacted as she kissed and caressed her way down until she rested comfortably between Lindsey's thighs. She reached up with her right hand to trace the letters of the tattoo.

Lindsey feared she would explode from the soft caress of Kendra's fingers across her skin, and felt her muscles begin to quiver with excitement.

She glanced up into Lindsey's face to find her watching closely as she gently opened her silky folds, gently probing her wetness with her tongue, lapping upward to softly stroke across her swollen clit. Kendra's hand moved to gently squeeze her left nipple, as she covered Lindsey's clit, sucking it into her mouth.

Lindsey threw her head back, her hands clawing at the bed linens, as she struggled for control. Kendra teased her body expertly, urging her excitement higher than she'd ever been before, beyond her control, and a cry ripped from her body. "Yes, Kendra," she nearly screamed as her juices flooded her lover's face.

163

Kendra crawled back into her arms and held her as tears of joy flowed down Lindsey's cheeks. No words were necessary between them for several long minutes.

When Lindsey's tears subsided, Kendra rolled onto her side next to her, still cuddling close.

"That was perfection," Lindsey finally spoke.

Kendra's laughter filled the cabin, until she grimaced and reached for her damaged cheek. Her fingers met wetness, and when she brought them down, she saw them covered in blood.

"Oh my God," Lindsey cried and grabbed her shirt.

"I'm okay. I think I laughed too hard, and broke the seal on the glue."

"Here, use this while I get the first aid kit." Lindsey handed her the shirt and then climbed from the bed. She started toward the galley and grinned as she felt a weakness in her legs from all the recent exertion. It had been a long time since a woman had left her body physically drained.

Returning, she opened the kit and pulled out sterile pads to clean the wound. Kendra was right, the outer end of the wound had broken open. She opened the glue to reseal the wound, and used fresh steri-strips to stabilize the skin.

"There, now no more laughing," said.

She closed the kit and dropped the used items in the trash. "Do you need anything?"

"Are there any brownies left?"

Lindsey smiled. "Yes, ma'am, would you like ice cream too?"

"No, just a big brownie, a glass of iced milk, and a couple Ibuprofen." She was still holding the now bloodied shirt. "You might want to go ahead and pre-treat this so the blood will wash out." She handed her the shirt.

"I'll be back in a few," Lindsey said slipping into her sweats.

She went to her bunk and pulled out a clean shirt, slipping it over her head, and then sprayed the bloodied shirt before returning to the galley. *Damn, I can't believe this is really happening.* She found herself smiling as she pulled out the carton of milk. She poured the milk, then picked up the plate with the last of the brownies, and carried them back to the cabin.

"Here we go." She sat in the recliner, and handed her a glass of milk.

Kendra picked up a brownie and took a large bite. "Thanks, these really hit the spot."

"Damn, I'll be right back." Lindsey went into the bathroom to retrieve the Ibuprofen.

"Thanks again. You're a great nurse maid," Kendra said before downing the pills.

"I've had lots of practice growing up on a shrimp boat."

"I hear ya."

Lindsey glanced up to see that Kendra had changed the television back to the Weather Channel, for the hurricane coverage. "Any changes?" she asked.

"She's dropped wind speed, so she's back to a Category 2, and she's moving faster, so hopefully as soon as she makes landfall, she'll drop strength fast."

"That's great news." She popped the last bite of brownie into her mouth, just as the phone rang. Lindsey handed Kendra the phone. "I'm going to check on the deck."

Kendra nodded, and answered the phone, "Hey, Dad."

†

Lindsey walked into the galley and pulled on a slicker before stepping outside and turning on the flashlight. The rain was falling, but not as hard as earlier, as she checked the security of the equipment. When she glanced over the railing she saw the beacon of the other shrimp boat several hundred yards away.

"Plenty distance between us," she spoke to the wind.

A look up in the sky found a near full moon, clouds pregnant with rain rushing past it as the winds were coming in from the northeast. *These would be the feeder bands directly from the storm.* She knew they would only grow stronger as she walked back to the galley.

Stripping out of the slicker, she decided to load their dishes into the dishwasher to give Kendra a few more minutes of privacy to talk with her dad. When she finished, she returned to the cabin to find Kendra nodding off.

Kendra's head snapped up. "Will you come snuggle with me?" she asked.

Lindsey kicked off her shoes and started for the bed.

Kendra smiled at her. "Can you lose those clothes?"

Lindsey undressed and climbed in beside her.

"Thanks. I want to feel your skin next to mine. Can I spoon you?"

"Absolutely." Lindsey grinned and turned onto her side.

Kendra snuggled into her back and draped an arm over Lindsey's waist. "You comfy?"

"Very much so." She covered Kendra's hand with her own. She felt Kendra's warm breath on her neck and then a soft purring as she drifted off to sleep. *Yeah, this must be what heaven feels like* she remembered thinking before sleep overtook her.

Hours later, the rocking of the boat intensified, waking Lindsey. Kendra had rolled over onto her back, so Lindsey crept out of the bed and walked into the wheelhouse. She sat down in the captain's seat and brought up the weather screen.

The winds had increased dramatically. "No wonder the boat's rocking." The latest satellite image showed that Dani was just a few miles from land, so the worst would hopefully be over by mid-afternoon at the latest. She sensed movement in the room and turned to see Kendra. "Did I wake you?"

"No, the bed got cold without my heater." She smiled and sat in Lindsey's lap. "What's it looking like? It's really rocking out there." Her hand began playing in Lindsey's hair.

"She's almost made landfall. We've had gusts up to ninety with sustained winds at seventy-five," Linsey reported.

"Too risky to go outside so let's go back to bed. I'll let you cook me breakfast when we wake up." Kendra grinned.

"You have a deal."

Kendra stood and took her hand.

Back in Kendra's quarters, Lindsey was lying flat on her back, with Kendra's head on her shoulder, when the winds began to howl around the boat.

†

When they woke next, the wind had died down. They scrambled to dress and get out on deck to check the boat while they had a short reprieve from the winds. It was past sunrise, but the brilliant rays that normally welcomed them were nowhere on the horizon. The clouds were a lighter shade of gray, but still too dense to allow the rays to burn through. A strange mist floated above the water as Lindsey stood at the railing, gazing across to where she had last seen the other boat. There was no sign of a beacon.

Kendra walked up behind Lindsey and wrapped her arms around her in a hug. "Eerie looking, isn't it?"

"Like something out of a sci-fi movie." Kendra's lips brushed against her neck, causing Lindsey to shiver with anticipation. "Last night was beautiful," she whispered.

"Yes, it was."

An explosion caught their attention as a bright green flash penetrated the gray from the shoreline.

"What the hell?" Lindsey yelled.

"A transformer just exploded. They light up like green lightning when they become overloaded," Kendra explained. A second, then a third transformer exploded in the distance. "I think that's our cue to move back inside. The winds are returning."

Lindsey turned in her arms and kissed her softly. "I did agree to cook you breakfast." She grinned as she took her hand, to lead her toward the galley.

A loud crash at the rear of the boat startled them. "What the hell?" Lindsey shrieked. Panic filled her eyes as they felt the boat sway from the impact. She rushed aft with Kendra.

A twenty-foot sailboat had slammed into the back of the boat, causing little damage to the shrimper, but the hull of the

167

sailboat was shattered. The winds pushed the boat against the metal hull of *Heaven Sent,* causing the fiberglass hull of the sailboat to cave in and take on water quickly. The winds whipped the rain into their eyes as they strained to see what was happening.

"Oh, dear God." Lindsey saw a body floating in the water. Without a second thought for her own safety, she took off at a dead run and leapt into the water.

Lindsey's heart was pounding with the adrenalin rushing through her as she reached the person floating in the water and rolled the body onto its back. It was a woman. Blood tainted the water from a gash in the woman's head as she floated unconsciously. The life jacket on her upper body was the only thing keeping her afloat. Lindsey wrapped an arm around the woman's chest, keeping her head above water as she struggled to swim back to the boat.

Lindsey thought she heard Kendra calling out to her, but she was concentrating on getting back to the boat. The dead weight of the woman's body was exhausting her rapidly since she could only use one arm to swim. A large wave slapped her in the face and when she spit out a mouthful of water, she found to her horror, that the woman was conscious and like a terrified animal was trying to escape her grasp. Panic had her eyes open wide as she flailed against Lindsey's efforts to swim them to safety.

"I've got you, but you have to relax or we're both going to drown," Lindsey warned her.

In her fright, the woman failed to comprehend what Lindsey was shouting, and she was nearing the point of knocking her out, when she felt the woman relax. She had passed out, so Lindsey swam as hard as she could toward the boat.

Kendra ran to the railing to find Lindsey swimming toward the body bobbing in the waves, which were growing in the increasing winds. She watched as Lindsey fought against the waves to reach the body, which was face down in the water. She rushed over to pick up the life ring and line to toss out to Lindsey when she got close enough to reach for it.

"Come on, baby," she called out to Lindsey.

Kendra watched as the boat began to sink as her eyes searched for anyone else occupying the sailboat. Finding no evidence that there was anyone else on board, she turned back to Lindsey. She could tell that her energy was draining quickly and she prayed Lindsey was close enough to reach the lifeline. She lifted the ring and flung it out as far as she could.

Kendra pulled the line with all her might, frustrated by the slow progress they were making toward the boat. The waves threatened to pull them underwater, as the winds howled around the boat.

"Come on, swim, baby, you can do this," Kendra spoke out loud, even knowing there was no way Lindsey could hear her.

Lindsey saw a flash of white light and looked to find the life ring floating toward her quickly. *Thank God. I'm just about drained.* She stopped swimming long enough to reach for the ring, pulling it toward her. She looked up to lock eyes with Kendra who began to retract the line.

Five feet from the boat, the woman regained consciousness, and wearily looked into Lindsey's eyes, but thankfully did not fight against her. "Is there anyone else on board?"

"No, it's just me," the woman managed to croak.

"Okay, relax, and we'll be on the boat in just a few minutes." *I can do this,* she repeated in her mind as her muscles began to burn with exhaustion.

Relieved to reach the boat, Lindsey looked at the woman. "Can you reach up and grab Kendra's hand if I help lift you up?"

"I...I think so, but I think my left arm is broken."

Lindsey saw Kendra tie the line to the railing and move as close as she could to reach out to the woman, bracing her body between the railings.

"Okay, we'll have to work with that, but we'll have you on board in no time." She looked up at Kendra and shouted to Kendra over the roar of the wind.

"Careful. Her left arm might be broken."

169

Kendra reached down as Lindsey used her remaining strength to lift the woman as high as she could. Kendra grabbed her right hand, and with both arms pulled with all her might.

Lindsey's right hand gripped the rope as she felt the woman's body begin to leave the water and felt the woman's foot on her left shoulder. She supported the woman's weight as she pulled on the rope to lift her high enough for Kendra to help the woman over the railing.

✝

The jarring of the woman's arm caused her to cry out in pain as they fell onto the deck.

"Owww," she hollered as she grabbed for her left arm.

"I'm sorry, I know it hurt, but that's the best I could do," Kendra said.

The woman gritted her teeth against the pain and nodded.

"Let me get Lindsey on board and we'll tend to your injuries." Kendra rushed back to the railing to find Lindsey struggling to climb the rope. She took her hands, and pulled her high enough to get her feet on deck and helped her over the railing. One look into her eyes and she knew Lindsey was exhausted. She guided her to sit on the deck. "You okay?"

Lindsey nodded. "Yeah, just tired. Take care of her."

They turned to look at the woman sitting on deck, holding her broken arm.

"I'm Kendra and this is Lindsey. How are you feeling?"

The woman grimaced in pain. "I'm Susan. Thank you both for saving me."

"Other than your arm and that nasty cut on your head, how do you feel? Is anything else hurting?"

"Not that I can feel. My arm is really hurting."

"I'm going to see if I can reach the Coast Guard, and I'll get the first aid kit." She looked at Lindsey. "Do you think you'll be strong enough in a minute to get you both inside?"

"Yeah, I can do that," Lindsey answered. She struggled to sit upright.

"I'll meet you in the galley as soon as I can."

"Okay, baby."

Kendra left Lindsey and the woman and rushed inside, grabbed the first aid kit, carried it into the galley, and placed it on the table. Lindsey would see it and hopefully would be able to stop the bleeding on the woman's head. Then she ran back through the galley to the wheelhouse and picked up the radio.

Kendra reached the dispatcher for the Coast Guard, explaining their situation and providing their location. Unfortunately, she learned, the weather prevented the Coast Guard helicopter from launching from Pensacola to take the injured woman for care. She and Lindsey would have to provide whatever medical care they could until the weather cleared enough to allow the helicopter to launch. Disappointed and concerned for the woman's health, she returned to the galley.

Lindsey watched Kendra rush toward the wheelhouse. As she struggled to her feet, the sky opened up. Lindsey looked up at the clouds. "Really, you don't think we're soaked enough already," she growled.

"Thank you," Susan told her. "If you hadn't been here, I would be dead by now."

Lindsey reached out to take her right hand. "I'm glad we were here. Let's get you inside."

With her help, Susan climbed to her feet, allowing Lindsey to guide her across the deck.

Lindsey's legs were shaking as she guided Susan into the galley. She saw the first aid kit on the table and helped the woman into a chair.

"Let's see if we can stop the bleeding." Lindsey rummaged through the kit for sterile pads and pressed a small stack of them onto the gash on Susan's head. The look in her eyes showed that Susan was falling into shock. The pain from her arm was probably the only thing keeping her alert.

"Do you think you can hold this and put pressure on it while I get a bandage ready?"

Susan reached for the thick stack of sterile pads, pressing them against her head as Lindsey sought out the supplies she needed.

Lindsey looked up and saw Kendra smiling at the women as she entered the galley.

"The Coast Guard can't launch in this weather. They will contact us when they get clearance to fly, but it probably won't be until tomorrow according to the dispatcher. We'll do what we can to make you comfortable."

"Thank you for everything you've done for me," Susan said, grimacing.

Lindsey shared a worried look with Kendra.

Lindsey was wrapping a pressure bandage around Susan's head. "I think we've got the bleeding stopped for now."

"That's good news. We need to figure how we can stabilize her arm," Kendra stated.

"Let's get her out of these wet clothes while we come up with a solution. Kendra, can you get a pair of my sweats, a shirt, and some socks? Bring a blanket, too. I think you're starting to go into shock," Lindsey told Susan.

Kendra nodded. "I'll be right back."

"I need to get this shirt off you. Would you mind if I cut it off? It will be less painful for you."

"Yes, thanks, that's fine."

Lindsey fished out a pair of scissors and began cutting the shirt from the woman. Do you have pain anywhere else?" She had noted some bruising on her left side.

"No, just my arm, and I'm getting a headache."

Kendra returned with the clothes and dry towels. "Can you get Susan some of your Ibuprofen for her pain?"

"Sure, I brought you some dry clothes, too."

"Thanks, baby."

Susan waited for Kendra to leave the room. "Is she your girlfriend?"

"Yes she is." Lindsey smiled.

"I really am lucky you two were here," Susan replied.

"I'm glad we were, too." Lindsey smiled at her. "Can you try to dry off some while I take a look at your arm? I'll try to be gentle."

Kendra raced back into the galley with the medicine and poured a glass of water. "Here you go." She handed Susan two pills and then the glass of water.

"What's the verdict on her arm?" Kendra asked.

"Definitely broken, but thankfully it didn't break through the skin. Can you get me a roll of duct tape?"

"Sure, what do you have in mind?"

"Don't laugh, but we're going to make splints out of some wooden spoons."

Kendra grinned. "That's clever, baby."

"Can you see if one of the crew has a pair of tube socks?"

"This is getting more curious by the minute," Susan said with a painful grimace.

"I'll be right back. See if you two can get into some dry clothes," Kendra suggested.

Kendra returned carrying a variety of items as Lindsey helped Susan get into dry clothing. "I'm going to change clothes. Will you get six wooden spoons if we have them?"

"I'm all over it, Doc."

"Place an ice pack on her arm while I'm gone, too, please?"

Kendra looked at Susan. "Do you prefer peas or carrots?"

Susan chuckled. "Peas, please."

Kendra took a bag of frozen peas from the freezer and laid them gently on her arm. "I prefer the peas, too." She pointed to her bruised cheek.

"What happened?"

"A buckle came loose during the storm last night, and clipped me when I was making rounds."

"That looks painful."

"It was, but Lindsey's a good nurse."

"I heard that," Lindsey called out.

"You can play doctor with me anytime." Kendra winked at Susan and then grimaced from the pain in her cheek. "Damn, that hurt."

Susan smiled at her. "You two make a cute couple."

"Thanks. I think so, too."

Susan looked at her with a frown. "I guess my boat's gone."

"I'm afraid so. It went down quickly. How did you end up in the water?"

"I was below deck getting ready to make some breakfast when I heard the crash. I got slammed into the cabinet. I hadn't realized that the anchor had broken free and that I was drifting in the water."

"The way the waves were kicking up, it's no wonder you couldn't feel you were moving," Lindsey said, as she took a seat at the table.

Susan looked up at her with wide eyes. "I'm not really sure what happened. I think I came up top to find out what was going on, and the boat slammed into your hull again, and I went overboard. Did I do much damage to your boat?"

"Just a few scratches, nothing bad. Fiberglass doesn't fare well against steel," Kendra said.

"I'm sorry. I thought I'd be safe to shelter here. I was on my way to Panama City to meet my girlfriend when I learned about the approaching storm."

"Would you like to give her a call?"

"That would be great. My cell and everything else was on the boat."

"I'll grab the satellite phone and be right back then."

Lindsey groaned when she stood to walk to the kitchen.

A grimace covered Susan's face. "Are you okay? I didn't even think about what you risked to save me."

"I'm fine, just chilled, and tired. You gave me a run for my money for a few minutes when you were panicked."

"I'm sorry. I could have hurt you."

174

"Don't worry about it. You were scared and disoriented. I'm happy we're both safe."

Kendra returned and handed Lindsey the blanket to wrap around Susan. "Is there a number I can dial for you?"

Kendra dialed the requested number and handed the phone to Susan. While Susan talked, Lindsey began making the splint.

"Will you pour us some coffee?" She asked Kendra. "I'm sure we could all use something warm." She looked at Susan. "I'm glad she got her friend."

"Me too. Hopefully she'll be able to come to the hospital to be with her."

"How far is it to Panama City?" Lindsey asked.

"Two to three hours, depending on traffic and road conditions."

"I don't envy her that drive."

"Me either, especially if this rain keeps up." Kendra reached over to push wet hair from Lindsey's face. "You okay?"

"Yeah, just physically wiped out. I thought I was in good shape, but damn that was tough."

"I'm very proud of you."

"Do you have any idea what hospital I'll go to?" Susan asked.

"I'll request Sacred Heart for you. That will be easy for your friend to find."

"Yes, she knows where that is. Thanks."

Kendra poured them coffee and returned to the table.

"Can you hold these for me?" Lindsey asked, holding out two of the spoons.

Kendra took the spoons and held them while Lindsey wrapped duct tape around the center and each end. "You are so clever," Kendra praised.

"Thanks."

"Would you mind talking to Kelly?" Susan asked Kendra.

"No, not at all." Kendra spoke to her for several minutes and explained that the Coast Guard would come as soon as they could get clearance, and she promised to call Kelly as soon as they were on the way. When Kendra finished, she handed the phone back to Susan.

"Yes, honey, I'm in good hands and will be all right. Love you too. See you tomorrow."

She ended the call and gave Kendra the phone. "Thanks."

"How's the ice working?" Lindsey asked her.

"My arm's not throbbing as badly as before."

"Good, because I can't promise you this won't be painful."

"I know you're doing your best and I'm grateful for that."

Lindsey slipped a pair of spoons into a sock and handed it to Kendra, and then fashioned the next two. When she finished, she carefully placed one splint under Susan's arm. "Can you hold this one Susan?"

Lindsey waited until Susan held the spoon and then placed another on each side of her damaged arm.

"Can you wrap the large ace bandage around these, as snug as Susan can tolerate, while we hold them?" she asked Kendra.

When they were done, Lindsey smiled at Susan. "It ain't pretty, but it should help."

"Thank you. It feels better already."

"We were about to have breakfast. Have you eaten yet?" Kendra asked.

"No, I was about to cook breakfast, too."

"Well, you two sit back and relax, and I'll have some French toast ready in a few," Kendra said.

"I promised to cook you breakfast," Lindsey said.

"I know, but you've done plenty, so please relax, and let me cook."

"I'm too tired to argue," Lindsey said.

"Good. You know I'd win anyhow." Kendra kissed her before leaving the table.

While they ate the wind began to howl. "You want to check the weather?" Lindsey asked.

Kendra walked over and turned the set on. "Damn, you've got to see this."

Lindsey walked over to Kendra. "Holy cow, how did that get there?"

"Apparently a twister picked up a sailboat and it landed in that old oak."

"How bad is the damage?"

"Not as bad as it could have been, but bad enough. The roofing contractors in the state will be busy for a while. Trees down, and forty thousand people are without power. FEMA is on the way, so hopefully, once the storm dies out, people can get to work picking up the pieces of their lives."

"Have you heard from any of the guys?" Lindsey asked.

"Not since Harvey called early last night. I thought after breakfast I'd give him a call."

✝

After getting Susan set up in Lindsey's berth, Kendra walked to the wheelhouse and picked up the receiver, delighted to hear she still had a signal from the satellite. She'd hoped they would still have a working tower in town. Kendra dialed Harvey's number and he picked up on the third ring.

"Hey, I'm glad you called."

"How are you and your family fairing?"

"We're good. Lost power last night, but the generator restored the power in less than a minute. I've talked to the rest of the crew and everyone is doing well. How are you doing on the boat?"

"We're safe and it hasn't been too bad. Last night had us rocking pretty good." Kendra grinned, remembering making love to Lindsey. She immediately regretted grinning that hard. The skin on her injured cheek was tight and smiling made it ache. "This morning got a little crazy though. A woman's sailboat crashed into the back of the boat and sank. Lindsey had to go into the water to save her from drowning. For a few long minutes, I wasn't sure either of them was going to make it back to the boat, because the woman panicked and was struggling against Lindsey. We patched her up the best we could with our limited supplies. The Coast Guard can't make it out until the weather clears to transport her to the hospital, so she's hanging with us."

"She's fortunate you two were out there, or she probably wouldn't be alive right now."

"Yeah. She gave us a good scare for a little while, but I think she'll heal well from her injuries."

"The two of y'all doing okay out there?" he asked.

"Yes, we're going to try to get some rest and head back in after the storm has passed through."

"I'm hoping by lunchtime tomorrow the worst will be over. I'll ride into town when it's safe, check on the house for you, and then give you a call."

"Thanks, Harvey, I'd appreciate that."

"No problem, Kendra. When can we expect you back in port?"

"Hopefully the day after tomorrow, if the winds return to normal."

"Great. I'll look forward to seeing you soon. Have you heard from your Dad?"

"Yes, we talked last night. Uncle Henry is doing well and is back at home. Dad's been chomping at the bit to come home, but I'm going to try to get him to stay a little longer."

Harvey chuckled. "Good luck with that. He's as stubborn as you."

It was her turn to laugh. "Yeah, he is."

"Be safe and I'll call you later. The wife's calling me to breakfast."

"Thanks again, Harvey."

"Did you get Harvey?" Lindsey asked when Kendra returned from the wheelhouse.

"Yes, so far everyone's doing well. He'll go by the house later today, or in the morning if this weather moves through, and give me a call."

"So what do we need to do today, boss?"

"I need a shower."

"I hear that."

"Do I smell that bad?"

"I didn't mean that and you know it. I need one, too."

"So, take one with me."

Lindsey nearly choked on a sip of coffee. She coughed several times and swallowed. "I'd love to."

"Am I putting too much pressure on you? I meant what I told you last night. I have fallen hard for you."

Kendra saw a blush rising to Lindsey's cheeks as she answered. "Not at all, I just have to pinch myself to remind me this isn't a dream."

"Oh, you are definitely a dream come true for me," Kendra replied. "Wow, that sounded kind of cheesy, didn't it?"

Lindsey chuckled. "Cheesy yes, but also very romantic." She reached over, covering Kendra's hand with her own. "Let me clean up here and we'll shower."

After a leisurely shower, Kendra convinced Lindsey to take a nap. She was exhausted from the morning's adrenalin rush and was grateful for a short rest. Kendra checked on Susan and went to the galley to watch the weather channel while the others rested.

✝

Two hours later, Susan walked into the galley and joined Kendra on the couch.

"How are you feeling?" Kendra asked.

"My arm's throbbing a bit, but not like it was at first."

"It's probably time for more painkillers. Let me get some pillows, too, to prop your arm on." Kendra placed several thick pillows under her arm.

"Thanks." Susan said. "Is Lindsey okay?"

"Yes, she's still napping." She handed Susan two pills and a glass of water.

"Have you two been together long?"

"No we've just begun a relationship. She came down from North Carolina to work on my shrimp boat for the summer, and we've fallen in love."

"Will she be staying after the summer?"

Kendra hadn't given it much thought. "I sure hope she will." She smiled.

"I hope so too."

Lindsey walked in, wiping the sleep from her eyes. "What's the latest on the storm?"

"She's stalled and is pounding the coastline with rain. She's causing tornadoes to the east all the way into south Georgia."

Lindsey sat next to Kendra, "Any more news from Harvey or your Dad?"

"Not yet." She looked at Susan. "Do you like shrimp?"

Susan grinned at her. "Is it raining outside?"

"I was thinking I'd boil some reds for dinner." Kendra looked at Lindsey. "Will you make some of your hushpuppies while I make a salad?"

"I'd love too. Would you ladies care for a glass of wine?"

"I think I'd better pass, but you two go right ahead," Susan said. "Is there anything I can do?"

"Nope, we've got this under control." Lindsey poured two glasses of wine. "Can I get you tea or something else to drink?"

"Tea would be great, thanks. I hope that you two will come to Panama City for a visit so I can return the favor and cook for y'all."

"I've never been to Panama City," Lindsey said.

"I think that can be arranged." Kendra smiled.

Lindsey stood and pulled on a slicker.

"Where are you going?"

"I'm going on deck to check the equipment before it gets dark out," she replied. "I'll be right back to start on dinner."

✝

Susan raved about the reds. "These shrimp are incredible. I've never had anything that tasted near this good."

"They are delicious," Kendra said, as she peeled several more for their injured guest.

"I need to get your recipe for these hushpuppies, too. I could make a meal of them alone."

"I think that could be arranged." Lindsey grinned.

"Are these some of the shrimp y'all harvest?"

"Yes, this is our first year of fishing reds. We hope it's going to be a good one."

"I will definitely have to see if we can get these at home. They're like baby lobsters."

Kendra chuckled. "Yes, that's why they are so prized along the gulf."

"How are you feeling?" Lindsey asked.

"My head is throbbing again and I'm suddenly tired."

Lindsey examined her eyes closely. "You probably have a slight concussion. If you don't mind, I'm going to wake you every few hours tonight to check on you. Hopefully, the chopper will be cleared in the morning to get you medical care."

"Do you really think that's necessary? You've done so much for me already I hate to impose on you further."

"I'd feel better."

"We can take turns and it's not an imposition. You're on board our boat, so you're our responsibility," Kendra said with a wink. "Ouch. Damn, I need to stop doing that."

"Will you go in for medical care for that cut?"

"It's been too long for stitches, and I think the glue is holding up well. I just need to remember to stop winking."

"That's hard to do for such a flirt," Lindsey chimed in.

Kendra grinned but didn't argue.

"If the weather clears tomorrow, will you head back to harbor?" Susan asked.

"I think we'll wait one more day to let the traffic settle a bit."

"If you two don't mind, I think it's time to lie down. Thanks again for saving me and giving me such good care. Is there anything I can do to repay your kindness?"

"Get well and get another boat. Don't let this experience spoil it for you," Kendra replied.

"Do you need anything before you lie down?" Lindsey asked.

"No, I think I'm good. Thanks."

"I'll see you in a few hours then." Lindsey smiled.

"Goodnight, ladies," Susan bade them and then left the galley.

"I think it's time for us to turn in as well," Kendra said.

"I'm right behind you, Captain." Lindsey stood to walk behind her. She laughed. "Damn nice view too."

"Come on, you," Kendra turned to reach for her hand.

†

Kendra laid her head on Lindsey's shoulder and snuggled in close.

"I've set my alarm for two hours, but I'll try not to wake you," she said as she ran her fingers through Kendra's hair.

"I'll take the next watch if you'll tell me what to look for," Kendra offered.

"Look at her pupils to see if they're different sizes or her eyes are unusually bloodshot. Also, check to see if she appears to be running a fever. If so, take her temperature and give her some Tylenol."

"That sounds simple enough. I'm impressed with your medical knowledge."

"I've picked up a lot from Dad over the years. He was a medic in Vietnam."

"I didn't realize that."

"Your dad probably doesn't talk about it much either."

"No, not often. He tries to stay positive and looking forward."

"Just like you." Lindsey kissed her softly. "Love you."

"I love you, too. I hope you get some rest. It's been a hectic day."

"Yes it has," Lindsey agreed and turned out the light.

†

They alternated checking on Susan throughout the night, and as the sun began peeking over the horizon, Lindsey started a pot of coffee. She was waiting to pour cups for herself and Kendra when the phone rang. It was the Coast Guard calling to notify her that they had received clearance to fly and would arrive in approximately thirty minutes. Kendra poured three cups and went to wake the others.

"The chopper will lower a gurney to the deck for you. Will you be able to lie down to be airlifted?" Lindsey asked.

Susan nodded her head. "That should be easy. I'm feeling stronger this morning."

"You might want to call Kelly, too, to let her know you're on the way," Lindsey suggested.

Twenty minutes later, they heard the helicopter approach.

"I'll go and guide them in, Kendra, if you'll get Susan on deck," Lindsey offered.

Lindsey waved the chopper to hover over the deck of the boat, and watched as one of the crew rode down on the gurney.

"Y'all made great time," she yelled, over the noise of the rotors.

"What do we have here?"

"An injured left arm, probably a break, and a head injury. We've got a pressure bandage on her head, and an improvised splint on her arm. We were afraid to attempt too much with her arm."

The man nodded. "Any loss of consciousness?"

"She was unconscious when I reached her in the water, but revived on the way to the boat, and she has been alert. There's a possibility that she's suffering from a concussion."

Lindsey looked up to see Kendra leading Susan, who was carefully guarding her arm.

"Let's get you settled on the gurney, ma'am." The crewmember offered Susan his arm. He looked into Kendra's bruised face. "You okay? That's a nasty looking bruise."

"I'm good, just caught the wrong end of a metal buckle in the storm. We've kept it clean and steri-stripped."

"You want me to take a look while I'm here?"

"No, I'm good. Thanks for offering." She nodded at Susan. "She's in some pain and needs to have that arm looked at. Will you take her to Sacred Heart? She has family that will meet her there."

"Most definitely. The worst is over, but be careful until you're back in port."

"We will," Kendra assured him. "Will you make a report on her boat? There was no saving it from sinking."

"Yes ma'am, we'll take care of that." As he finished strapping Susan onto the gurney, another crewmember dropped a line down for him and prepared to lift the gurney. He reached into his bag and pulled out a tube of ointment. "Put this on that cut several times a day. It'll help with the pain and minimize scarring."

"Thanks," Kendra told him, taking the tube.

"Thank you for everything," Susan told them as the gurney lifted off the deck.

"We'll take good care of her," the medic promised, and followed the gurney to the helicopter. He waved to them, and the craft lifted and flew away.

Kendra wrapped an arm around Lindsey's shoulder as they watched the helicopter disappear. "I'll start some breakfast if you're hungry. After we eat, I think you need some rest. I'm very proud of you."

"Thanks," Lindsey grinned as they started to the galley. "How about ham and cheese omelets?"

"That sounds wonderful."

"When we get home, I'd like to take a long, hot bubble bath with you," Kendra said while they ate.

"Looking forward to that," Lindsey grinned. "Call your Dad while I clean up, so we won't have any distractions."

"Very good idea," Kendra agreed, and cleaned her plate.

✝

"I need a shower," Lindsey stated after she finished cleaning the galley.

"You mind some company?

Lindsey grinned and stepped into the shower. She held out her hand to Kendra, and pulled her into an embrace as they stepped under the flow of the water. She was mesmerized by watching the water soak into Kendra's thick hair, then sliding down her smooth skin in small rivers.

Lindsey kissed her softly, and then knelt down before Kendra, her tongue chasing a drop of water as it raced down her body. Lindsey looked into Kendra's eyes to find them dark with desire, smiled, and used the tip of her tongue to tease her lips as her hands spread her thighs apart. She slipped first one, and then a second finger, inside the silky wetness as her lips enclosed the swollen clit, sucking it slowly in and out of her mouth.

"Oh yes," Kendra cried out, and braced her arms on the shower walls as her body began trembling.

Lindsey reached up with one hand to take a firm nipple between her fingers, twisting it slowly as her other hand stroked the inside of Kendra's body.

Kendra's hips rocked in motion with Lindsey's fingers as they drove her wild with need. "Faster," she groaned, and her moans echoed in the shower.

Lindsey's fingers picked up speed as Kendra's moans grew louder, and with a scream of pleasure, Kendra grabbed the back of Lindsey's head, holding her in place as her orgasm raced through her.

Kendra lowered herself to her knees, her arms resting on Lindsey's shoulders as she caught her breath. Her eyes glowed with excitement as she leaned forward and kissed Lindsey. Tasting herself on her lover's lips made her heart skip a beat.

Lindsey parted her lips, and pulled Kendra close for a deeper kiss.

When they broke the kiss, Kendra smiled. "We better hurry and bathe before we lose the hot water."

†

Lindsey tended to Kendra's wound and then led her lover to the bed. They spent the rest of the morning there, making love and talking.

"This has been wonderful, having you all to myself, but what happens when we return to the real world?" Lindsey asked.

"That depends on you."

"Why me?" Lindsey asked.

"Are you comfortable being out as my lover in front of the crew?"

"Yes, I have no problem with that. What about your dad?"

"He thinks you will make a great partner for me." Kendra smiled.

"What?"

"He noticed our attraction to each other before I did."

"So he's okay with us?"

"He'd be very proud to call you the newest addition to his family."

"I wish my family was that accommodating," Lindsey replied with a frown.

"Give them some time. I'm sure they only want you to be happy." Kendra smiled, and kissed the frown from Lindsey's face.

They snuggled until Kendra's stomach growled. Lindsey chuckled. "I think your stomach's telling us it's time to eat."

"I hope Susan is resting well and is reunited with her girlfriend."

"Do you find it ironic that she crashed into our boat? As big as the bay is, why did she crash into us?"

Kendra frowned. "Does seem a bit odd, doesn't it, but I'm glad you were able to save her. You're such a handsome hero, my love."

Chuckling at the remark, Lindsey kissed the top of Kendra's head.

"Let's go outside to check the weather, and then find something to eat," Kendra suggested, and offered her hand.

†

They stepped out into the first sunshine they had seen in days.

"This is spectacular," Kendra said as they walked around the deck.

"If we didn't know better you'd think we've had perfect weather," Lindsey remarked as they walked over to the rail.

There was activity on the deck of the other shrimp boat that suggested they were making plans to leave the protected harbor. "Looks like someone is preparing to leave for home," Kendra stated.

Disappointed that their time alone together was coming to an end Lindsey looked into Kendra's eyes. "What about us?"

"Nope, we're staying put until tomorrow, unless you want to go back today."

"Hell no. I want every minute alone with you I can get."

"I was hoping you'd say that, so I took steaks out of the freezer last night. I think it's time we had a meal topside tonight."

"Fantastic, but what do you need to hold you over?"

"Will you make us sandwiches and chips while I set up out here? Later we can work on dinner together."

Lindsey kissed her tenderly and stepped back. "I'll be waiting for you inside."

"See you soon." Kendra watched her disappear into the galley.

Kendra removed the grill from storage, and checked to make sure there was gas and that the racks were clean.

She would grill some link sausage as an appetizer that they could munch on while watching the sunset, and then grill the steaks.

Lindsey made them a plate of ham and turkey sandwiches then pulled out a bag of chips from the pantry, before pouring glasses of tea. She surveyed the contents of the pantry and freezer for items to accompany steaks for dinner. She placed several potatoes and onions on the counter. There was a bag of corn on the cob in the freezer that she could wrap together with sliced potatoes and onions in foil to cook on the grill.

She turned to see Kendra walking inside and washing her hands in the sink. "I'm starving. Those sandwiches look great."

"What would you like for dessert tonight?"

"You did well last night, so surprise me." Kendra sat at the table for lunch, took a sandwich, and bit into it.

"I can do that." Lindsey crunched on a chip. "Will we go back out on Monday?"

"I'd like to, if nobody has major storm damage to deal with. I'd like to make the most out of every outing this season."

"I'm sure you won't get any argument from the rest of the crew. We all enjoy getting those nice paychecks."

"It's great to see everyone so pleased."

"Are you all set up outside?"

Kendra smiled. "I've got one more thing I need to do."

"You need some help?"

"Nope, I've got this."

"I thought you could grill some vegetables to go with the steaks."

"Potatoes, onions and corn," Kendra asked?

"That's what I was thinking. I'll wrap them in some foil, add some butter and seasonings."

"If we slice the potatoes and boil the corn a bit they'll cook faster."

Lindsey smiled at her. "I was thinking that too. I'll get that started while you finish outside."

"Would you like a salad to go with the meal?"

"Oh yeah, sounds great," Lindsey replied.

†

Kendra walked into the small storage area and located the two lounge chairs she hoped were still useable. It had been a while since she had them out, but they appeared in good shape. She carried the chairs to the front of the boat, and returned for a small table to place beside them. Tonight would probably be the last opportunity for them to have some privacy on the boat, and she wanted the night to be special. After dinner, they would take a bottle of wine, stretch out, and gaze at the stars until they were ready to retire.

She smiled, pleased with her idea, and returned to the galley to help prepare dinner.

"I thought I'd grill some sausage for us to munch on while we watch the sunset." Kendra showed the package she'd taken from the freezer.

"I'm all over that." Lindsey smiled.

Kendra whipped up some honey mustard for dipping while Lindsey chopped the potatoes, and boiled the corn. "I can put the veggies on while I cook the sausage. That should give them plenty time to cook."

"I can taste them already."

Kendra left the galley for a few minutes and returned with a bottle of wine and two glasses. "Can I interest you in a glass of wine?"

"Please." Lindsey wiped tears from her eyes caused by slicing onions for the grill.

Kendra poured their wine and placed one beside Lindsey, then leaned against the counter next to her. She grinned at her lover. "What do you think about turning this boat into a pirate ship, and the two of us heading out to sea?"

Lindsey chuckled as she picked up her glass. "That would be fun." She lifted her glass. "To the booty," she toasted.

Kendra grinned back at her and tipped her glass. "I've already found the best booty."

"You say the sweetest things for a pirate captain,"

"I must admit, you bring out the best in me."

Lindsey sat her glass on the counter and took Kendra in her arms. "A part of me wishes this day could last forever. I've enjoyed our time together."

"We've only just begun," Kendra promised and kissed her. "Umm, this wine tastes even better on your lips."

"I'm surprised at how romantic you are. Pleasantly though."

Kendra felt her eyes watering. "You make me feel so…unbelievably good. I want to share everything I am with you." A tear slid down her injured cheek. "What I'm trying to say here is, I love you."

Lindsey used her thumb to gently wipe the tear from Kendra's cheek. Her eyes sparkled with excitement. "I love you, Kendra. I've never told anyone that before, because until you, I never knew how good it could feel to constantly crave someone's touch and smile. And the way you kiss me just melts my insides."

Kendra grinned so wide at Lindsey's admission that she winced.

"Pretty sore today, huh?"

"Yes, but worth every ounce of pain to hear you talk that way."

Lindsey took her hand and placed it over her heart. "I hope you know my words come from here." She tapped her chest with their joined hands.

"We better stop there or I'm going to be a blubbering mess." Kendra leaned in to rest her forehead against Lindsey's as her hands encircled Lindsey's waist.

They stood together for several minutes.

"I guess I'd better start making our salad now." Kendra stepped away from Lindsey.

"I'll finish getting the veggies ready to go."

They worked together in the kitchen, and after Kendra placed the salad in to chill, she took a sip of wine. "I'm going to get the grill going. I'll be back shortly."

†

They shared the wine and sausage appetizers while watching the sunset. The robin's egg blue sky was cloudless after the storm, and the setting sun lit the horizon with beautiful hues of red, gold, and orange.

"Does it seem strange that the sky is so beautiful after such a harrowing storm?" Kendra asked.

"I know we're still out on the water, so we don't know about damage on shore, but it's hard to believe a hurricane just came through the area."

"I guess we should be grateful we didn't experience any more problems on the boat. It certainly could have been much worse."

Lindsey reached over to place her hand on Kendra's, entwining their fingers. "I'm very thankful for the time I've shared with you. It's been great to get to know you better."

Kendra returned her smile. "That won't stop once we return to work."

"Maybe, but I know I won't be able to spend the time with you like we've had these last two days, or kiss you whenever I want. I have to go back to sharing you." Lindsey shrugged.

"There's nothing stopping you right now." Kendra leaned over to kiss Lindsey.

"You know what I mean."

"I do, and I promise to make as much time for us to be together as possible. Would you feel comfortable sleeping in my cabin?"

"I'd love that, if you don't think it will cause problems with the crew."

"I don't think they will care one bit."

Lindsey smiled and picked up a slice of sausage and popped it into her mouth. "This is good, but I can't wait for the steaks."

"I can take a hint, are you all set inside?"

"I've got to finish dessert, but other than that, yes, I'm ready."

"Will you do that while I grill the steaks?"

"You betcha," Lindsey said and followed Kendra into the galley.

"I don't know what you're cooking up, but it sure smells good in here." Kendra took the steaks from the refrigerator. "See you soon." She kissed Lindsey and left the galley.

†

After finishing dinner and a delicious dessert, Kendra took Lindsey by the hand and picked up the bottle of wine.

"Come with me," she requested, and led Lindsey to the loungers. She sat the bottle on the table. "I thought we'd relax and enjoy some star gazing tonight. It may be the last truly relaxing night we get for a few days."

Lindsey stretched out on the lounger and took a fresh glass of wine from Kendra. "Thanks."

The lack of artificial light made the stars sparkle across the sky. A cool breeze blew and the lapping of the water against the boat was the only sound.

"It's so peaceful." Kendra reached over and took Lindsey's hand.

They enjoyed the serenity of the night and finished the wine before retiring for the evening. Lindsey snuggled into Kendra after they made love, content to be in her arms. Kendra kissed the top of her head. "Sweet dreams, my love."

"You too, Kendra," Lindsey said with a sleepy voice, and she burrowed under the covers to sink into the warm bed.

Chapter Fifteen

Lindsey joined Kendra in the wheelhouse after cleaning the kitchen, and Kendra guided the boat through the narrow pass. As the beachfront homes came into view, the presence of blue tarps secured to roofs began telling the story of the damage that Dani had left in her wake. Several of the homes had evidence of water damage from the storm surge, and the dunes had taken a beating, showing significant signs of erosion.

Concerned for her crew, Kendra reached for the phone to call Harvey. "Hey, Harvey, how did everyone survive the storm?"

"No major damages, Captain. A few downed trees and the town is still without power, but the generators are doing their jobs. I went by your home and, other than some broken branches, the house seems to have fared well."

"Do you think we can get back on the water Monday?"

"Monday may be pushing it, but Tuesday should be a go."

"That will give us time to restock supplies."

"Great. Several of us are going out to Charlie's later today. He lost quite a few trees so we're going to help him clear his drive. He won't need firewood for a few years." Harvey chuckled.

"No damage to his home, though, right?"

"One broken window and some missing shingles, but nothing we can't handle."

"Do you need help?"

"Thanks, Captain, but we've got this. Get some rest and we'll be ready to go Tuesday morning. I'll let the crew know."

"Thanks, Harvey."

She turned to Lindsey. "So, it looks like you're stuck with me for another day."

Lindsey grinned. "Time for that long hot bath in your tub."

"That's an excellent idea."

"Uh oh, we have a casualty." Lindsey frowned, nodding toward the jetties where a small sailboat had crashed into the rocks, causing significant hull damage.

"That didn't have to happen. That boat is small enough to have been put in dry dock somewhere."

"I'd be sick if that had been mine." Lindsey shook her head.

"You'd have known better."

"Yeah, I would have. Still, such as waste."

Lindsey saw the relief written on Kendra's face when she pulled into the boat's slip and looked up the street to see her house. As Harvey had reported, there were limbs down from nearby trees, but no other signs of damage.

Kendra eased the boat into the slip while Lindsey tossed the mooring lines onto the dock. She stepped off the deck, securing the lines as Kendra closed up the wheelhouse. She looked up to see Kendra walking across the deck, wearing a beautiful smile, and her heart melted. *God I love it when she looks at me like that.* She held out her hand to Kendra as she stepped off the boat. Her heart soared when Kendra failed to let her hand go.

Lindsey looked up to see two women approaching the pier. She smiled when she recognized Susan with her arm secured in a cast and sling.

"Well look at you," Lindsey smiled. "How are you?"

"Alive and kicking, thanks to you. Lindsey, this is my girlfriend, Kelly."

"Susan has told me how much you two did for her, and I can't tell you what that means to both of us," Kelly said.

"I'm just glad we were there to help out." Lindsey smiled at the two women.

"Well, hey there, stranger," Kendra said. "You're looking good."

"Thanks, I'm feeling better too." Susan took the two bags Kelly was holding and handed one to each of them. "I'm returning your clothes freshly laundered," she told Lindsey.

"You didn't have to do that."

Kendra opened her bag and began laughing. She pulled out a handful of wooden spoons.

Susan returned her grin. "The doc in the ER said the use of the spoons was nothing short of genius, but I'm afraid he didn't save them, so we bought you new ones. Hopefully, you won't need them for future splints."

"Thank you." Kendra stepped forward to hug her. "Are you two staying in the area?"

"No, we just wanted to take a chance and stop to thank you both. We're heading home. I do hope you'll keep a future visit in mind, though."

"We definitely will," Kendra promised.

"Thank you again for everything. I know you're eager to check on your home so we won't keep you. It's time for some medicine and a nap while Kelly drives us home."

"Be safe, and call us to let us know how you're doing," Lindsey said as they walked Susan and Kelly back to the car.

"Will do." Susan exchanged hugs with them before getting in the car.

Kendra turned to Lindsey. "Let's go home."

They walked up the hill and Kendra let out a deep breath. "That's a relief. I was afraid it would be worse."

"Do you have a chainsaw?"

"Yeah, we've got one in the garage."

"I can use it to cut the limbs into manageable sections while you check the inside of the house. You can call your dad to report in."

"Ummm, sexy, and you can use power tools, too?" Kendra teased.

"Oh yes, ma'am, I'm a woman of many hidden talents." Lindsay wiggled her eyebrows for effect.

Kendra laughed. "I'm going to love discovering those," she said with a smirk.

Relieved that there were only a few limbs that they would need to cut into sections, Kendra kissed Lindsey. "Be careful, I'll be out to help as soon as I've inspected everything and called Dad."

"Take your time. I can handle this."

"I know, but maybe you're not the only one who loves power tools."

"I'll save you one," Lindsey said with a chuckle.

Kendra entered the house, heard the gentle humming of the generator, and knew the power was still out. She began checking to make sure the refrigerator was still receiving power, and then moved through the house, checking for signs of any leaks and finding none. Upstairs, she began opening the shutters. She smiled when she saw Lindsey walk out of the garage wearing safety glasses and gloves, carrying the chainsaw. There was nothing about her that Kendra didn't love.

She dialed her dad as the roar of the chainsaw filled the air. She walked away from the window and farther into the house.

"Hey, honey," her dad answered. "Is that a chainsaw?"

"Yes, Dad, we had a few limbs down, so Lindsey's going to cut them into sections. We'll carry them to the woodpile and the brush to the curb."

"No other damage though?"

"Not even a lost shingle that I can see. I'm inside the house and everything looks good. So relax, things are fine here. How are you doing?"

"I'm good and Henry is settling into therapy well, so I'm flying home tomorrow. Can you pick me up at three?"

"No problem. Mobile or Pensacola?"

"Mobile. The airport in Pensacola is still closed. They must have had some serious damage there."

"It'll be good to have you home. I'll be there to pick you up at three."

"I can't wait. It's great to visit, and I'm glad Henry is making progress, but there's no place like home."

"I know exactly how you feel. See you soon. Love you."

"Love you too, sweetie. Tell Lindsey hello for me."

"Will do, Dad,"

Kevin ended the call wearing a huge smile. It had been a long time since he had heard the happiness in his daughter's voice that he had just heard. He knew something had happened to trigger the change, and he couldn't wait to get home to find out what it was. He prayed that the spark he had witnessed between Kendra and Lindsey had finally ignited and they realized they had fallen in love.

†

Lindsey was like a kid with a new toy. She cut the oak branches into two-foot sections after trimming the smaller branches. She had cut through all but one of the downed branches when she saw Kendra coming over to her. She flipped the switch to kill the engine on the chainsaw.

"See, I saved you one as promised." Lindsey motioned to the largest branch.

"So I see. You looked like you were having fun."

"What's not to like about a chainsaw?"

"Go ahead and finish cutting. I'll grab some gloves and the wheelbarrow, and start taking the sections around back."

"Are you sure?"

"Absolutely."

"Deal." Lindsey pulled the cord to restart the saw.

Kendra smiled and turned toward the garage.

When they finished stacking the cut wood, they had a sizeable pile. "This will make some nice fires in the outdoor fireplace this winter," Kendra said.

"I can't wait."

Kendra squealed with excitement. "Does that mean you're staying?"

"I've received an offer too good to pass up, and found me a woman I'm head over heels for, so yes, if you still want me, I'm yours."

Kendra grabbed her in a bear hug and kissed her passionately.

"You make me a happy woman."

"I'm kinda pleased myself, ma'am."

"Are you up for a ride downtown? I'd like to stop and place an order with Hank, if he's open, and maybe we can find some lunch. I'm starved."

"I could eat, too."

†

"Hey, ladies, I'm glad to see you weathered the storm well." Hank was happy to see them enter the store.

"We rode it out up in the bay. Did you have any damage?" Kendra asked.

"A few broken windows at home and some water damage here, but nothing serious."

"That's good to hear. Are you up for some business?"

"I'd love something to keep me busy for the rest of the day. It's been quiet. I did have some folks come in earlier for some plywood and a few bundles of roof shingles."

"The town seemed to fare well," Kendra said.

"Not bad, but the road east is washed out."

"What about west? I've got to pick Dad up in Mobile tomorrow?"

"May be a bit rough, but you should make it. Some spots are down to one lane."

"Anything open for food?"

198

"The burger joint's running on generator power, but still slinging burgers and fries."

Kendra looked at Lindsey, who shrugged. "Sounds good to me."

"Can we bring you anything, Hank?"

"Thanks, but the wife packed me some sandwiches."

Kendra passed over her list. "Can we get a delivery in the morning?"

He studied the list. "Will ten o'clock be soon enough?"

"That will be perfect. Thanks, Hank, just send me a bill."

"I will, Kendra. Thanks for the business."

"Always a pleasure, Hank."

"Oh, and thanks for the shrimp. They were awesome."

"Ready for another batch?" she asked.

"Anytime you have a few extras, I'll gladly take them off your hands."

"I'll see you next weekend then." Kendra grinned and left the store with Lindsey.

Kendra looked at Lindsey. "What do you think about grabbing a few bags of burgers and fries, and riding out to Charlie's place to check on the boys? I'd also like to deliver these." She handed Lindsey a check. "I was able to revise the totals from this week's haul and I'm sure everyone could use the extra money to help with storm repairs."

"Fine with me." Lindsey grinned.

"What's the grin for?"

"Because you're such a considerate boss," she answered.

"I have the best crew a captain could ask for and I plan to keep it that way," Kendra answered honestly as they climbed into the Jeep.

†

The crew was nearly finished when they reached Charlie's, and Lindsey had the opportunity to sit back and watch how Kendra interacted with them. It was obvious they loved and respected her as she passed out the burgers and fries. She also handed each one

199

of them a check to make up the difference in their pay. To the last man, they hugged her, some even kissing her on the cheek to show their affection for her.

Harvey walked over to Lindsey.

"Hey, Harvey, how you doing?"

"I'm doing great thanks, and you? What happened with her cheek?"

"She had a run in with a flying buckle during the storm. Scared the hell out of me, but otherwise, I couldn't be better." She smiled as she watched Kendra with her crew.

Harvey took a bite of his burger. "You two finally figured it out?"

Lindsey looked at him. "Figured what out? What are you talking about, Harvey?"

"What the rest of us have known for a few weeks now." He chuckled.

"Known what?"

"That the two of you were meant to be together. I've never seen Kendra so happy. There's a connection between the two of you. It's like a magnet, pulling you two together."

She looked at him and smiled.

"Even now, you can't keep your eyes off her."

Lindsey blushed. "Are you okay with us being together?"

"We were all just wondering how long it was gonna take y'all to figure it out," he teased. "Me and the boys are happy for both of you."

Tears filled her eyes as he hugged her. "Thanks, Harvey."

Kendra looked over to see Lindsey hugging Harvey. "I wonder what that's all about."

"Harvey's probably giving her the talk," Charlie answered.

Kendra whipped her head around to look at him. "What are you talking about?"

"You know, the talk," he said making quotation marks in the air with his fingers. "The one where he warns her about breaking your heart, and finding herself fish bait if she does."

"What…" she stammered.

"Someone has to tell you two, it's okay with us if you're in love."

"Is it that obvious?"

"Apparently to everyone except for the two of y'all. We've known for weeks now."

She shook her head and chuckled. "Thanks, Charlie. The acceptance of the crew means a lot to us."

"Well, both of you mean a lot to us. Personally, I've never worked for someone who treated me like family the way you do," he said, choking back emotions.

"You are my family, Charlie, always have been, always will be."

"We want y'all to feel comfortable around us and just be who you are."

It was Kendra's turn to wipe tears back. She winced when she wiped her right cheek.

"By the way, what happened to your face? Did Lindsey have to smack you to finally get you to notice her?"

"What?"

"That's one heck of a shiner you're sporting."

"No, smart ass, a buckle came free during the storm and sliced open my cheek."

"Uh huh, likely story," he teased.

Kendra shook her head, but chuckled.

"Are we heading back out in the morning?"

"Nope, we're going to wait until Tuesday. We thought everyone might need another day at home. I've got supplies being delivered tomorrow, so we'll be ready to head out early the next day."

"We'll be there, Captain. Do you need help tomorrow?"

"Thanks, but no. It'll give me something to do before I go collect Dad at the airport."

"If you change your mind, just give me a call."

"I will, Charlie, thanks."

She caught Lindsey's eyes and smiled. "I think it's time for us to head back into town."

Charlie chuckled. "I reckon so."

✝

"I think it's time for our bath," Kendra announced when they pulled into the drive.

Lindsey smiled at her. "That sounds good to me."

They climbed the stairs and Kendra started the water in her tub. "Do you mind some bubbles?"

"Not at all," Lindsey called from her bedroom.

Kendra chuckled. "Did you get the same third degree from Harvey that I did from Charlie, about us taking so long to realize we were in love?"

"Yeah. Harvey said they were beginning to wonder what they needed to do to bring it to our attention. You know, I think it's so cool that the guys are so accepting of our relationship. I'm not so sure that would happen on Dad's boat."

"We have the best crew ever," Kendra reminded her.

"That we do."

Kendra stepped into the tub and looked at Lindsey. "Do you want front or back?"

"I'll take the front." Lindsey climbed into the tub and settled into the warm water and laid her head back on Kendra's shoulder. "This was a great idea. The water is heavenly."

"I can't imagine heaven would be any better than this."

"I'll take this spot just south of heaven any day then," Lindsey purred as Kendra's arms wrapped around her body.

Kendra chuckled. "Just south of heaven. That sounds like a good name for a boat."

"Always thinking like a captain." Lindsey turned her head to look up at Kendra.

"Not always." Kendra smiled, and leaned down to kiss her softly.

✝

202

The fire that ignited from their kisses spilled over to the bedroom. They took advantage of the luxury of time to explore one another's bodies as they made love into the night.

Lindsey rested her chin atop her hands spread across Kendra's chest. "Will it always be this special between us?"

"I think we can only grow closer. We have a great start to build on." Kendra smiled. "For the first time in a long time, I regret making a decision to jump right back into the routine of work." She locked eyes with Lindsey. "I would love a few weeks alone with you."

Lindsey felt a tear slide down her cheek. "We will have our time, but for now we've got a season to finish. It's important for the entire crew and our futures to do well on our first season."

Kendra wiped away the tear with her thumb. "I promise at the end of red season we will have that time together."

"I'm gonna hold you to that, Captain."

"I'm thinking some time spent in the mountains out west could be fun."

"That sounds wonderful to me. I've never taken a true vacation."

"We'll have to make that happen." Kendra pulled Lindsey into her arms.

Chapter Sixteen

The morning dawned beautifully. Kendra woke to find Lindsey watching her closely. "Have you been awake long?"

"No, not really, just a few minutes. I love waking up next to you."

Kendra took Lindsey in her arms. "Do you think you could handle this for the next fifty years or so?"

Lindsey snuggled into her warmth. "Ask me again in ten years."

Kendra grinned. "I can't imagine waking up to anyone else now." Her fingers played in Lindsey's short hair. In the quiet, she could hear their breathing, each breath in unison as they lay together. She smiled to herself thinking how perfectly matched they had turned out to be. Everything seemed to be falling into place, and man, did she feel good about life.

Lindsey could feel the beating of Kendra's heart as her head rested on her chest. Lindsey's hand reached to cover a breast and she felt Kendra's heart begin to race. She tossed a leg over Kendra's and propped her head on her hand as she looked into Kendra's sparkling green eyes.

"I get so lost looking into your eyes."

"You're right here with me, baby." Kendra's fingertips traced down Lindsey's strong jaw, "Right where you're meant to be."

Lindsey let her hand drift slowly down Kendra's body until she reached her center. Wetness coated her curls, betraying Kendra's excitement as she moaned softly in anticipation. Lindsey's fingertips gently parted the velvety folds, drawing the wetness upward as her thumb circled Kendra's swollen clit. She planted a tender kiss on Kendra's lips, which deepened into a fevered kiss as Kendra's lips parted, inviting her inside. Lindsey's other hand gently cupped a breast as her mouth left a molten trail of kisses down Kendra's neck until her tongue lavished the hardened nipple. Lindsey's fingers glided easily through her wetness. Kendra's muscles welcomed her fingers, closing tightly around them as they worked deeper inside.

Kendra's hips moved in rhythm with Lindsey's fingers as her arousal soared. The heat of Lindsey's breath on her skin left her body feverish with desire. She could feel a swarm of butterflies taking flight deep in her stomach as her muscles began to quiver with the approach of her climax. Her hand roamed across Lindsey's back and down her hip to rest over her heated mound.

Lindsey moaned deeply as fingers penetrated her, matching the rhythm of their lovemaking. Lindsey felt her arousal cresting and lifted her mouth from Kendra's breast. "Come with me, Kendra," she groaned.

"I'm right there with you, baby," Kendra answered and with a final thrust she cried out in pleasure. "Oh God, yes, Lindsey."

The sound of Kendra's desire was all Lindsey needed to topple over the edge of desire and she filled her hand with warm juices as she released.

"Damn, that felt good," she purred as she locked eyes with Kendra.

Lindsey kissed her sweetly and propped her head on her hand as she smiled down at Kendra. "I know it's impossible, but I'd love to start every morning like this."

"We'll make as many of them happen as we can," Kendra promised. She ran her fingers through Lindsey's hair. The alarm rang, shattering their tender moment. Kendra chuckled and reached over to smack it.

"Duty calls," she growled, then pulled Lindsey down for another kiss. "Will you shower with me?"

"I'd love to. Will we have time for lunch before you leave to pick up your dad?"

"I think so, but I have a different idea. Let's shower and walk down to the boat. You can make us some of your monster omelets while I work on deck."

"That does sound good to me."

Kendra noticed the stillness of the house when they came downstairs. The generator, which had softly hummed as it powered the house, was silent. Realizing that the power had returned, she reached over and flipped the light switch. "Let there be light." She grinned.

"Does that mean the power has been restored to the rest of town?"

"Probably so," Kendra answered. "We bounce back pretty quickly in these parts."

"Good to know. Come on, I'm starving."

"I'm right behind you." Kendra slipped her cell phone in its holster and followed Lindsey out the door.

†

"Can we share a peaceful cup of coffee before we get busy?" Lindsey asked.

"I think we've got time for that." Kendra slipped into a chair in the galley.

Lindsey brought them cups and sat across from Kendra. "You're sure wearing a beautiful smile today."

Kendra reached across the table and held her hand. "That's because you make me a very happy woman."

"I second that. My heart has never felt this full before." Lindsey took a sip of her coffee. "Do you plan to tell your dad about us today?"

"He already knows something is happening between us, so it may be more confirmation for him. He really likes you, too."

Lindsey sighed. "I wish my dad was as willing to accept my sexuality."

Kendra squeezed her hand. "Hopefully he'll come around eventually. I wouldn't be surprised if Dad talks to him at some point, to break the ice a bit."

"You're blessed to have him as a father."

"Yeah, I am. He's been my best friend for most of my life."

✝

Kendra began removing the gear from storage while Lindsey cooked breakfast. They would have just enough time to eat before the supplies arrived. When Lindsey called her inside to eat, her stomach answered the call with a loud growl in anticipation of the meal.

"Would you like juice or more coffee, Kendra?"

"Both actually."

"That sounds good to me, too." Lindsey brought the coffee pot over to refill their cups and then poured glasses of juice.

"I think I'll start doubling the egg order. These omelets are fantastic," Kendra said.

"It's a good way to use leftovers when we have them."

"With Charlie around, we don't have to worry about them often."

"Did I hear my name being called?" Charlie stuck his head inside the galley.

"Hey, Charlie. We were just talking about leftovers or the lack thereof," Lindsey teased.

"Mama always told me to clean my plate." He grinned sheepishly.

"You learned that lesson well. What are you doing here today?" Kendra asked.

207

He shuffled his feet. "I've got a case of cabin fever, so I thought I'd come down and see if you needed any help."

"We have supplies coming soon, and I want to get the rest of the equipment back in place," Kendra told him.

"Would you mind some help?"

"I'd love to have your help. Did you have breakfast?"

"Yes, ma'am, but those omelets sure look good."

"Pour yourself a cup and you can split this one with me, and if you're still hungry, I'll cook us another," Lindsey offered.

"I don't want to take your breakfast, Lindsey."

"Just let me grab another plate."

Charlie poured a cup of coffee and joined them at the table. He watched as Lindsey cut more than half of her omelet and passed it to him. From the way he ravenously attacked the food, Kendra suspected that Charlie's wife wasn't much of a cook, or they didn't have much in the way of groceries. At least during the week she knew he would eat well.

"This is really good, Lindsey."

"Eat up and I'll fix another," she told him.

Lindsey cooked him an even larger omelet and four slices of toast.

Kendra was surprised to see that Charlie eyes had tears in them when Lindsey placed the plate in front of him. She nodded her head toward the door as she locked eyes with Lindsey, who nodded an answer to her wordless question.

"I'm going to check something in the wheelhouse. I'll see you on deck when you finish eating." Kendra stood.

"Yes, ma'am," Charlie answered between bites.

Lindsey returned to her seat at the table after Kendra left the galley. She looked at Charlie. "You can tell me to mind my own business, but is everything all right at home, Charlie?"

Charlie shocked her by breaking down in tears.

She rushed to place her arm around his shoulders. "I didn't mean to upset you, Charlie."

"It's not you, Lindsey. I'm sorry. Things have just been hectic at home."

"I'm sorry. Is there anything I can do to help?"

"It's my fault," he sniffled. "I should have paid closer attention to our finances, but I thought Lucy was paying the bills, until I came home early and found a pile of past due notices. It's taken everything I've made these last few weeks to catch up on the bills. I can barely feed my wife and son." He broke down in tears.

"Are you caught up yet?"

"I made the last payment Saturday, but it's left almost nothing for groceries. I feel guilty for eating this breakfast, but I haven't eaten much since we got home."

Lindsey reached into her pocket and pulled out her wallet, removing four one-hundred-dollar bills, and placing them on the table beside him. "I want you to finish your meal then go buy some groceries for your family. Kendra and I can handle what needs to be done here."

"I promise I will pay you back," he replied, choking back his tears.

"A little bit at a time, but make sure you cover your bills and groceries first," she instructed him.

"I'm embarrassed to take this from you."

"You are family to me, Charlie. All you need to do is ask if you need help. We've all had our ups and downs. It's okay to ask for help," she said in a comforting tone.

"I didn't come down here to beg, but I could kiss you."

"Whoa, Charlie, no need for that." Lindsey patted his hand. "This will stay between us. There's no need for anyone else to know."

He looked at her curiously. "What about the captain?"

"We've got this covered between you and me, so there's no need to bring her into this unless you think it's necessary."

"Thanks, Lindsey. I hate taking money from you, but I'm at my wits' end."

"Just make sure you stay on top of things moving forward. We're going to make enough money this summer to allow you to put some back in savings."

"If it weren't for the checks we've gotten from the reds, I'd probably be losing my house."

"We won't allow that to happen, I promise."

He gobbled down the last bite and took to his feet. "Thank you so much."

"You're welcome. Now go get that shopping done. I'll see you in the morning."

"See you, Lindsey."

She watched him wave to Kendra as he rushed across the deck. Then she took the dishes to the sink to wash them.

†

Kendra looked up from her task to see Charlie exiting the galley. He smiled and waved at her before rushing off the boat. She returned his wave and finished the task she was working on. When Lindsey didn't follow him from the galley, she went in search of her.

Lindsey was standing at the sink, washing the dishes from breakfast when she entered the galley. "Charlie left out of here like he was on fire." Kendra walked over next to her.

"He had something come up that he needed to take care of, so I told him we could handle re-stocking the boat."

"There's more to it than that, but you aren't going to tell me, are you?"

"We handled a situation, so there's no need to bring you into it and cause him embarrassment."

Kendra wrapped her arms around Lindsey's waist, hugging her from behind. "Thank you," she whispered in her ear.

"You'd do the same thing, but you're welcome. We're family and have to take care of one another."

"Yes, we are, and yes, we do."

Kendra heard the squeal of brakes and looked out the window to see the delivery truck arriving.

"I guess it's time for us to get to work." Lindsey placed the dishtowel on the counter before turning in Kendra's arms for a quick kiss.

Kendra smiled. "I'm blessed that you've come into my life."

"We are both well blessed by fate," Lindsey stated. "Would you mind if I cook some dinner while you're gone after your dad? I'm sure he'll be starved by the time you get home."

"That would be great. Thanks."

†

When they returned to the house, Kendra said, "I think I'm going to take a quick shower before I leave for the airport."

"Is it okay if I take your Jeep to the store before you go?"

"Go ahead. Do you need some money?"

"No, ma'am, I've got this."

"I'll see you in a few then."

Lindsey watched Kendra climb the stairs before picking up the keys and heading for the garage. Lindsey hated missing an opportunity to shower with Kendra, but it was so much easier to carry groceries in the Jeep than on her bike. She wanted to cook a hearty meal to welcome Kevin home, and knew exactly what she needed. The shopping went quickly. She returned home, placed the groceries in the refrigerator, and just as she was finishing, Kendra was walking into the kitchen.

"Are you all set?"

"Yes, ma'am. I'll have a hot meal waiting on y'all when you return."

"Are you going to tell me what to expect?"

"No, ma'am, it will be a surprise. You'll be home around four thirty, right?"

"If he arrives on time, yes. I'll call you if there's any delay."

Lindsey took her in her arms and kissed her softly. "Be safe, but hurry home to me."

"I'll be back as quick as possible." Kendra plucked the keys from the table and went out the back door.

Lindsey watched her go before brewing a fresh pot of tea and placing it into the refrigerator to chill. She prepared the supplies she needed for the meal and set the table. With plenty of time before she needed to start cooking, she decided to call home and talk with her dad.

She debated about telling her dad about her decision to stay in Florida, and the reason for her decision, but she couldn't get the words out of her mouth. Instead, they chatted about the storm and made small talk about the season's catch. When he asked how she was doing, she couldn't help but smile as she thought about Kendra and their growing relationship. Then her dad dropped a bomb on her.

"Kevin asked me to come down next weekend. I'm going to let your brother take over and come for a visit."

"That sounds great, Dad. Could I ask you to bring more of my clothes with you?"

"Sure. I'll pack up what I can and bring it with me."

"Thanks, Dad. I especially need some jeans and work shirts."

"Not a problem. Just let me know if there's anything else."

"I will, Dad. Thanks, and drive safely."

Wow, I wonder what Kevin and Dad are cooking up? She doubted Kendra had any idea her dad was coming to visit either. She drained her glass of tea and returned to the kitchen to begin the meal.

✝

Heeding Harvey's warning about the highway damages from the storm, Kendra decided to head north to pick up the Interstate. She left with plenty time to reach the airport even if it took extra time to get through the tunnel in Mobile. The bright sun beat down on the pavement and she dropped her shades to cover her eyes. The wind blew through her hair as she picked up speed on the nearly vacant highway. *I'll be lucky if traffic stays this light.*

She arrived at the airport early, pulled the Jeep into the parking lot, and walked inside the small terminal. She saw Kevin's flight would arrive on time. *A miracle.* She grinned and went in search of something to drink.

She watched as air traffic arrived and departed. When they announced Kevin's flight had arrived, she walked to the baggage claim to wait on him.

Her dad's face lit up when he saw her and wrapped her in an embrace. "Hey, honey. What happened to your cheek?"

"A little accident during the storm, but it's healing well."

"Henry sends his love. He's doing great at home and his doctors are amazed by his recovery."

"It's those strong Drake genes."

"That must be it." He grinned and reached for his bag.

"You want me to get that?"

"Nope, I'm still capable of handling a bag."

Kendra threw up her hands. "Handle away."

They walked into the bright sunshine. "Hello, humidity."

"I imagine it was very different in Arizona."

"It was hot, but it was a dry heat." He chuckled at using the worn old cliché.

They walked to the Jeep and Kendra placed his bag in the back.

"Where's Lindsey?"

"She's at home, cooking a special meal just for you."

He rubbed his hands in anticipation. "What's she cooking?"

"I have no clue. She didn't say, but you can guarantee it will be good."

He nodded as he buckled his seat belt. "Yep, she's a good cook."

"That she is." Kendra backed the Jeep from the parking spot. "Home, here we come."

"It's great to be home. How are you two doing?"

"Things are going great, Dad." She smiled.

"Perfect." He leaned back in his seat for the ride home.

†

Lindsey was pulling out a pan of biscuits as she heard the Jeep turn into the driveway. "That's pretty good timing." She grinned as she turned back to stir the gravy. A bowl of rice and a platter of pork chops were waiting on the counter.

She watched out the window as Kendra grabbed her dad's bag from the back of the Jeep and they headed for the back door.

"Something smells delicious," Kevin said as he stepped inside the door.

"Welcome home. I thought you might be hungry."

"You figured right. My in-flight peanuts are long gone."

"Let me drop Dad's bag in his room and I'll be back to help." Kendra stopped to kiss Lindsey before walking away.

Lindsey blushed and Kevin chuckled. "What can I do to help?"

"Um, you can pour some tea," she managed to say, as she walked past him with the gravy and rice.

Kendra returned to the kitchen and took the platter of pork chops to the table. "Is there anything else we need?"

"Nope, we're good."

"Thanks for cooking such a great meal." Kevin speared a pork chop and passed the platter to Lindsey. "I haven't had rice and gravy in ages."

"I think it makes a good combination with the pork chops," Lindsey replied.

Kendra moaned as she took a bite. "I'll have to agree with you on that."

They made small talk during the meal, and when they were all stuffed, Kevin pushed his chair back. "I probably should have talked to you both before now, but I've invited Lindsey's dad, Paul, down for the weekend."

"Dad told me earlier when I called to check in with him," Lindsey said.

Kendra looked at Lindsey and then at her dad. "I feel like I'm missing something here."

Lindsey smiled at her. "That makes two of us."

"Okay, Dad, spill it. What are you up to?"

"What? I can't invite an old friend down for a visit?" he protested.

"Of course you can, but that twinkle in your eyes tells me you have an ulterior motive for this particular visit."

"Well, for starters, I think it's time for Paul and I to have a Dad to Dad talk about our daughters' happiness and their choice of life partners. Even an old dog like me can see how much you love one another."

"Well, I'll admit that would be an easier conversation to have in person," Kendra agreed. She looked at Lindsey. "Are you okay with this?"

"It's a conversation we'll have to have eventually. I also need to tell him I'm not coming home at the end of summer, so yeah, I'm good with it. Nervous about it, but I'll deal with my nerves."

Kevin beamed. "I'm hoping that once he sees the two of you together, it won't matter to him about your sexuality. All I want is for the two of you to be happy, and you seem to do that for one another pretty well."

Kendra reached over and covered Lindsey's hand. "We do, Dad. Thanks for your support."

Lindsey looked at her with tears welling in her eyes. "I just want both of you to be prepared. Dad won't take the news well."

"That's where I hope my experience will come in handy." Kevin grinned.

"He may be glad I've decided to stay here when he realizes my sexual orientation isn't just a phase I'm going through."

"Don't judge him too harshly yet. He may be upset, but you're still his daughter and firstborn," Kevin soothed.

Kendra was silent for a few minutes. "With our late start this week, we probably won't be in until late Friday."

"That will give us a chance to catch up on life and maybe break some ice on the relationship issue."

"I trust that you know what you're doing."

Kevin grinned at them. "Let's clean the kitchen, then have a couple cold ones out on the back porch."

They chatted about their experience of riding out the storm. "It sounds like you did everything just the way I taught you."

"I did, Dad. There were a few tense moments clearing the narrows in the channel, but after that, I thought all went well."

He looked at Lindsey. "That was really your first experience riding out a storm?"

"Yes. Dad usually sends me in to care for the house."

"I'm actually pleased we had this storm," Kevin said. "It seems to have brought the two of you together."

"It has," Kendra agreed. "I think the time alone together was what we needed."

"Now she's stuck with me, at least until next year's red season," Lindsey replied. "Then you'll have to deal with me moping around the house until she comes back in."

"It just so happens I've been thinking about that. With the second boat, we can run both until red season starts," Kevin said.

"Yeah, we should do well on the local runs with two boats," Kendra agreed.

"I've got an idea I'd like to run by you. I'll have been retired for a year by then, and I can only play so much golf. What would you think of me using the boat for fishing tours during the red season?"

Kendra looked at him and then Lindsey. "Wow, Dad, that's a great idea."

"I've spent all my life on the water, and I think it'd be fun taking folks out to some of the local fishing spots. It won't take much to equip the boat, and it'll give me something productive to do for at least a few months each year."

"We'll need to hire you a crew," Kendra stated.

"Hank has a couple of teenage boys who would be perfect."

"You really have thought this out?" Kendra asked.

"I had a lot of thinking time while I was in Arizona."

Kendra looked at Lindsey who wore a huge smile. Lindsey nodded. "I like it. I could go out with you for red season, so we'd be together."

"Start doing your homework on the license, equipment, and marketing then, Dad."

†

They retired early to be fresh for the morning ahead of them. Lindsey was snuggled in Kendra's arms.

"Everything seems to be happening so fast. Are you okay with everything Dad has planned for us?"

"Ask me again when my head stops spinning," Lindsey replied.

"I'm serious. If we're moving too fast, just say so."

"It's just a lot to take in at once. I agree with his thinking completely, but there is one thing I'm very pleased about."

"What's that?"

"That I get to spend every night with you and wake up next to you every morning."

Kendra chuckled. "I love you."

"I love you too, Captain Drake."

Chapter Seventeen

The week passed quickly. Kendra had worried the storm may have sent the reds to deeper water, but when they reached their grid, the nets filled with every run. They started for home early Friday morning fully loaded and it took all day to get there.

With the deck cleaned and the equipment stored, the crew decided to play some cards on the ride into the harbor. Lindsey played with them for a while before going to the wheelhouse to visit with Kendra.

"You're stressing over your dad's visit aren't you?"

"Yeah, I guess I am, even though I'm trying to be calm."

"You didn't rest well last night. You were tossing and turning in your sleep."

"I'm sorry if I kept you awake."

"You didn't. I just wrapped my arms around you and we slept like that for a while."

"Is there anything I can do? I'm a bit stir crazy."

"Why don't you take over here? I'll go ahead and run the calculations to write out the week's paychecks."

"That sounds good to me."

They swapped seats and Kendra began running the numbers for the week's catch. Lindsey focused her attention on the water ahead, leaving her worries behind, at least for a short time.

"This has been another good week," Kendra announced as she tore out the first check and handed it to Lindsey.

"Wow, you aren't kidding," Lindsey replied when her eyes landed on the check. "Thanks. I guess I need to ask your dad to set up a bank account for me so I can start depositing some of these."

"I'm sure he would do that for you. You'll probably have to sign some papers, but he can get it set up for you." Kendra continued writing out checks. "If you're okay here, I'll go pay the guys and make some lunch. Do you have any special requests?"

"Yes, make us a batch of brownies. There's ice cream in the freezer."

"That does sound good. I'll be back soon." Kendra kissed her and left the wheelhouse.

†

After passing out paychecks to the appreciative crew, Kendra began mixing a batch of brownies while Harvey and Charlie made sandwiches.

"It's such a beautiful morning, why don't we eat on deck?" Harvey suggested.

"I won't argue with that." Charlie turned to the two other crewmembers. "Tim and Bobby, will you set up a table and chairs for us on deck?"

"Sure thing," Tim answered.

†

Lindsey watched as the guys set up a table and chairs. Tim turned to smile at her and she smiled and waved back.

When the sandwiches were ready, the crew carried them out to the table. Charlie and Tim brought out drinks for everyone. Kendra walked into the wheelhouse. "Let's set the auto pilot so you can join us for lunch."

"Are you sure? I don't mind eating in here."

Kendra chuckled. "Have you seen anything other than water in front of you lately?"

"Only a few sea birds."

"I think we can trust the auto pilot to keep us on course long enough for us to eat."

"You're the boss." Lindsey followed her to the deck.

"Is there anything else I can do while we're heading in? I'm tired of cards," Harvey asked.

"Tired of losing you mean," Charlie countered.

"Yeah, that too." Harvey smiled.

"Why don't you and the boys come up with a new menu for next week and make me a shopping list?" Kendra suggested.

"We can do that, and I'll drop it off to Hank for you on my way home tonight," Harvey said.

"We need to give thought to some other activities for you guys for the travel time. I agree there's only so much poker a person can handle."

"I'll pick up some new movies when I go out this weekend," Tim volunteered.

"If we add more baking supplies, I can make cookies or cakes for our desserts," Charlie added.

"It's a good thing we burn a lot of calories," Lindsey said.

"I've got a ton of paperbacks I can bring in, if anyone else likes to read," Bobby offered.

"Starting a small library would be a great idea," Kendra agreed. "I'll buy a few tablets too, so we can download eBooks as well."

"You'll probably have to teach us how to use that," Charlie said.

"That won't take but just a few minutes," Lindsey promised.

"Sounds like we've got a plan. If anyone comes up with anything else, just let me know." Kendra turned to Lindsey. "I'll take over the wheelhouse if you want to catch a nap. I have a feeling our dads will keep us up talking tonight."

"That's probably not a bad idea. I'll help get cleaned up from lunch and then go crash for a bit."

"Go ahead, Lindsey, we can handle this," Charlie said with a warm smile.

"Captain, will you let us know when we're close enough to home to start getting the shrimp ready to offload?" Harvey asked.

"Not a problem," Kendra answered before returning to the wheelhouse.

Lindsey followed her and stopped for a quick kiss. "Don't let me sleep the afternoon away."

"I'll wake you in a couple of hours if for nothing else than to get another kiss."

"You can have all of those you want." Lindsey grinned and kissed her again.

✝

Kevin heard the approach of the boat and turned to Paul. "That will be our girls returning to port. Would you like to walk down to greet them?"

"That would be great."

They walked to the pier just as the crew was tying off the mooring lines. They stood back and watched the crew while they unloaded the shrimp.

"Damn, that's a lot of shrimp," Paul remarked as bin after bin was loaded onto the delivery truck.

"They've had great luck on the reds so far this season," Kevin replied proudly. "Even with this week being a short week for them, it looks like they've managed their quota again."

No one apparently noticed that they were there, so Paul watched as Lindsey worked with the rest of the crew. He saw the smile on her face and she appeared happy to be working with the men. When the wheelhouse opened and a taller woman walked out to join them, he saw firsthand the change in his daughter's expression. Her smile changed to a look of complete adoration as she watched the captain approach. *Kevin is right. They really do love one another. I've never seen that look of contentment on Lindsey's face.* "That must be Kendra."

"Yes, it is, and I couldn't be more proud of anyone. She's grown into a remarkable captain."

"I'm sure you taught her well."

"Yes, but there's some things you cannot teach. She's got such a great relationship with the crew that they'd run through walls for her if needed."

✝

Lindsey looked up to see her dad and Kendra's father standing at the end of the pier. Both men were smiling. *Hopefully that's a good sign.* She motioned with her head to Kendra, who turned to see them as well.

"Go ahead. I'll finish up here and join you in a minute," Kendra said.

Lindsey stepped onto the dock and strode confidently down the pier toward her dad. Her insides were quivering like Jell-O, but she smiled and hugged her dad when she reached them.

"Hey, Dad," she said and kissed him on the cheek before releasing him. "It's good to see you."

"You're looking really well. You seem to be enjoying yourself here, too."

"I am, very much."

"It looks like you had another good run," Kevin said.

"We did. Kendra got us on the shrimp right away, and our nets were stuffed with shrimp on every run."

"She's got good instincts."

"Yes, sir, she does. How long have you been here, Dad?"

"Since about midmorning yesterday. Kevin and I've been doing a lot of catching up while we waited on y'all to arrive."

Lindsey watched and saw his eyes fix on Kendra, who was signing the receipt for the driver.

"I hope you have something good planned for dinner. I'm starved," Lindsey said.

"I've got steaks ready to grill, a salad in the fridge, and potatoes baking in the oven," Kevin told her.

"You sure know how to welcome us home. I can taste that steak already." Lindsey grinned at Kevin.

"We can all relax and have a few beers while the steaks cook. Y'all must be tired from the hard week."

"A good cold beer sounds good right now."

"Why don't you and your dad head on up to the house and I'll wait on Kendra. We won't be too far behind you."

"Yes, sir." Lindsey took her dad's arm and walked with him down the pier.

"You look very happy here," Paul commented as they walked together.

"I am, Dad. The fishing has been great, and Captain Drake and Kendra have been wonderful to me."

He could see the sparkle in her clear blue eyes as they passed a street lamp. "Kevin and I had a long talk about the two of you this afternoon. I have to admit, while I don't understand the nature of your relationship, you're still my daughter and I just want to see you happy." He wrapped his arm around her shoulder. "Kendra appears to make you very happy."

"She's an incredible woman, Dad. I've never felt this way with anyone before."

"I just don't want to see you get your heart broken."

"Dad, I'd run that risk if I were with a man or a woman," she gently reminded him.

"I know, I know, but I'm still your dad, so it's my right to worry."

Lindsey chuckled. "Yes, it is, but I feel at home in her arms."

He stopped walking and turned to look at her. Even in the growing darkness, he knew she could see the tears shining in his eyes. "I said the same thing about your mother. I loved her with all my heart and miss her every day. All I could ask for is that you find someone who makes you feel that way."

"I have, Dad." Lindsey wrapped her arm around his waist as they continued to walk to the house.

†

Kendra looked up to find her dad watching Lindsey and Paul walk to the house. When he turned back to her, he was still smiling. She walked over to him and hugged him tightly. "I love you, Dad."

"I love you, too, and I'm glad you're home safe. It looks like you've had another great haul."

She chuckled. "The shrimp couldn't wait to jump into our nets."

"Let's hope that lasts for a long, long time."

"How do you think the visit is going to go?" She motioned to the couple walking toward the house. "Lindsey has really been stressing over his being here."

"Better than any of us could hope for. He doesn't understand the attraction between you two, but I think the more he sees the two of you together, he'll realize how much you're in love."

"You know what?"

"What's that?"

"I couldn't have asked for a better dad. You've never questioned my sexual orientation and you've always accepted the women in my life."

He chuckled and draped an arm around her shoulder as they turned to walk home. "That's true, but this one, I think, is a keeper."

"Me too, Dad. Me too." She placed an arm around his waist and they walked home.

†

Kevin grilled some link sausage for them to munch on while they drank a few beers.

Paul took the opportunity to watch Lindsey and Kendra interact, and the more he watched, the more comfortable he felt about their love for one another.

"If I eat another bite, I swear I'm going to explode," Kendra groaned and pushed back from her plate. "That was the perfect meal to come home to. Thanks."

"My pleasure and I'm glad you enjoyed it."

"You can cook for me anytime, old friend," Paul told him.

"I was thinking we could boil up a batch of crabs tomorrow."

"We've barely finished supper and you're already planning tomorrow night's meal. I love that about you, Dad."

"I've had a good week, too, and with some of those reds you've been bringing home, I'd say we could cook up a feast."

"I'll make some slaw and Lindsey can cook us some of her famous hush puppies," Kendra added.

In the silence that followed, Kevin's stomach growled loudly. They all broke out laughing.

"See, my stomach approves of the plan," he joked.

After another round of beer, Kendra stretched and tried to stifle a yawn. "I hope y'all don't mind, but it's been a long week. I'm going to shower and hit the sack."

"No problem, honey. I've got Paul set up in Lindsey's old room."

She chuckled at his comment. "I'll see you all in the morning."

"I was thinking French toast and bacon in the morning," Kevin announced as she stood.

"I can hardly wait," Kendra grinned and bent down to kiss his cheek. "Goodnight everyone."

Paul watched how Lindsey's eyes followed Kendra's every move and smiled. "Kevin and I were talking about a little friendly fishing competition tomorrow," he told Lindsey.

"Are you going to give us the opportunity to win our money back from last time?" Lindsey asked.

"Sure am, unless you want to sweeten the pot."

"Not the way you catch fish. You should have seen the size of that grouper, Dad. it was huge."

"So he wasn't telling me a fish tale?"

"No. Remind me to show you the picture tomorrow. That was the biggest grouper I've ever seen." She looked up at Kevin. "Would you mind if Charlie went with us? He's been a bit down, and I'm sure he'd appreciate any fish we could send home with him."

Kevin smiled. "That's fine with me. The more the merrier. I bet with five of us fishing we can send him home with plenty to eat."

"Good, I'll go call him. What time do you want to leave?"

"Nine should give us plenty of time to get ready."

"Okay, I'll be right back."

Kevin watched her leave and smiled. "You raised a good one with her."

"I think we both did right by our daughters. They're strong, independent women."

"That they are. Can you do one more round?"

"I do believe I can," Paul answered and handed him an empty bottle.

"Charlie was tickled to be invited and will meet us at nine," Lindsey told them when she returned.

"Good. Your dad and I are going to have another round before we call it a night. Do you want to join us?"

"Thanks, but I think I'm going to call it a night. I need to rest up if I'm going to out fish you tomorrow."

"Goodnight, baby girl," Paul told her. "I love you."

"Love you too, Dad. See y'all in the morning."

✝

Kendra stood wrapped in a towel and brushing her teeth when Lindsey entered the bathroom.

"Darn, I was hoping to catch you still in the shower."

"Sorry, baby, it sure felt good though."

"We need to rest up. We're going fishing tomorrow at nine. I hope you don't mind, but I invited Charlie. Our freezer's still full, so I was hoping we could fill his up with a nice catch tomorrow."

226

"That's very sweet of you. I appreciate your asking him. We'll have a great time."

"I think so too. I'll hit the shower and see you soon."

"I'll keep the bed warm."

Lindsey rushed through her shower, but when she entered the bedroom, Kendra was already asleep. She watched her beautiful lover sleep for several seconds, then turned off the lamp and crawled into bed.

Kendra stirred long enough to cuddle into Lindsey's body. "You smell good," she whispered, and then immediately started purring in her sleep.

Chapter Eighteen

Charlie was already on board when they arrived at the boat. "Good morning," he called out, looking up from the table where he was cutting bait. "I remembered we had a few bait fish in the wet well, so I thought I'd go ahead and cut it."

"Thanks, Charlie," Kendra replied and introduced him to Paul. "Do you want to take us out to your honey spot, Dad?" she asked, holding up the keys to the wheelhouse.

"Sure thing. You want to come with me?" he asked Paul.

"I'm right behind you, Captain Drake."

"Let's get a few chairs set out while Charlie finishes up the bait. We can load the bait buckets, and then set out rags and rods when he's done."

"I went ahead and put a case of beer in the freezer, too," Charlie grinned.

By the end of the afternoon, Charlie had two coolers of grouper filets to take home with him. He also had the pot of eighty bucks for catching the largest fish, and he tried to give it to Lindsey.

"No way, you won it fair and square."

"I know, but I owe you four hundred," he whispered.

"Which you can start repaying next week, but today that's yours to enjoy."

Kendra helped him carry the heavy coolers to the back of his truck. "Can I come help restock tomorrow?"

"Absolutely," she replied. "I'll see you in the morning."

✝

The rest of the weekend passed in a blur. On Monday, Kevin and Paul were sitting up drinking coffee when Kendra and Lindsey came down the stairs.

"Good morning," Kevin stated. "I know y'all won't eat, but will you have a cup of coffee with us before you go?"

"Sure, Dad," Kendra replied.

"When are you planning on leaving?" Lindsey asked Paul.

"Later this morning. If I don't make it all the way, I may lay over in Atlanta."

"Please be careful and let me know when you've made it home."

"You sound just like a mother," he said.

"Very funny," she replied, but grinned at him. "I'm glad you came for a visit."

"I am too, and I hope later in the fall, you all will come for a visit."

"I'd like that," Kevin and Kendra both answered at the same time.

"I guess that's settled then."

When Kendra and Lindsey stood to leave, they all hugged one another. Paul whispered in Kendra's ear and she smiled before saying, "Thanks, I will forever."

She turned back to her dad. "We'll see you Friday, love ya."

"Love y'all too. Be safe."

Kendra draped an arm across Lindsey's shoulder as they walked down to the boat. "That went better than expected," she commented.

"Yes, it was a great weekend. I have to know, though, what did Dad whisper to you."

229

Kendra stopped and turned to face her. "He told me welcome to the family, then told me to love and care for his little girl."

Lindsey smiled. "I didn't hear what you told him."

"I said thanks, I will forever."

"Forever," Lindsey echoed, smiling.

"Or as long as you'll have me."

"Forever may not be long enough."

Recipes by Ali

Several readers have asked me to begin including recipes of some of the foods I describe in my books, so this will be the first. My dad, Charlie, frequently had cookouts or fish fries for the customers he served. One of his most loved dishes was his hush puppies. You definitely couldn't eat just one. Here is a basic recipe that I hope you enjoy.

Charlie's Southern Boy Hush Puppies

1 bag hush puppy mix – Preferably Dixie Lily in the red bag
1 finely chopped sweet Vidalia onion
1 can drained whole kernel corn
1 can Ro-tele tomatoes
1 can Budweiser beer
1 tablespoon ketchup
A pinch of Cayenne pepper

Mix all ingredients together in a large mixing bowl. Add additional beer as needed to make a moist batter. Using a teaspoon, mound the batter on the spoon and carefully slide the batter from the spoon into a deep fryer with oil heated to 350 degrees. The batter will sink until it begins to cook. When done it will float to the top and be beautifully browned on all surfaces. Remove carefully and drain until cooled. Salt to taste while still warm. For a bit of spice, you could add diced jalapeno peppers.

Best served with seafood. Can be dipped in a variety of sauces or eaten plain. Highly addictive, so consider yourself forewarned!

Ali

About the Author

Author

Ali Spooner, a native of Florida, calls Pensacola her forever home. Ali has been writing for many years as a hobby, and with the assistance of the Affinity team, she has taken her love of storytelling to a new level.

Ali's characters range from cowgirls and psychics to a healthy dose of supernatural beings. She has written stand-alone titles as well as series. Ali is an avid reader and her other hobbies include photography, outdoor activities, and watching college sports.

Other Books from Affinity eBook Press

Catch to Release by Lacey Schmidt
On the verge of finally releasing her own record label, lesbian folk-rock star, Shay Greenaura, finds herself caught up in more than just her music. Addison Weller, a former Diplomatic Security Services agent is called in to assess the threats against Shay. Follow this fast-paced adventure to its surprising romantic conclusion.

Ready for Love by Erin O'Reilly
Kylie Wilcox's life dramatically changed with the death of her husband. Dr. LJ Evans, a renowned archaeologist, needed and wanted nothing but her work for her happiness. Their worlds are about to collide and lives will be altered forever.

Neptune's Ring by Ali Spooner
In the sequel to *Venus Rising*, Nat and Liz, owners of Venus Rising, invite Levi and Vanessa to join them in a venture for a new club on another island. They find the perfect place in an unfinished resort Neptune's Ring. While on the island, Levi is drawn into a mystery involving secret compartments and a murder. Join the characters in this page-turning adventure, filled with steamy romance, intrigue and an unsolved murder.

The Ultimate Betrayal by Annette Mori
Lara is a successful, beautiful, charming, financier. She is also a total control freak, so whatever Lara wants, Lara makes sure she gets. Rachel is Lara's fun loving, charming, irresistible wife. Sophia's surprise visit to see Lara sets in motion a number of life changing events for them all. Hell has no fury like a woman scorned.

It's in Her Kiss by Various Affinity Authors
A collection of various holiday stories dedicated to anyone and everyone that reads it. Young, old, lesbian, gay, bisexual, and transgender. We are all the same inside, and want the same things outside…love, happiness and that special someone to spend all of our holidays with.

Keeping Faith by TJ Vertigo
Join the antics of Reece, Faith, Cori, Vi, and even The Animal, one last time in *Keeping Faith*. Faith has finally made the big screen, but how will Reece handle her success? Will the love that they share be enough to save their relationship and soothe The Animal?

Bound by Ali Spooner
A rogue master vampire threatens the existence of the New Orleans vampire clan. Lord Jordan enlists Devin Benoit, sister of the Baton Rouge Alpha, and her witch lover, Tia, to assist with cleansing the city from potential disaster.

The Circle Dance by Jen Silver
Jamie Steele has moved to another town, trying to forget the heartbreak of losing her lover of six years. Sasha Fairfield finds her thoughts taken up with her ex-lover and thinks she wants Jamie back. Follow this captivating romance as love dances through the lives of these women to its surprising conclusion.

Search for the White Moon by Natalie London
Kathryn Austin, a government agent, is given opera singer, Adriana Desi, as her new assignment. Their lives and futures are in danger as the White Moon terrorists hunt them. Immerse yourself in this fast-paced romantic thriller by debut author Natalie London.

Take Me As I Am by JM Dragon & Erin O'Reilly
When Jo Lackerly and Thea Danvers meet, an unexpected friendship develops, proving a catalyst for both women to change their lives irrevocably. Follow them on a journey of discovery that will have your heart smiling, blood boiling, and senses entangled in a wonderful romance.

Carved in Stone by Jen Silver
Join the characters from *Starting Over* and *Arc Over Time* in this final book from the Starling Hill trilogy. Ellie Winters thinks she might be going mad when the ancient queen wants a proper burial for herself and her consort. *Carved in Stone* has romance, adventure, a treasure hunt, and a happy endings for all, living and dead.

Anywhere, Everywhere by Renee MacKenzie
Gwen Martin's life in the Ten Thousand Islands area changes irrevocably when Piper Jackson comes into her life. Without trust, can the budding relationship between Gwen and Piper survive? Or will the answers to the questions continue to haunt them?

Venus Rising by Ali Spooner
Levi Johnson arrives at Venus Rising, an exclusive lesbian-only tropical resort in the Virgin Islands and finds more than she expected—a sizzling hot love triangle. Torn between her attraction to two women, she struggles to choose the right woman to share her life.

The Devil's Tree by Ali Spooner
Torn between her love for the pack and her need to find what's missing in her life, Devin Benoit travels to New Orleans. Will the previous happenings at the Devil's Tree help or hinder Devin in the fight of her life, and the life of Tia, the woman who now owns her heart?

The Beggars' Coppice by Erica Lawson
Edda Case is a woman in crisis who discovers that things are not as they seem. Is it truly a message for her from beyond the grave or is something more sinister taking place? Can Edda solve the mystery of *The Beggars' Coppice*?

Locked Inside by Annette Mori
How much does the power of love matter to someone who must overcome obstacles far greater than most people face in a lifetime.

Line of Sight by Ali Spooner
Sasha and her lover Kara are back. Continue the thrilling adventures of this couple from the Sasha Thibodaux series.

Against All Odds by JM Dragon
From award-winning and bestselling author JM Dragon, with significant updates by Erin O'Reilly, comes an original tale of romance where everything seems to be stacked against two women whose destinies bring them together. Life however takes a twisted path, setting both Steph and Louise in directions they never thought possible. Will love win out against all odds or will love be forever lost?

The Settlement by Ali Spooner
The outpouring of love and friendship toward Cadin helps her on her path to healing and learning to trust her heart to love once again. Join bestselling author Ali Spooner on this sensational journey that ends with a heartwarming romance.

E-Books, Print, Free e-books

Visit our website for more publications available online.

www.affinityebooks.com

Published by Affinity E-Book Press NZ LTD
Canterbury, New Zealand

Registered Company 2517228